CAN SNOW LEOPARDS ROAR?

Amelia Lionheart

2nd Edition – 2014

Amelia Lionheart
Can Snow Leopards Roar?
978-0-9937493-6-0 *softcover*
978-0-9937740-0-3 *ebook (mobi)*
978-0-9937493-7-7 *ebook (epub)*

Printing
Minuteman Press (Calgary North), Alberta
Information and Sales: info@mmpresscgy.com
Printed & bound in Canada

The paper used in the publication of this book is from responsible forest
management sources.

Other titles in this series:
Peacock Feathers
The Dolphin Heptad
An Elephant Never Forgets
The Humming Grizzly Bear Cubs

To, Michelle & David,
There are lots of colours in this book!
of endless
Warmly,
In conservation,
Lionheart
11 May 2019

Website: http://www.jeacs.com

Dedicated to

The JEACs – CAC – Groups

Thank you, members of the *JEACs – CAC – Groups*!
May you continue to create awareness of conservation and
environmental issues, and fundraise to support established
conservation groups in Canada.

FOREWORD
by
Dr. Doug Whiteside

"In the end we will conserve only what we love.
We will love only what we understand.
We will understand only what we are taught."
~Baba Dioum

Known as the "ghost cats of the Himalayas", snow leopards (*Panthera uncia*) are among the most beautiful of the big cats with their characteristic thick grey spotted fur and long bushy tails. While snow leopards can growl, chuff, hiss, mew and wail, unlike other relatives such as lions and tigers, they cannot roar. Their range in the high mountains of central Asia extends across twelve countries, covering approximately 2 million square kilometres. Unfortunately it is estimated that as few as 3,500 of these magnificent cats remain in the wild. Fragmentation and loss of their habitat, illegal poaching for their hides or bones, a reduction in their natural prey due to illegal hunting, and killing in retribution for when they prey on domestic livestock, have led to the snow leopard being placed on the endangered species list by the International Union for the Conservation of Nature.

Approximately 1 in 7 species on earth that are threatened with extinction are now protected in zoos and aquariums. In some cases the genetic diversity that exists within these conservation institutions is greater than that which exists in the wild. But protecting them in a captive environment is not enough. Accredited zoos such as the Calgary Zoo extend that protection to the natural homes of these species by contributing to in-situ conservation programs. Canadian accredited zoos participate in approximately 800 conservation science programs locally, nationally, and globally. And their contribution to endangered species breeding and reintroduction programs is significant; black-footed ferrets, swift fox, Vancouver Island marmots, whooping cranes, Puerto Rican crested toads, eastern loggerhead shrikes, and Przewalski's horses have been born in Canadian zoos and released into the wild.

Accredited zoos also play an important role in connecting the public with nature and educating about the importance of global biodiversity, conservation, and environmental sustainability. Through exploration of such issues, people re-examine their lifestyle choices and consumption habits and the impact that these choices and habits may have on their environment. This often inspires them to make better choices in their day-to-day lives.

The survival of snow leopards is dependent on partnerships between conservation organizations such as International Snow Leopard Trust, the Snow Leopard Conservancy, and Panthera, as well as other captive conservation institutions such as accredited zoological facilities. There are approximately 650 snow leopards in accredited zoological institutions around the world. This partnership extends far beyond just maintaining a genetic refuge for the species in zoos; it also serves to partner with local people to protect habitat, protect against poaching, and support researchers who study the species in the wild. In addition, this partnership allows for bridging of knowledge gaps between wild and captive populations of snow leopards.

In her book *Can Snow Leopards Roar?* Amelia Lionheart introduces her readers to the issues that imperil these magnificent cats. Amelia is passionate about the conservation of wildlife and wild spaces. Even more so, through the creation of the Junior Environmentalists and Conservationists (JEACs), she is impassioned to educate and engage today's youth to develop a better tomorrow for species threatened with extinction. The JEACs continue to expand globally and are a great example of how we as a species will embrace change that we help to create.

Dr. Doug Whiteside
Senior Staff Veterinarian, Calgary Zoo
Clinical Associate Professor, University of Calgary Faculty of Veterinary Medicine

ACKNOWLEDGEMENTS

I would like to extend my sincere gratitude to the following wonderful people who have contributed generously to the production of this book. In this *second* edition, my thanks go to:

Dr. Doug Whiteside, DVM, DVSc, Dipl. ACZM, Senior Staff Veterinarian at the Calgary Zoo. As you will gather, after reading his foreword to this book, Dr. Whiteside is a highly qualified expert in the protection of wildlife, and speaks at numerous conferences. Dr. Whiteside set aside many hours of his limited time, meeting with me and assisting me in understanding the technicalities of tranquillizers; reading the manuscript and ensuring that all technical information was accurate; and providing helpful insights and suggestions in order to make the story more plausible. Thank you, Dr. Doug, for honouring me by writing the foreword.

Joanne Bennett, for editorial assistance;
Glenn C. Boyd, for handling the printing of the books and production of all marketing materials in his consistently exceptional and efficient manner;
Mary Anna and Warren Harbeck, for editorial assistance and excellent suggestions;
Michael Hartnett, for know-how and business advice;
Grace and Hubert Howe, for assistance in innumerable ways;
Sarah Lawrence, for her advice, and dedication in bringing this book to publication;
Elaine Phillips, my cheerful editor, who proofread yet another book;
Robin Phillips, for business advice;

and, once more, **my family and many friends**, for their encouragement and support.

Finally, in 2012, 2013 and 2014, I have done, and am booked for, close to 200 book signings – at Indigo, Chapters and Coles book shops, Monkeyshines Children's Books, and Bentleys Books, located in Calgary, Edmonton and Cochrane. This page of acknowledgements would be incomplete if I did not extend my appreciation to the owners, managers and staff of all the book shops – thank you for opening your doors to me and making the JEACs' series such a success.

YOU
CAN MAKE A DIFFERENCE

You are UNIQUE! This means YOU have special gifts to help change the world. Talk to your parents about ways in which you can recycle or conserve at home. Ask the wonderful folk at zoos and conservations close to you how you can get involved in all kinds of fun and educational activities. Get your friends and neighbours involved. Look up websites for zoos and wildlife conservations, and check out what's going on around the world!

THEME SONG

Jun-ior Environ-menta-lists and Con-ser-vation-ists!

When we think about our world, all the animals and birds
Who are losing their homes day by day
If each person does their part, it will cheer up every heart
So let's take a stand and act without delay!

We've decided we will strive to keep birds and beasts alive
And to make CONSER-VA-TION our theme
We will talk to all our friends, try to help them understand
That our world must come awake and not just dream!

All the creatures that we love, from the ele-phant to dove,
Must be cared for and well protected, too
So all humans, young and old, have to speak up and be **bold**
Or we'll end up with an 'only human' zoo!

Where environment's concerned, in our studies we have learned
That composting at home can be a start
And recycling's very good, each and every person should
Be aware of how we all can do our part.

To the JEACs we belong, and we hope it won't be long
Till our peers and our friends all will say
They believe that con-ser-vation and environ-menta-lism
Is the only way to save our world today!

Will you come and join our band? Will you lend a helping hand?
Though it's serious, it can be great fun!
Tell your friends about it all, let them join up, big and small
And our fight against destruction will be won!
Jun-ior Environ-menta-lists and Con-ser-vation-ists!

ABOUT THE JEACs

The JEACs (*Junior Environmentalists and Conservationists*), a group created by *Amelia Lionheart* in the first book of her series, attempts to enlighten children – through the means of adventure stories – about conservation and environmental issues. The author is delighted that the JEACs, once only a figment of her imagination, have become a reality in recent years.

The JEACs firmly believe that some of the key factors in **saving our planet** are:

- **Participation**
- **Awareness**
- **Co-operation**
- **Education**

****

JEACs' MISSION STATEMENT AND GOALS

We are an international group of Junior Environmentalists and Conservationists who long to **save our planet** from destruction. We will work towards this by:

- educating ourselves on the importance and necessity:

  o of protecting *all wildlife* – especially endangered species – and the techniques used by conservation groups all over the world to reach this goal;

  o of preventing our *global environment* from further damage, and finding out how we can participate in this endeavour;

- creating awareness of these issues among our peers and by sharing knowledge with them, encouraging more volunteers to join our group;

- becoming members of zoos, conservations and environmental groups in our region, actively participating in events organized by them and, through donations and fundraising efforts, contributing towards their work.

Table of Contents

CHAPTER 1

Catching Up

'Up one more floor,' said Umedh, racing up the stairs.

'Right behind you, yaar,' said Rohan. 'It's a good thing we're fit. Why didn't we take the lift?'

'Because you're too fat,' chuckled Umedh.

'Huh, still not as fat as you,' teased Rohan. Both boys were fairly thin because of their spurt of growth over the past six months.

'Quit gabbing and hurry up,' said Amy, who was behind Rohan. 'We don't have much time to catch up before joining the APs at dinner.'

'Here we are,' said Umedh, opening the door to a large, cosily furnished room on the sixth floor. The JEACs settled down on the carpet, in front of a large fire.

'Did you sleep well?' asked Anu, looking at Amy and Michelle.

'Like logs,' said Amy. 'What about you folks?'

'Rested and raring to go,' said Rohan.

'I can't believe we're actually together again,' said Amy. 'Mich and I really missed you all.' Michelle was known as 'Mich' to family and friends.

'We missed you, too – despite keeping in touch via the internet. It's like a dream come true – we're in London, England!' said Anu, giving Amy a quick hug. 'What are the plans, Umedh? When do we tour London, Glasgow, Edinburgh, and visit Loch Ness to look for the monster?'

'Yes, please tell us,' chorused the others, turning eagerly to the boy.

'Whoa! Slow down, folks,' said Umedh.

'Sorry, yaar,' laughed Nimal. 'We're so excited that we can't stop bombarding you with questions – especially since you got here yesterday and know the itinerary.'

'True – and I was so impatient for your arrival that my aunt told me my eye would wear out if I kept checking my watch so often.'

Umedh Ghosh, Rohan's best friend, was born with only one eye. His uncle and aunt managed 'The Welcome Inn' – a small hotel in the heart of London. Umedh lived in India with his parents, went to boarding school with Rohan and Nimal, and had arrived in London on the fourteenth of December.

The Larkins – Amy, Mich and their mother, Janet – had arrived early that morning, travelling from Canada; the Patels – Rohan, Anu and Gina, along with their cousin, Nimal (their fathers were brothers) – had arrived from India around noon that afternoon, accompanied by their respective mothers, Dilki and Jo.

'Unfortunately, I don't know the exact itinerary,' continued Umedh, 'but Jay will be here around 8:30 this evening; she'll give us details.'

Although Jay was Umedh's aunt (his mother's youngest sister), she was only ten years older than Umedh, so they were more like siblings. She had asked him, when he entered his teens, to drop the 'aunt' since it made her feel ancient to be called Aunty Jay by someone who was at least seven inches taller than her. Almost a year before, she had married Dan MacDonald, manager of the Kinnaird Wildlife Conservation Centre in Scotland.

'When do we go to the Centre?' asked Nimal eagerly.

'Early tomorrow morning,' said Umedh. 'The fundraising event is on the twentieth, which gives us four days to help out. After Christmas, we explore Scotland before returning here on the twenty-ninth, and that's when we visit Madame Tussauds, the museums, take in a show, and do tons of sightseeing.'

'And the book shops – right?' added Anu, and Umedh nodded.

'Now, young ladies,' Umedh said, turning to Mich and Gina, 'will you survive until dinner at 8:30, or are you hungry?'

'We're fine, thanks, Umedh, but we're worried about Nimal. You know what he's like when he's hungry and . . .' Mich trailed off with a shriek, as Nimal grabbed her and Gina (who was giggling madly and egging her on), and proceeded to tickle them.

'Little wretches,' growled Nimal. 'Just wait until we're in the mountains – I'll bury you both in snow.'

The girls escaped him by rolling in opposite directions, and then pounced on him, tickling him in return.

Nimal, though much bigger than they were, had a tough job holding them off since he could not use his full strength. The others laughed and begged them to watch out for the fire.

'Pax! Pax!' panted Nimal.

'Promise you won't bury us in snow,' said Gina sitting on one of his legs.

'And promise you'll make friends with *every* animal so that we can pet them,' said Mich, sitting on his other leg. She was Gina's age, but slightly taller, and both girls were gymnasts.

'I promise,' gasped Nimal. 'Please get off my legs, mes amis – I can't feel them anymore.'

The girls tumbled off and he sat up, rubbing his legs ruefully. 'Man – they may be small, but they're fast and strong.'

'Only *you* would attempt to take them on, yaar,' said Rohan, grinning at the girls.

'*Nobody* loves me,' sighed Nimal tragically. 'It's one of the saddest . . .'

'. . . stories of your life,' chorused the others.

Nimal chuckled. 'Just wait until I've got my black belt. I've already had a wonderful *karate-spooky* match with Mohan – and, man, was he petrified!'

'Spooky? What happened?' asked Amy and Mich, as the others laughed. They loved hearing about Nimal's hilarious episodes at school.

'Anu, you're on,' said Rohan.

Everyone looked at Anu expectantly – she was their storyteller.

'Right,' said Anu. 'You remember Mohan – the pompous chap in Nimal's class?'

'Of course,' said Amy and Mich.

'Well, he also takes karate lessons and, being who he is, believes that he's not only *the best* in school, but also knows more than the instructors.

'One day the karate instructor was sick and the young new English Lit. teacher, who has his black belt, was asked to fill in. Although brilliant in his subject and excellent at karate, he was nervous about taking the session, and Mohan, realizing this, was rude and cheeky to him.

'The other boys were frothing mad, and after the session they put their heads together, agreeing that Mohan needed to be taught a lesson and made to apologize to the teacher. Nimal, naturally, came up with the idea of being the "ghost of karate instructors past", and it was hilarious.' Anu told them the tale and had them in fits of laughter.

'Oh, Nimal,' said Amy, she and Mich wiping away tears of mirth, 'will you *ever* stop playing practical jokes?'

'I was as good as gold,' said Nimal, grinning cheekily. 'It isn't *my* fault that Mohan's petrified of ghosts.'

They caught up on other news, thrilled to be together again, reminiscing about their summer trip to Sri Lanka and their adventure with the elephants at the Alighasa Wildlife Conservation Centre.

'Who else is joining us at the Kinnaird Wildlife Conservation Centre, or KWCC for short?' asked Amy. 'Anyone from Sri Lanka?'

'The Sri Lankan contingent can't make it to the conference on Endangered Species, here in London, since Priyani broke her leg,' said Rohan. 'Those attending and then coming on to KWCC on the twenty-third are Uncle Jack and Helen from Australia, Uncle Greg, your father, Amy, and mine. Hopefully, Mike and Monique will arrive on the same day. It's a pity your parents couldn't join us, Umedh.'

'Yeah,' said Umedh, 'but the mater's older sister isn't well, and they'll spend a quiet Christmas with her. By the way, when are Mike and Monique getting married?'

'Their initial wedding date was set for November, but they postponed it to the seventeenth, the day after tomorrow,' said Amy. 'After a small church wedding, they'll take a long honeymoon, visiting friends and relatives: first India; then here for Christmas and the New Year; on to France to visit Monique's relatives; to Sri Lanka, Canada and back to Australia. It's so exciting.'

'That's some trip,' said Nimal. 'It'll be super to see them again.'

'Yes, and we can plan a lovely wedding party for them. We'll be a merry group at KWCC,' said Anu. 'Luckily for us, so many things panned out, and here we are.'

'How did it come together, Anu?' asked Mich.

Gina and Mich had not, so far, assimilated the details.

'Firstly, Uncle Greg got that unexpected large bonus when he finished a complicated job in Dubai earlier this month; secondly, he and Aunty Jo wanted all of us to visit KWCC to learn about breeding endangered species and, since he's setting up a computer program for them in January, he thought it would be a great Christmas holiday for the whole group; then there's this big conference in London that our dads, Uncle Greg, Uncle Jack and Helen, were coming to. Finally, just when it seemed impossible for us to come here until the twenty-second – due to lack of space at KWCC – a large group cancelled their visit due to an epidemic of measles which broke out at the school – so we lucked out.'

'I'm sorry for the kids who had to cancel,' said Nimal, 'but I'm thrilled that the APs get these brilliant ideas, not to mention thumping bonuses.'

'True, and it's wonderful that they believe it's worth spending Uncle Greg's hard-earned bonuses on educating us JEACs on different aspects of conservation all over the world,' said Rohan gratefully. 'Three cheers for Uncle Greg and Aunty Jo,' he yelled.

As they raised the roof with their cheers, Andrina, one of the hotel staff, entered the room and invited them to dinner. The JEACs followed her downstairs to the private dining room.

'Has my aunt arrived, Andrina?' asked Umedh.

'She'll be here in twenty minutes.'

'Is Scotland far away?' asked Gina.

'It's a long drive, love, but a short flight,' replied Andrina. 'You'll land at a small airport in Scotland, and board a helicopter which will transport you to the Centre.'

'Yippee!' yelled Mich and Gina. 'We've never been in a helicopter before.'

'Isn't KWCC accessible by road?' asked Anu. 'Do you know much about it and Scotland, Andrina?'

'I surely do, lassie,' laughed Andrina. 'I'm Scottish and hail from a little town at the foot of the Cairngorms. KWCC is in the Cairngorm mountain range and since it's situated on one of the peaks – the name *Kinnaird* means a summit or peak – it's only accessible by helicopter.'

'It sounds extremely remote and isolated,' said Nimal. 'How high are the Cairngorms? Also, I'm sure I read, somewhere, that *Cairn Gorm* is a specific mountain, lying at one end of the Cairngorm mountain range – is that correct?'

'Absolutely, Nimal,' said Andrina. 'But most people just refer to the *Cairngorms*, which includes the whole range. The range varies in height, but KWCC is approximately 1,070 metres high,' said Andrina. 'Some of the other peaks are over 1,220 metres high.'

'What about the "Grey Man" – the creature which resembles the Yeti?' asked Umedh. 'Is it true that he lives in the Cairngorms?'

Andrina chuckled and said, 'Who knows, laddie, but don't you go looking for him – he's dangerous. Some say he lives on the *Ben Macdui* summit, which is around 1,310 metres high, close to the *Cairn Gorm*.'

'Gee, what does he look like?' asked Mich, wide-eyed.

'You'll see pictures of him at KWCC – they have a fine gallery and one section is devoted to mythical creatures like the Grey Man and the Loch Ness Monster,' said Andrina. 'But don't be scared – he stays in his area. And here's the dining room.'

'What's for dinner?' said Nimal, sniffing hungrily. 'Something smells yum-a-licious, and I'm . . .'

'*Starving!*' shrieked Gina and Mich, running ahead into the room.

'Dinner will be served in five minutes,' Andrina assured them.

The three mothers were already seated at the table, and smiled to see the youngsters in such high spirits.

Led by Rohan, they cheered Nimal's mother; Amy and Mich, who were meeting her for the first time on this trip, hugged and thanked her and her husband for their wonderful gift.

'You're welcome, JEACs,' said Jo, smiling at the group. 'I'm glad you've recovered from jet lag.'

'How about you, Mum, Aunty Dilki and Aunty Janet?' asked Nimal, giving his mother a hug as he sat down beside her.

He was thrilled to have her around. His parents travelled the world – Greg Patel, a renowned and busy computer consultant, was rarely at home and, since his wife accompanied him on his trips, Nimal had lived with his cousins from a very young age. Both families lived at the Patiyak Wildlife Conservation Centre, in India, where Jim Patel, Rohan's father, was the manager. Nimal loved living with his cousins but, naturally, missed his parents, although they were in constant touch via email and telephone.

'We're fine, thanks,' answered Dilki. 'Are you folks ready to help with the fundraiser?'

'Definitely, Aunty Dilki,' said Amy, 'and it's superfantabulous to be together again.'

Everyone took a seat and the conversation turned to Jay's arrival.

'I'm looking forward to meeting her,' said Janet.

'Us, too, Mum,' said Amy. 'I guess we three Canucks are the only ones who haven't met her. What's she like, Umedh?'

'Incorrigible,' said Umedh. 'She lived with us and used to get *me* into trouble because of her craze for animals. When I was four, she found an injured duck and was determined to keep it in her room until it was healed. Mum, who loves animals but prefers only dogs or cats in the house, had given Jay firm instructions about animals in her room – this was after she'd discovered a grass snake, comfortably ensconced in a shoe box in Jay's cupboard.'

There was a shout of laughter, and Umedh continued. 'Mum was out, so Jay smuggled the duck into her room and called me to have a look. She was worried that the duck would be discovered, so I was given strict orders: "Whenever the duck quacks, Umedh, you must quack too – several times, so that your mum thinks it's you making the noise – now, let's practise." And we did.'

When the laughter subsided, Umedh said, 'I adored Jay, so I practised quacking till Mum came home and we were summoned to lunch. The duck fell asleep, comfortably settled on one of Jay's party dresses.

After the meal, Jay and I went to her room, and the duck immediately began quacking loudly. Mum called out, asking Jay what that noise was. Jay, quick as a wink, put me, and the duck, into her cupboard, and whispered that I must pretend to be the duck when it quacked. So, when Mum, wondering what the rumpus was about, came to investigate, yours truly was following orders.

'"What's all that quacking?" queried Mum. "Just Umedh and I playing a game," said Jay, striving to look innocent. Fortunately, the duck had subsided when Mum opened the door, but Mum, suspicious of Jay's innocent look, questioned her about the nature of the game and my whereabouts. Jay began telling her that I was hiding and she had to discover my whereabouts by the sounds I made, when the duck, fed up with being in a cupboard with a quacking human, fluttered its wings and tried to get out, banging its head on the door. In a flash, Mum opened the cupboard door and the duck, slightly dazed, waddled past her, while yours truly, a little startled, but hoping that Mum had *not* seen the duck, continued to quack until Mum pulled me out and told me, firmly, to stop that noise. To cut a long story short, I was given a long time out and no dessert that day, while Jay had to forego her next party – not that *she* cared. As for my mater, she managed to keep a straight face until we were out of sight.'

'That's hilarious,' gasped Nimal, as everyone wiped away tears of mirth. 'How come you remember it so well?'

'The story came out at Jay and Dan's wedding reception,' said Umedh. 'Dan nearly choked when Mum told the tale.'

'And here's the lady of the hour,' said Rohan, as Jay walked in.

'What's the joke?' she begged, as everyone burst out laughing and rose to greet her.

They told her, and she chuckled. 'Telling tales out of school are we, Umedh? Just wait till I tell them about you.'

She hugged everyone, and when the meal arrived the JEACs ate hungrily, while asking Jay questions.

'Do you mind telling us about Hunter, first?' asked Nimal.

'Of course,' said Jay. 'He's having a wonderful time. He pined for you the first week – but we kept talking about you. He's so intelligent that I'm sure he senses your arrival imminently.'

'Good-o!' said everyone. They all loved the beautiful, clever Alsatian dog, which belonged to the Patels.

'Thanks, Jay. Please tell us about the Centre and the fundraiser,' said Anu. 'We know it's called the *Kinnaird Wildlife Conservation Centre*, KWCC for short; it's situated in the Cairngorms, you have a breeding programme for endangered species, and we get there by helicopter.'

Jay looked around the table thoughtfully and said, 'There's a lot going on just now, so I'll begin with the basics. KWCC is six years old, and we're fortunate in our founder and patron, Robert MacCale, a wealthy philanthropist who's passionate about conservation. Ten years ago, Robert put forward a proposal to the government, and they leased him a large area in the Cairngorms, which already had several buildings and a boundary wall – mostly in excellent condition. It was teeming with wildlife: birds such as ptarmigan, dotterel, golden eagle, snowy owl, capercaillie, Scottish crossbill; and animals like the red deer, roe deer, mountain hare, pine marten, red squirrel, wildcat and otter, as well as reindeer – to name a few of the species.'

'Does Mr. MacCale live at KWCC?' asked Amy.

'No. He's handicapped – lost an arm and a leg in the war and has various other problems which necessitate him having to stay in town, near a hospital. He's amazing and you'll enjoy meeting him.'

'It'll be an honour,' said Umedh. 'How did he set up KWCC?'

'He brought in experts, and once it was operational, Robert paid all salaries for five years, until KWCC was stable and in a position to support itself. He persuaded several large corporations to become involved and, together, they donated two helicopters and cover the running and maintenance costs. Robert's very keen on educating the world about the critical need to save our planet, and that's another strong focus for us.'

'What types of educational programmes do you run?' asked Anu.

'All sorts,' said Jay. 'We encourage child participation from an early age. Groups of young people from schools love coming over to live in tents during the summer months, and in the buildings in the winter, and depending on the age group, they stay from a week to a month. In living the experience, by pure osmosis, they absorb a great deal of information about conservation and environmental issues. We involve them in caring for the animals, show them videos, and hold classes with fun, practical lessons and games. We also want to specialize in breeding endangered species, under carefully controlled conditions – we've only been doing this for two years.

'Also, at the upcoming fundraiser, we'd like you to speak to the young people about your group, the JEACs.'

'We'd love to do that, Jay,' said Amy, and the others nodded.

'Your branches are currently in India, Canada, Australia and Sri Lanka, and your website is www.jeacs.com, right?'

'Correct,' said Rohan.

'Tell us more about the breeding programme,' said Nimal.

'The proper name is "captive breeding", and although there's some controversy about trying to breed animals out of their natural environment, as we know, it's sometimes the only way in which some of the endangered species can breed and survive. Once KWCC was well established, Robert and Dan, inspired by the success of other conservation centres, explored the feasibility of starting up a programme at KWCC. Then, at a conference in Glasgow, Dan met Luag Abercrombie, who was an expert in the field, and invited him to take charge of our captive breeding programme – and that's how we began.'

'Which animals do you breed?' asked Nimal.

'Well, one wildlife conservation park succeeded in breeding Asian short-clawed otters and the red panda, so we decided to start with those two species as well. So far, we've managed to breed two otter kits – which are nearly three months old, and one red panda cub, who's a month old.'

'Oooh – they must be so cute,' said Gina, clapping her hands.

'Will we be able to play with them?' asked Mich.

'The otter kits and baby panda are being bred for release when they're older, so you won't be able to play with them, but you can see them. However, our biggest success is with the *Panthera uncia*, commonly known as snow leopards, which, unfortunately, brings me to the problems surrounding them.'

'What problems, Jay?' asked Rohan.

'Snow leopards are an endangered species,' began Jay.

Just then a waiter entered the room to clear away the dishes and Janet Larkin, looking at her watch, said, 'Good grief – it's nearly 11 o'clock. What time do we leave tomorrow, Jay?'

'By five, to avoid traffic,' said Jay. 'We must get some sleep.'

'But you were going to tell us about the problem with the snow leopards,' protested the older JEACs, who were eager to learn more.

'Sorry, folks – I'll explain on the plane,' said Jay.

'Okay,' said Nimal, seeing Mich and Gina stifle yawns.

The others agreed, and everyone went to bed, eager to start their trip in the morning.

Chapter 2

Three Weeks Ago

The next morning, the sixteenth of December, the JEACs rose at four, and after a glass of hot milk, were ready for anything.

'We're going to see Hunter,' sang Mich and Gina, as they climbed into the van which would take them to the airport.

'You must sing your JEACs' theme song for me, girls. I hear that you wrote the words, Gina, and you drew the cartoons, Mich,' said Jay.

'Sure, Jay,' said Gina.

'But the others must join in, too,' added Mich.

'We will, kiddos,' said Rohan, 'and we'll be happy to sing any other new songs the two of you produce.'

Once the small aircraft had taken off, and they could see nothing but clouds, Rohan asked Jay about the snow leopards.

'We obtained four pairs from Central Asia, which has the largest population of these beautiful creatures. These snow leopards, which had been preying on herds of sheep and cows, were captured at various times by a conservation centre in the region, who didn't want them euthanized. The centre was only too willing to send the animals to us. Prior to bringing them over, Luag and his team consulted with experts, to ensure that we could provide a good breeding environment, and once the animals arrived, we observed them carefully and continually improved their enclosures. It was a lot of work, so you can imagine our joy when, nine months ago, one of the females delivered three cubs.'

'They must have been adorable,' said Amy.

'They were. Then, a month and a half ago, another female gave birth to four cubs – we now had a total of seven cubs.

'Our programme was a success, and three weeks ago we had a huge celebration – everybody who supported KWCC was invited. The event was well attended, and we celebrated at Ruthven, which is where we have our events, and took groups of visitors to Burns to see the new cubs. However, the next morning we discovered that the three older cubs, and their parents, were missing.'

'Oh, *no!*' gasped everyone.

'What happened?' asked Rohan.

'Unfortunately, nobody saw anything suspicious,' said Jay. 'The police arrived, but found nothing unusual around the enclosures – visitors had not been taken to see the older cubs. All the boundaries were checked, but there was no damage to the high walls surrounding KWCC.'

'But . . . was absolutely *nothing* discovered about their disappearance?' said Umedh.

'Yes – but it was horrible,' said Jay, tears glistening in her eyes. 'Ten days ago, a man named Huang, travelling to China, was arrested at the airport. Craig – a senior airport official who's one of our volunteers and bitterly mourned the loss of the snow leopards – happened to be in the office when a customs official called a co-worker to check about permits for snow leopard skins being taken out of the country. Craig called back the customs officer immediately, and instructed him to take Huang to a private room and keep him there. Huang's baggage was to be sent to Craig's office.'

'What happened next?' asked Rohan.

'Craig, and a colleague, opened Huang's bags and found the pelts of an adult snow leopard and one cub. The bag was ripped apart and they discovered a number of bones, sewn into a thick blanket, which, in turn, was sewn into the suitcase to look like part of the bag. Huang was brought into Craig's office and questioned. But he was a tough character and merely said that he had bought the bag and pelts in Hackney, in East London. He refused to answer any questions about the bones.

'Huang was handed over to the police, who requested the airport management not to publicize this discovery just now, since there were still three snow leopards to be accounted for. The police contacted Dan and

Luag, and the three of us rushed to the airport, where Luag confirmed that these were the pelts of our missing male and one cub – each snow leopard coat pattern is unique, like our fingerprints. It was quite upsetting, and we went to the police station, with Craig. Inspector Jeffries, who's in charge of our case, requested us, at this stage, not to discuss it even with our staff. We reluctantly agreed.'

'What next?' asked Nimal.

'Craig promised to ensure that every single piece of luggage which had any kind of animal pelt, whether genuine or fake, would be checked by him or Brenda, another airport official who's also a volunteer. The next day, Brenda called Dan, at 2 a.m., asking us to come over immediately. Three more snow leopard pelts and bones were quickly identified as belonging to the other KWCC snow leopards.'

'Who was caught this time?' asked Umedh.

'A woman named Rizana,' said Jay. 'She was flying to Delhi with a piece of luggage similar to Huang's. When the scanner discovered animal skins, Rizana was taken to a private office; her bags were placed in another room, and Brenda found the pelts and bones. She contacted us, Craig and Inspector Jeffries. Once Luag had confirmed that they were our snow leopards, Rizana was brought into the room, and the Inspector arrested her.'

'Gee whizz! What happened?' said Amy.

'Rizana made a huge scene, screaming and shouting that she was innocent, that she was carrying the pelts for a friend, that she didn't know about the bones, that it was a friend's suitcase she had borrowed, et cetera. Jeffries stated that they had been tipped off about her. Rizana assumed Huang had betrayed her, and blamed him and a man called Zulfikar; Jeffries questioned her further. She finally admitted that Zulfikar had given her an airline ticket and the suitcase, already packed, and told her that she was to hand it over to someone in Delhi, who would contact her and pay her a good fee – she didn't have a name or phone number. It was apparent that she was simply a go-between. The inspector then admitted that he had merely made his statement to see her reaction, and she had fallen into the trap.'

'Excellent,' said Rohan. 'What did she say to that?'

'She was stunned,' said Jay. 'She gaped at him, realized her folly, and went quietly when they took her away. It was agreed that we should now publicize our findings, and it was in the news the same day. Jeffries would continue with the investigation, and try to find Zulfikar.'

'So, what's the current status?' asked Nimal.

'Our staff, eager to prevent another loss, agreed that the snow leopard enclosures should be guarded carefully during events, and that our rangers should patrol that area at least three times during the night,' concluded Jay.

Gina and Mich were quite upset, and their mothers comforted them as best they could; but the older JEACs were also angry.

'How can people destroy innocent animals?' growled Nimal. 'It's wicked and cruel.'

'What's been discovered as to how two fully grown snow leopards and three cubs were removed from KWCC, Jay – especially with so many people around for your event?' said Rohan.

'Brian . . .' began Jay, and was interrupted by an announcement that they would be landing in a few minutes. As she fastened her seat belt, she continued, 'We're hoping you'll be able to solve this problem for us, the way you've solved several others – we want our snow leopards to stay safe. Get further details from Luag's son, Brian. He's furious, and determined to catch the crooks – but he's stuck in a wheelchair.'

'What happened to him, Jay, and how old is he?' asked Anu.

'Twelve on the twenty-second of December. The poor kid lost his mother, and both his legs – they're amputated from just below the knees – in a car accident – ten months ago – hit by a drunk driver in Glasgow. They were visiting Biddie's mother. Biddie died on the spot, as did the driver of the van, and Brian was in critical condition for weeks. Poor Luag was shattered – they were a very close family. Brian, naturally, suffered from acute depression and shock, and although we got him a puppy as a welcome-home gift, nothing seemed to take him out of his misery until the snow leopard cubs appeared, and then they, along with his dad and dog, became the centre of his life – all the cubs love him.'

'Poor child,' said Jo.

The girls had tears in their eyes.

'We're hoping he'll befriend you. He was a jolly, active lad who loved sports, had a great sense of humour and a deep love for animals. Now he's uncomfortable with the children who visit KWCC because they're either too sympathetic, which he resents, or they're thoughtless and ask him insensitive questions. He needs to wait a while before they can give him prosthetics – you know, artificial limbs. His best friends visit him as often as possible, but they can't stay long, and he's lonely – the other kids at KWCC are very young – under three.'

'Leave him to us, Jay,' said Umedh, and the JEACs agreed, each vowing to themselves that they would make Brian feel comfortable and welcome in their group. They could only imagine what it would be like to suddenly lose their mother, as well as both legs, and their hearts went out to the boy.

'Here we are,' said Jay, a few minutes later. 'Welcome to Scotland!'

The plane landed smoothly at a tiny airport, taxied off the runway, and stopped near two helicopters.

The JEACs climbed into one helicopter while the adults got into the other, and the helicopters whirled away. Everyone looked out of the windows, admiring the beautiful scenery as they rose above the Cairngorms.

CHAPTER 3

Castles Galore

The flight was a short one, and soon the helicopters were descending rapidly, guided by spotlights around the helipads. It was still dark and the JEACs stared out of the windows, gazing at a huge building close by.

'It's a real castle!' gasped Gina. 'Like the ones I've seen in books.'

'I wonder if it has dungeons and secret passages,' squealed Mich. 'Are we going to live in it, Amy?'

'Don't know, hon,' said Amy. 'It's awesome – Umedh, did you know that Jay lived in a castle?'

'No,' said Umedh, laughing as he added, 'but now I understand why she wouldn't describe KWCC or send pictures of her *little cottage in the woods*, as she refers to it. She said it would be a surprise – and it is.'

'I think,' said Anu, gazing dreamily at the castle, 'that my next story will be based here . . .' She trailed off as the others burst out laughing.

The pilot opened their door, and they jumped out. The surrounding grounds were covered in snow, but a well-lit pathway had been cleared from the helipads to the castle.

Dan MacDonald, Jay's husband, welcomed them and, although he had not met any of them, except for Umedh, greeted them by name. 'Jay assured us that you'd be pretty hungry,' he said, leading them through a long hallway, 'so, Nilini's organized a hot breakfast and you'll meet a few of the staff.'

'Thanks, Mr. MacDonald,' chorused the JEACs.

'Please call me Dan – we're quite informal,' he said, ushering them into a large room.

'Hunter!' yelled the JEACs as a large jet-black Alsatian dog barked loudly and leapt to greet them, his tail wagging nineteen to the dozen; he whined excitedly as he tried to lick everybody at once.

'Oh, Hunter,' said Gina and Mich, hugging the dog exuberantly, 'we've missed you sooo much.'

Hunter washed everyone's face with his tongue, as the others knelt to hug him, too.

A series of sharp, excited, little yaps parted the group around Hunter, and as Nimal sat back on his heels, a tiny, soft bundle of dog, jumped into his arms.

'And who are you?' said Nimal, laughing as the puppy licked him lavishly. 'Aren't you a lovely little chap?'

The puppy squirmed with joy, and tumbling out of Nimal's arms, leapt up at Hunter. He was a cocker spaniel, with long, floppy ears and a lovely, golden coat. Hunter licked him, and the others crowded around the puppy, petting him and crooning over both dogs.

'His name's Tumbler,' said a voice, 'and he's mine – he's three months old.'

The JEACs turned to greet the boy in a wheelchair, just outside their group.

'Hello, you must be Brian,' said Nimal, shaking hands as he introduced himself. 'Tumbler's a super friend for Hunter. We've been looking forward to meeting you – another C-ite, right?'

'I'm Brian Abercrombie – but what's a "C-ite"?'

'Yes,' said Mich, looking puzzled. 'I've never heard it before either.'

'Sorry,' said Nimal with a laugh, 'I just made it up – it means anyone who lives on a conservation centre. We're exceptionally fortunate – and all of us, except for poor Umedh, are C-ites.'

Brian chuckled. 'Nice word – it's great to meet other C-ites.'

The others crowded around, introducing themselves, and Brian had no time to feel shy or awkward.

'And let me introduce more C-ites,' said Dan. 'This is Luag, Brian's father, and head of the breeding programme; Saroj and Nilini Ramanathan – they're twins even though they look so different, and they work in the office; the couple wearing tall, white hats, are our chefs, as they like to be called – Ceana and Drostan McArdle – they have degrees in the culinary arts, but prefer to work here rather than in the large hotels, since they're avid conservationists.'

'Thanks to their delicious meals, I've put on nearly ten kilograms since I arrived,' said Jay.

'Well, lassie,' said Ceana, smiling at the slim woman, 'since you were nearly anorexic, we *had* to feed you.'

Dan invited the visitors to serve themselves and sit wherever they wished. 'Welcome to KWCC. We're delighted to have you and thank you for agreeing to assist with our fundraiser. It's particularly great to have Dilki and Janet, experts at fundraising, to advise us; and a special thanks to Jo and Greg, who made this trip possible. JEACs, KWCC is thrilled to hear about your group and hope you'll start a branch in Scotland. All questions are welcome, and please make yourselves at home,' concluded Dan.

'Thanks, Dan,' said Jo. 'We're happy to be here. I do have one immediate question – why did nobody tell us that you live in a castle?'

'I hate to disappoint you – but it's not actually a castle – just built to look like one from the outside,' said Dan. He smiled at the JEACs' groan of disappointment, and continued, 'The original owner of the land loved castles and, therefore, all original buildings in KWCC, look like castles – and this is the largest – named *Ruthven Lodge*. It's the main building and the vast grounds surrounding it are perfect for our fundraising events. We did extensive renovations to the buildings, which were palatial homes, but unsuitable for our needs. At Ruthven we have several apartment suites, offices, a library, picture gallery, gift shop, fundraising room which doubles as a meeting room, lounge and theatre – on this floor. On the next floor we have an auditorium which holds over 2,000 people, and several conference rooms for smaller groups. On the top floor, we have more accommodation – a few bedrooms, and five dormitories – groups of school children, between the ages of six and ten, are housed here, sometimes for two weeks at a stretch.'

'It's humongous,' said Umedh. 'Does it have a cellar too?

'Yes – our large freezers are in one section, and storage in the other,' said Jay.

'How many more castles are there?' asked Anu.

'Three more,' said Luag. '*Burns Taigh* – Taigh means house – is where we have the breeding programme, and Brian and I live there, along with four others. Burns also has a helipad, so that animals can be transported quickly to Glasgow for specialized treatment.'

'How large is the area for the breeding programme?' asked Dilki.

'About twenty acres,' said Luag, 'and we have extra enclosures for injured animals. Also, we're only twenty minutes away from *Cairns Taigh* – an ancient building which – you'll be happy to hear – *was* a real castle built by one of the early kings of Scotland. It's made entirely out of stone. One section of the building is a pile of rubble, but the rest of it is safe, and we often house groups of older children at Cairns. It's right on one of our boundaries.'

'The last original building is *Knox Dachaigh* – Dachaigh means home,' said Dan. 'We have a petting zoo, and families with small children love spending a weekend or holiday there. We have many extra buildings, connected to the four main ones, mainly for housing purposes – KWCC is very popular.'

'It's fascinating! Do you think . . .' began Amy impulsively. She stopped and looked at the older JEACs, who were nodding eagerly, '. . . we could stay at Cairns? It would be super, and we promise to be completely responsible.'

The adults burst out laughing, and Jay said, 'We knew you'd want to stay there, and arrangements have already been made. We'll take you over, shortly.'

'Hurray! Three cheers for KWCC!' yelled the JEACs.

'And you'll join us, won't you, Brian?' said Umedh, turning to the silent boy.

'Oh, yes – you've *got* to come,' said Gina.

Brian looked at his father.

'It's your choice, son,' said Luag. 'He does need assistance with some things,' he added.

'We'd be happy to help,' said Rohan. 'Brian, we'd really like you to join us – just tell us what you need.'

'*Please* come, Brian,' said Anu. 'You know so much about KWCC and we want to hear everything about the snow leopards.'

'I hear the cubs love you, and we're longing to play with them,' added Nimal.

'It won't be fun without you,' said Amy.

'*Do come*, Brian,' said Mich, shy, but eager to show that she wanted to be friends, too.

Brian laughed and nodded, pleased with their obvious sincerity. He would enjoy spending time with these friendly children, none of whom seemed to be bothered by the fact that he was in a wheelchair.

'I'd like to, Dad,' he said eagerly. 'I'll take my crutches – and Tumbler.'

'Sure, son,' said Luag, delighted to see the brightness in the boy's face and his willingness to make friends. His request for his crutches was a positive sign – he had been reluctant to use them after a couple of children had referred to them as false legs.

'Has everyone had enough to eat?' asked Ceana.

'Yes, thanks – it was superfantabulous!' chorused the JEACs.

'Good,' said Ceana. 'We've stocked up tons of food at Cairns, but if you run short, let us know and we'll bring over another load. There's food for Tumbler and Hunter, too.'

'Thanks, Ceana,' said Nimal, politely. 'I have a modest appetite, but the rest of the crowd – well – they'll eat you out of house and home.'

'Only the last part of his sentence is true, Ceana – we do have *extremely* healthy appetites,' said Rohan, 'but Nimal's definition of "modest" should be taken with a whole *bagful* of salt. Nimal's appetite is considerably more *modest* than all the others put together.'

'Of all the cheek . . .' began Nimal, but the others agreed vociferously with Rohan.

'No bickering, JEACs,' laughed Drostan. 'You remind me of my noisy family. There were eleven of us, and we were always joking around – my dad's a comedian. Now, stop picking on the wee laddie before he bursts into tears.'

'Thank you, Drostan,' said Nimal pathetically. 'It's good to have *somebody* on my side. The torture I suffer – it's one of the saddest stories of my life.'

'I feel for you, laddie, and I'll drop you a postcard with my condolences,' said Drostan, thumping him on the back. 'And if I believed you, I'd be writing fairytales,' he added sotto voce.

'Right, JEACs,' said Dan with a laugh. 'Jay will brief you on KWCC, give you a map, and tell you what the programme is for the next week.'

'Thanks, Dan,' said everyone.

'This way, JEACs and ladies,' said Jay.

'Nimal, why does everyone call you *JEACs*?' asked Brian, as they followed Jay.

'It's the acronym for a group we founded,' explained Nimal. 'It stands for *Junior Environmentalists and Conservationists*. We'll tell you about it – I'm sure you'll want to join up.'

'It sounds great,' said Brian, eagerly. 'Are all of you in the group?'

'Yes – and we have branches in Canada, India, Australia and Sri Lanka. It would be great if you started one here,' said Nimal.

'I think you'll be an excellent advocate for the group, Brian,' said Anu. 'Our members are eager to protect animals, especially endangered species, and save our planet from being destroyed. We've even got a website.'

'Cool,' said Brian. 'I can't wait to hear more.'

Once they were seated in the lounge, Jay handed out maps of KWCC, which showed the trails, waterholes and facilities.

'Brian knows everything, so I won't go into details,' said Jay. 'He has a mobile phone, and here's an extra one in case you split up, but the network coverage isn't always good, especially in bad weather, so we've left walkie-talkie units at Cairns.

'We rely mainly on ATVs – sorry, Gina and Mich – ATV stands for *All Terrain Vehicles*, and they're perfect for the rough terrain at KWCC. We use snowmobiles, skis, toboggans and sleds to get around during the winter, as well as snow tracs – which are about the size of a car. We have ski-doos and several large snowmobiles, three of which are at

Cairns; Gavan will teach Umedh, Rohan and Nimal how to drive them – they're not difficult, just rather heavy.'

'What's the difference between a snowmobile and a ski-doo?' asked Gina.

'A *ski-doo* is a *type* of snowmobile – and some of them are light and easy to handle,' explained Jay. 'Like you have lots of cars, but different makes – we keep lots of smaller ski-doos so that visitors, including children, can ride them in the winter.'

'Thanks, Jay,' said Gina. 'I would love to learn how to ride a ski-doo.'

'I'm longing to learn how to skate and ski, and I'd love to go tobogganing,' said Anu.

'There are plenty of toboggans, sleds, snowshoes, skis, skates and ski-doos, in the sheds at Cairns, and you're welcome to try anything you like,' said Jay. 'I know you Canadians girls, and Umedh, have done most of these things, and can teach the others, so my only request is that you wait for Gavan to give you a quick demonstration of our ski-doos and other ATVs.'

'Of course, Jay,' agreed the JEACs.

'And I'm sure Brian will help us,' said Nimal. Brian's face was sombre as he realized that he would be unable to join in their activities and Nimal continued quickly, 'Although he can't participate in skating and skiing, he'll be the perfect person to give us instructions because he's done it before.'

'Exactimo,' said Rohan, placing a hand on Brian's shoulder. When the boy looked at him uncertainly, he shook him gently and said, 'You *will* teach us, won't you, Brian?'

'Okay, but I'll be *very strict*, especially with Nimal,' said Brian, cheering up instantly when he realized that they wanted to include him in everything.

'Hey!' yelped Nimal, glaring at him mockingly. 'If *you* start picking on me, Brian, I'll go and live in the wild – become one of the wildlife – at least they won't mock me.'

'You'll be the *only* species that's likely to become *extinct*, rapidly,' teased Amy, tweaking his ear affectionately.

'And none of us will mind,' added Rohan, as everyone chuckled at the look of mock indignation mixed with laughter, on Nimal's face.

'I'm *so* glad you've cottoned on that Nimal's the worst of the lot,' said Anu, sighing in exaggerated relief. 'The tales I could, and *will*, tell you about how he makes life miserable for everyone.'

'Beasts,' muttered Nimal, 'though, actually, beasts are much nicer than you lot. Now, if you *kids* would refrain from talking nonsense, we can revert to serious matters.'

'Definitely, *Uncle*, before you get verbal diarrhoea,' teased Umedh. 'Jay, please tell us about the fundraising event.'

'It's on the twentieth – four days left – including today,' said Jay. 'We have a plethora of wonderful volunteers – many of whom arrive tomorrow morning, with a small batch arriving in the afternoon – and now that you three ladies, and you JEACs, are here to assist, I'm sure it'll be a roaring success.'

'What type of an event is it?' asked Anu.

'Everything to do with winter fun – it'll be a full day and night affair, with lots of shows, competitions and educational sessions. Robert persuaded corporate donors to fund the cost of eleven large helicopters for the day, and two of these will also be available the day before, to bring out our volunteers. On the twentieth, the helicopters will transport people to and from KWCC, all day. Robert, and some of our special guests, will stay overnight, and leave the following day.'

'What types of competitions will there be?' asked Rohan.

'Skating, tobogganing and ski-doo races, for all age groups,' said Jay. 'We have entertainment in the form of Scottish reels, the highland fling, and great music – everything provided on a voluntary basis; there are ice sculpting displays, carnival games, crafts and lots of good food and hot drinks. We'll have games and contests for younger children, and for the little ones, we have experts in face painting and balloons. We offer crèche facilities so that parents can participate in some of the events; and, naturally, the petting zoo is a popular venue. The entrance fee is minimal, and our visitors make generous donations.'

'Do you have many school children attending the fundraiser, Jay?' asked Jo.

'We expect as many as a thousand, ranging from six to eighteen,' said Jay, 'and that, JEACs, brings me to your role.'

'May I join in, too?' asked Brian anxiously.

'Naturally, hon. I include you automatically, when I say JEACs, because you're so like them, even though you haven't *officially* joined them yet,' smiled Jay.

Brian beamed at her and high-fived Nimal.

'We have an educational event which takes place ten times during the day, and all youngsters have the opportunity to attend a session. When it was confirmed that you were coming, we planned the sessions around the JEACs. I'll leave our volunteers to give you details at tomorrow's meeting – which we'd like you to attend.'

'Sound's fun and we'd love to participate, Jay,' said Anu, and the others nodded.

'That's fantastic, everyone,' said Jay.

'Isn't there anything else you'd like us to do?' asked Amy.

'Thanks, folks, but we'd like you to participate in the events and enjoy the day. Also, since Amy, Rohan and Umedh have just finished strenuous exams, and the rest of you have been working hard, too, we thought you deserved to relax on this holiday. We have more than enough volunteers, so if you'll look after the educational programme, we'll be grateful.'

'We'll do our best,' the JEACs assured her.

'Great,' said Jay. 'It's nearly 8:30, and here's Luag to take you to Cairns. Ladies, would you like to see them settled in or would you rather stay here? Unfortunately, I can't go.'

'How long will it take to get there and back, Luag?' asked Janet.

'We're going to Burns Taigh first, to see the snow leopards,' said Luag. 'By the time they drool over the snow leopard cubs and we collect Brian's gear, it'll probably be close to noon when we reach Cairns after de-icing waterholes for the animals. Then we need to show the JEACs everything, so it'll be at least a couple more hours before you return here.'

'I think we'll stay and help you, Jay,' said Dilki. 'They're an independent bunch.'

'Thanks, Mum,' said Rohan. 'Being the oldest, I promise to keep everyone in line, especially Mich and Gina, who are absolutely incorrigible.'

'We're not!' shouted the girls, dancing around him and exciting the dogs so that they joined in the mad dance, barking loudly and jumping up at them.

'Put on your winter gear, JEACs,' said Luag, grinning at them, 'and I'll bring the ATV to the front porch in five minutes.'

CHAPTER 4

Panthera Uncia

The JEACs bundled up quickly and joined Luag outside.

'Climb in, folks,' he said, 'and I'll get Brian.'

'I'll carry Brian, if he doesn't mind,' said Rohan. Brian agreed and Rohan continued, 'Okay, now tell me the best way to carry you. Since you'll be with us, Umedh, Nimal and I need to know how to avoid hurting you.'

'One arm under my back and the other under my knees,' said Brian.

Rohan picked him up easily – the boy was very light – and carefully placed him in the ATV, asking anxiously, 'Did I hurt you?'

'Not at all, thanks, Rohan,' smiled Brian.

Umedh collapsed the wheelchair and loaded it into the vehicle, while the others piled in the bags and clambered inside. There was a special section at the back for animals, but naturally, the dogs jumped in with the children.

'All set? Seat belts on?' asked Luag, delighted that his son was making friends with the group and was willing to let them do things for him without becoming embarrassed.

'Yes, sir!' chorused the JEACs.

'Then hang on to your toques,' said Luag, starting the vehicle.

Waving goodbye to the others, they set off, and a few minutes later, Gina broke into song, the tune similar to that of 'I grieved my Lord' – and since it was easy, the others joined in where they could.

Oh, JEACs all (*Oh, JEACs all*)
Please sing with me (*Please sing with me*)
In Scotland fair (*In Scotland fair*)
At KWCC (*At KWCC*).
And in this land we know we'll meet
New animals – oh, what a treat!
We'll greet them all with joy and glee.

Snow leopard cubs, small reindeer, too,
And badger babes – just to name a few.
We'll play with all and feed them well,
They'll fall right under Nimal's spell,
It's so much fun for me and you.

Bri-an we all will count on you
To tell us how to ride a ski-doo.
And when we can, we know we'll be
The fastest team at KWCC
Let's hurry up, there's tons to do!

Hunter and Tumbler, what a pair,
They'll join our games, in all they'll share.
In ATVs they'll ride with us
Whate'er we do, there'll be no fuss,
There's simply nothing they won't dare.

New friends and old, luc-ky are we
We'll have a blast, at KWCC.
The big event is drawing near,
We'll dress up warm in winter gear
And join the games, yip, yip, YIPPEE!

'Gosh, Gina,' said Brian, 'I've never heard that song before – so how come I'm in it, too? Where did you learn it?'

'I . . . er,' began Gina, rolling an anxious eye at Anu.

'She just made it up, Brian,' said Anu, smiling at Gina.

'She makes up lots of songs, and teaches them to us,' added Mich. 'Let's sing it again.'

'Excellent, Gina,' said Luag, as Brian appeared stunned.

'Sing it again, honey,' coaxed Amy.

Everyone sang, and the dogs joined in with barks. By the time they had sung it several times, they knew the words by heart.

'That was fun,' said Brian, who loved singing. 'Do you sing a lot?'

'Yes,' said Anu. 'And you're excellent – I heard you harmonizing. Do you sing in a choir?'

'At school – we had a super choir master,' said Brian. 'But . . .' He trailed off and then continued bravely, 'This year's been a bit of a challenge, but Dad said I could go back to school next year.'

The others asked him eager questions; as the boy answered them, he lost his fear at the idea of returning to school.

'We have several boys at our school, also in wheelchairs,' said Nimal. 'Man, the way they zip around on those wheels while playing basketball – I tried it once and nearly broke my neck. They're incredible!'

'And I'm sure you've seen the Special Olympics for challenged kids, right?' said Amy. Brian nodded. 'One of my classmates won a gold – we're so proud of her. She's such an all-rounder. I wish I was half as good at my studies as she is,' and Amy sighed. She was not an academic, though she worked hard and did well.

'Cheer up, Amy,' said Rohan, giving her a hug. 'You're pretty okay.'

'Is she *pretty* or is she *okay*, yaar?' teased Nimal immediately.

'Put a sock in it, yaar,' said Rohan, used to the teasing and not shy about the fact that he thought the world of Amy.

'But I can't *find* my socks just now,' began Nimal. 'Perhaps . . .'

'Whisht now, laddies, whisht,' said Luag with a chuckle. 'And what, pray, does *yaar* mean?'

'It means buddy or mate. But, sir, do tell us about the snow leopards,' begged Nimal eagerly.

'Yes, please, sir,' said the others.

'Okay – but only if you stop calling me *sir* and call me *Luag* – deal?' As the JEACs laughed and agreed, he continued, 'Do you know why they're an endangered species?'

'Partly because of poaching and loss of habitat,' said Anu.

'Why do poachers want them?' asked Gina.

'For their fur and bones,' said Nimal.

'Oh?' said Mich. 'I can imagine people wanting their fur, but why bones?'

'Their bones are used in certain areas of Asia, to make medicine,' said Rohan. 'It's tragic, but almost every species of wildcat, as well as other animals, are poached for their bones. Some people believe that the medicine is excellent treatment for pain and inflammation.'

'And also that it strengthens human muscles, tendons and bones,' said Brian. 'One of the chaps who works here – he's a nasty – told Dad that it would help me to get stronger muscles quickly. As if I would *ever* want to get better by using medicine made from the bones of snow leopards, or any other animals.' He stopped abruptly, striving to control his indignation.

Rohan punched him gently. 'Good for you, Brian. I'd feel exactly the same if I were in your shoes.'

'How can someone who works in a *conservation centre* say such things?' asked Amy, quite appalled.

'Because he's a . . .' began Brian, but his father interrupted him.

'Whisht now, laddie. I know you don't like Beiste, but he's a hard worker. He's different – not what I'd call a *true conservationist*, but he's attempting to learn about conservation and wants to work here.'

The JEACs, horrified that anyone working with wildlife could be so insensitive, agreed with Brian's reaction. However, the older ones realized that some people learnt by experience and could eventually become almost fanatical about conservation.

'We don't, at the moment, know many details about snow leopards,' said Rohan, tactfully bringing the conversation back to the animals. 'Please tell us more.'

'Go ahead, son,' said Luag.

'They're grand creatures,' said Brian. 'One rarely sees them in the wild, since their habitat is harsh and not easily accessible. They live in

Central Asia, in rocky, mountain ranges, usually between 3,350 and 6,700 metres above sea level. It's amazing how their bodies are adapted for living in mountainous regimes – well developed chests, short front legs and long back legs, enabling them to leap easily, from rock to rock, and a long tail to help them balance. Their paws, being so large, are perfect for walking on snow – just like snowshoes.'

'I've seen pictures of a snow leopard covering its face with its tail,' said Amy.

'Yes, the tail is extremely thick and they often wrap it around their bodies and faces for warmth,' said Brian. 'Their fur is well adapted for the cold – long and sort of woolly underneath.'

'Their nasal cavity is enlarged, so they can breathe easily in high altitudes,' added Luag.

'In pictures, they don't appear to be very big, like tigers and lions,' said Anu.

'True – they're medium size and the adults weigh between 30 and 60 kilograms,' said Brian. 'Sometimes their tails are almost as long as their bodies and can be nearly a metre long.'

'Are they white?' asked Gina.

'Some of them are lighter in colour and look white, but mostly their fur is smoky-grey, with a pattern of darker grey, open rosettes. Because of their colouring, they're barely visible against the rocks.'

'What do they eat?' asked Mich.

'Other animals – like sheep, goat, hare, and some of the larger birds like the snow cock and chukor. Also, if they get a chance, they'll attack animals in a herd. Then, naturally, the herders get mad and kill them – so we lose even more snow leopards, unless they're rescued, like ours were.'

'Another reason why they're endangered,' added Luag, 'is because snow leopards don't remain in one area, but cover vast ranges – the influx of people and livestock breaks up their range, and when snow leopards become isolated, they can easily be killed.'

'Do they move in groups – actually, is there a word for a group of snow leopards?' asked Umedh.

'No, to both questions – they're loners,' said Brian. 'The only time you see a few of them together, is when there are cubs – then the females stay with their young until they're independent of her.'

'Tell us about the cubs,' asked Gina.

'They're born just over three months after mating,' said Brian, 'and the female can have between one and five cubs at a time. By the time they're one-and-a-half years old, or sometimes a little older, the cubs become independent and move away from their mother. At birth, they weigh between 300 and 700 grams, and they are adorable. It's fun to watch our cubs, since they're as playful as kittens or pups and make little mock growls.'

'Will your cubs be released when they've grown up?' asked Nimal.

'Not this litter – they'll remain in the captive breeding programme,' said Luag. 'Their mother isn't producing milk – so we bottle-feed them, which, needless to say, Brian loves doing. You can play with them. They recognize Brian, and come rushing to greet him.'

'Aren't they scared of people?' asked Gina.

'They're still pretty young and, since they were born here, they haven't learnt to be scared of us,' said Luag. 'Also, like any cat – they're curious. Nimal, Jay told me that all animals are attracted to you and quite unafraid. I'm looking forward to seeing you with the cubs, and also their mother, who is *not* tame. She's a good mother and wants lots of interaction with her cubs. So we installed a *creep* in the enclosure so that we can get the cubs away from her when we want to feed them.'

'What's a creep?' said Mich.

'A feeding enclosure for young animals, with a long, narrow entrance so the mother can't get through,' explained Luag. 'And here we are.'

He drove into a clearing, brought the vehicle to a halt in front of the largest castle-like building, and everyone scrambled out. Umedh pulled out Brian's wheelchair, set it up, and Nimal placed him in it.

'Welcome to Burns Taigh,' said Luag. 'Come and meet whoever's around, and then we'll visit the cubs.' He led them into a dining room where a young woman was filling a knapsack with bottles of milk.

'Hello, lassie,' said Luag. 'Meet the JEACs – JEACs, this is Doilidh Ennis, a woman of many talents, and my right hand at Burns. She won't mind if you call her Dolly, which is the anglicized pronunciation of her name.'

'And a right welcome it is, JEACs,' said Doilidh merrily, shaking hands with the boys and hugging the girls. She turned to Hunter, who was licking her enthusiastically, 'And have you been a good cu today?' She hugged both dogs, who obviously adored her.

'Does *cu* mean dog, in, er . . . Scottish?' asked Gina.

'It does, lassie,' said Doilidh, 'but the language is called "the Gaelic" by us Scots, and is pronounced *Gal-lik*. Now you try it.'

They did, and though Doilidh, Luag and Brian laughed a little at their accent, they assured them that their pronunciation was excellent.

'Would you JEACs like to help me feed the cubs?' asked Doilidh.

'Yes, please,' they said.

'I'll join you as soon as I've put together Brian's gear,' said Luag. 'Doilidh, Nimal's the boy Jay spoke about – I assume you have the video camera?'

'Surely,' said Doilidh, patting her knapsack. 'Luag, Gavan noticed that Gràinne was limping – her left leg appears to be injured – but she's hiding in the back-most cave; Taran wants to examine her, so could you come as soon as possible?'

'Poor thing,' said Luag. 'I'll go immediately. She's the mother of the cubs, JEACs. Leave the dogs behind – let's not upset Gràinne further.'

Hurriedly shutting the protesting dogs into the house, everyone followed Luag down the path.

'How do you pronounce the snow leopard's name, Brian?' asked Nimal.

'It's *GRAW nya*,' said Brian slowly. The JEACs tried it several times, and finally managed to pronounce it to Brian's satisfaction. 'And the father's name is Niall – he's in a separate enclosure.'

'How do you manage with the snow, Brian?' asked Umedh, as the boy wheeled quickly along the wide pathway.

'The paths to the enclosures are cleared immediately after a snowfall,' said Brian. 'But if it's snowing, I have to go in the side-car of a ski-doo – I haven't tried to ride mine since the accident. Although the controls are in the handle bars, like in a motorcycle, the seat won't work for me, since I can't brace myself without my legs.'

'Hmmm – I'm sure we can fix that,' said Umedh.

'He's a genius – he'll invent something for you, Brian,' said Rohan.

'Seriously?' asked Brian. 'It would be fabulous to ride a ski-doo again. Is it possible, Umedh?'

'Nothing's impossible,' said Umedh cheerfully. 'But I first need to examine a ski-doo, ask you a few questions about your flexibility and strength, and then fiddle around a bit.'

'Wow! That would be great,' said Brian, his face lighting up at the idea of increased mobility. 'But won't it take a long time to fix?'

'Give him a few hours, mate,' said Rohan with a laugh. 'I promise you – he's brilliant.'

'Dry up, yaar,' said Umedh. 'Your chatter is distracting me from logical thought.'

Brian and Rohan laughed, but fell silent obediently.

It took them fifteen minutes along the path before they came to the first buildings where some of the animals were housed. They didn't stop, since Luag and Doilidh were obviously anxious to reach the snow leopards.

'Taran, what's the status?' called Luag ten minutes later. His colleague was standing inside a large enclosure, blow pipe in hand, peering anxiously through the metal slide which separated the main enclosure from a smaller section. Strong mesh surrounded the huge enclosure, which curved out of sight.

'Taran's the vet,' explained Doilidh to the JEACs, as they bunched around, looking eagerly for the snow leopard.

'She's hiding in her cave,' said Taran, coming to the mesh. 'Hello, youngsters – pleased to meet you.' He turned back to Luag and said, 'Gavan tried to coax her out, tempting her with various delicacies, so I could get a shot at her rump, but she's in so much pain that she won't budge an inch and just growls. And you know Gavan usually succeeds when the rest of us fail. It's her left, front leg. We managed to entice the cubs into the creep.'

'Where are Gavan and Beiste?' asked Luag.

'Beiste's gone to get more meat; Gavan's trying to calm Gràinne, but he's not having much luck – can you hear her snarls of rage? Here he comes.'

'Hi, folks,' said a young man, nodding at the youngsters, but turning immediately to Taran and Luag. 'It's no use – she won't even listen to me.'

'Is there anything I can do, Luag?' inquired Nimal. 'I know she's in pain, but if you tell me what might help, I'd be happy to try.'

'This is Nimal, Gavan,' said Luag.

'Oh – perfect timing,' said Gavan, shaking hands with him. 'We've heard lots about you – come with me. Luag, since Beiste's not back, could you manage the partition?'

'Sure,' said Luag.

Gavan led Nimal around the enclosure, and pointed to the heavily barred window set into the back of the cave. Nimal, peering through, could see the snow leopard crouching in a corner, glaring at them.

'This cave is connected to the small enclosure,' explained Gavan. 'To attend to the animals, we lure them into the small enclosure and block the cave entrance. If we can calm her down, she might be tempted out to eat some food, but at the moment, the poor thing's mad with pain.'

'Okay,' said Nimal.

Gavan backed away from the window and Nimal began to speak to Gràinne in the special voice he used for animals. 'Hello, Gràinne, you beautiful creature – you have such a lovely coat, and the most incredible tail. Are you in pain? Is your paw hurting you or is it your leg?'

The big cat snarled angrily, but as the boy continued to speak to her, she gradually quietened down and appeared to be listening to him. A gentle breeze from behind Nimal wafted his scent to Gràinne, and she sniffed curiously and then limped slowly towards the window, wondering who spoke to her so lovingly and smelt so friendly. His voice and scent were mesmerizing.

She listened intently, butting her head against the window, and made a soft sound, deep in her throat. Nimal kept talking, and glanced at Gavan who was grinning with delight.

'Move away slowly, Nimal,' whispered Gavan. As Nimal joined him, Gavan continued, 'Brilliant, laddie – she's calm now. Try calling her from outside the small enclosure.'

'She's gorgeous,' said Nimal, following him quickly.

'Everyone move away from the enclosure and don't make a sound,' said Gavan. He let Nimal into the large enclosure and closed the door.

Nimal called Gràinne a couple of times, and when she poked her head out of the cave, he spoke to her once more. Gràinne hesitated when she saw Taran and Luag, but as Nimal continued to talk to her, and the men didn't move, she decided to ignore them. Focusing completely on Nimal, she limped slowly out of the cave, and went right up to where the boy's hand was against the mesh. The snow leopard first sniffed at his hand and then rubbed her head against it as if she was, in fact, just a big cat.

Luag didn't want to drop the slide, which would make a noise and startle Gràinne, but Taran, although astonished, quickly shot a dart into the snow leopard's rump. In a few minutes, the animal was down, and Nimal, entering the enclosure, spoke to her as she dropped off rapidly.

'Och, now – will ye look at that!' exclaimed Taran, kneeling beside Nimal and giving the boy a friendly punch. 'That's a rare gift you have, laddie.'

The KWCC folk were astounded, and Gavan said, 'There's something extraordinarily special about you that makes a *wild* animal calm down like that. God bless you, laddie.'

'And I've recorded it on the video cam,' said Doilidh, happily.

'Why don't you go and see the cubs,' said Luag, as he and Taran lifted Gràinne onto a stretcher. 'We need to attend to her quickly. Thanks, Nimal.'

'Come along, lads and lassies,' said Doilidh.

They followed her around the enclosure to the creep, which contained a little pond. There were plenty of rocks, in varying sizes, scattered around. There were also some large sticks and a big red ball, which one of the cubs was playing with. He would first push it with his head, and when it rolled away, he would prowl after it and pounce on top of it, looking very surprised when he slid off.

'Oh, they're such darlings,' whispered Anu, as they watched the cubs playing with the ball, the sticks and one another.

'Brian, Nimal and I will enter first,' suggested Doilidh. She took a thick, heavy rug from a hook on the door, and continued, 'I'll spread out the rug and you lift Brian onto it, but you'll have to be fast because the minute the cubs hear the door opening, they'll come charging over to investigate. There are usually three of us to deal with them.'

'I could carry Brian,' said Rohan, 'while Nimal distracts the cubs. They'll go straight for him anyway.'

Doilidh hesitated, but Brian, understanding her concern, said quickly, 'That's a good idea, Rohan. Don't worry, Doilidh, Nimal can handle the cubs.'

'Okay,' said Doilidh. 'Once we've settled Brian, the rest of you come in.'

'Sure, Dolly,' said Umedh. 'Give me your video cam.'

'Here you go,' said Doilidh.

Rohan lifted Brian out of the wheelchair, and the four of them went in, Amy quickly pulling the door closed.

Nimal was in front and, sure enough, the cubs came rushing up to investigate. The boy squatted on the ground, held out his hands and began to speak to them. They came right up to Nimal, making little mewing sounds and rubbing affectionately against him; within seconds, they were all over him.

He was thrilled, and so were the onlookers, who breathed sighs of delight.

'Pick one up, Nimal,' said Brian, comfortably settled on the rug, delighted at the way in which his precious cubs responded to his new friend.

Nimal rose, with one of the cubs in his arms, and walked towards Brian. The other three cubs followed him, and when they saw Brian, they rushed over to the boy, nudging him eagerly for the milk they knew he would give them, making funny little noises of love.

He picked up a cub and held it out to Rohan, saying, 'Sit beside me and hold her. Doilidh will give you a bottle.' He called the others and said, 'Come in – we'll take turns feeding them.'

They trooped in, closing the door carefully behind them. Brian watched his friends pet and feed the cubs, assuring them that he fed them regularly and was happy to let everyone else have a chance.

Doilidh took back the video cam from Umedh, and he took a turn at feeding the cubs.

'Do they have names?' asked Mich.

'Yes,' said Brian. 'You're holding Sorcha; Gina has Catan – who's the smallest; Umedh has Failbhe; Amy has Beathag. Sorcha and Beathag are female.'

'I love them,' said Gina, rubbing her face against Catan's head. 'He's a little heavier than a grown-up cat, but I can easily hold him when I'm seated.'

Once the cubs were satiated with milk, they started playing with the JEACs.

'They seem to bounce instead of run,' laughed Mich, watching the cubs race after the red ball.

'I know what you mean, and I think it's because they actually lope along, in leaps and bounds, when they're older. And the heights they can leap to – see that rock over there – Failbhe can already jump onto it,' said Brian, pointing at the tallest rock.

'But that must be nearly two metres high,' said Amy in amazement.

'Just watch,' said Brian, eager to show off the cubs' skills. 'Nimal, since they'll follow you immediately, could you put the ball on top of the rock?'

Nimal did as requested, and everyone watched in amazement as the cubs leapt to try and reach the ball. Then Failbhe, using his tail as a spring, leapt up onto the rock and knocked the ball down.

'No wonder all their enclosures have roofs,' said Nimal, laughing as the cub sprang off the rock and bounced after the ball.

Doilidh's mobile telephone rang. She answered it and said to the JEACs, 'It's almost noon, and we should get you to Cairns. That was Luag – he's at Burns putting together your gear, Brian. Gavan's with him, and I need to go and assist Taran – Gavan will take you to Cairns.'

'Would you like some help with the cubs, Dolly?' asked Nimal.

'No thanks, love,' said Doilidh. 'Beiste will come and help me.'

'He's too rough with them,' growled Brian.

'Don't worry, laddie,' said Doilidh. 'I'll make sure he handles them gently. Nice to meet you, JEACs – see you again, soon.'

The youngsters left reluctantly, and Doilidh sat on the rug, holding on to the cubs, who were trying to follow the children. The JEACs shut the door carefully and made their way along the path, to the house.

'I have a silly question, Brian,' said Anu. 'Can snow leopards roar? I didn't hear Gràinne roar, even when she was angry.'

Brian laughed and said, 'It's not silly at all, Anu, and the answer is – no, they *can't* roar. But they mew, spit, chuff, moan, yowl, hiss and growl.'

Everyone looked surprised, and Anu said, 'That's most interesting – thanks, Brian.'

Halfway to the house, they met Beiste, and Brian made the introductions.

Beiste was of medium height, broad-shouldered, and strong. He had long, dirty-blond hair and blue eyes set close together. He beamed and shook hands with everyone.

'We're delighted to have you,' he said. The JEACs smiled politely, and he continued, 'It's great for young Brian to have company – poor laddie, stuck in that wheelchair. It's hard to lose your legs and be dependent on others.'

'He does a lot by himself,' began Amy, indignantly, but stopped when Anu nudged her gently.

'Actually, we find him incredibly independent,' said Umedh smoothly, laying a reassuring hand on Brian's shoulder.

'Definitely,' agreed Rohan. 'I'm afraid we can't chat just now – they're waiting for us. Goodbye, see you later.'

'Oh, of course,' said Beiste, slightly taken aback at their defence of Brian. 'It was a pleasure meeting you kids. See you around.'

He walked off, and the JEACs carried on, not saying anything until the man was out of earshot.

'Thanks for stopping me, Anu,' said Amy, squeezing her friend's arm. 'I don't like him – he's too sugary.'

'I didn't take to him, either,' said Rohan. 'But I'm glad you didn't give him a piece of your mind, Amy – it would've been awkward.'

'I guess,' sighed Amy. 'I hate people talking down to others – I *am* trying to control my temper though, and thanks to Anu's warning, I managed it. Sorry, Brian, I didn't mean to make you uncomfortable.'

'You didn't,' said Brian promptly. 'I can't stand the man. I . . .' he trailed off as they reached the house and found Gavan waiting for them in the doorway.

'We'll have a good talk later on,' said Rohan, curious about what Brian had to say.

'Hello, again, JEACs. I didn't mean to be rude, earlier, and ignore you,' said Gavan, ushering them into the house where Hunter and Tumbler greeted them joyfully. Luag was on the telephone.

'No problemo, Gavan,' said Umedh, shaking hands. 'It was a tricky situation with Gràinne – how is she?'

'Poorly, but Taran will fix her up. Thanks to Nimal, we got her tranquillized quickly. And it's Amy, Anu, Rohan, Mich and Gina – right?' They nodded and shook hands. 'Help yourselves to a hot drink,' he added, pointing to a tray. 'I'll deal with a couple of things, grab my jacket, and we'll leave shortly – make yourselves at home.'

They each took a mug of hot chocolate and settled down on the carpet, wrapping their hands gratefully around the warm mugs.

Luag finished his call and joined them, saying, 'And how did you like the cubs?'

He smiled as they told him they would like to play with them all day, and about the way the cubs had responded to Nimal.

'Well, after Gràinne's reaction to him, I'm not surprised,' said Luag. 'I'm afraid I can't come to Cairns as I must assist Taran, so Gavan's going to take you over and show you how to operate the larger ATVs; Brian will brief you on everything else. Any questions?'

'Are there any smaller ski-doos we can use?' asked Umedh.

'Yes, I'll show you how those operate, too,' said Gavan, joining them.

'Dad, Gav, Umedh's going to see if he can adjust a ski-doo so that I can ride it. Is there one he can experiment on?'

'I'll make sure it's safe, Luag,' said Umedh, realizing that he would be anxious about his son but wouldn't want to say so in front of the boy.

'Jay mentioned that you were brilliant at inventing things, Umedh,' said Luag, 'and I'm confident you won't take unnecessary risks. There's a new model of ski-doo – out last month – extremely light, and easy to handle, and there are twelve of them at Cairns. Brian, choose one and Umedh can experiment with it.'

'Wow, Dad!' shouted Brian, his eyes blazing with joy. 'You mean I can have a new one?'

'Yes, son, it'll be an early birthday gift from Gavan and me,' said Luag.

'Thanks, Dad and Gav,' said Brian gratefully.

The others were thrilled for Brian, and Luag was overjoyed to see his son so comfortable with these new friends. It was a turning point for the boy.

'Time to go, folks,' said Gavan, leading the way outside.

Everyone, including the dogs, clambered into the vehicle; waving goodbye to Luag, the group set off.

CHAPTER 5

Sharing Information

They drove along the track, the ATV moving easily along the rough, snow-covered terrain.

'Do you mind if we stop at a few waterholes and break up the ice for the animals?' asked Gavan. 'There are three on the way to Cairns and two close to it. I won't take more than a few minutes at each.'

'Of course not, Gavan,' said Rohan. 'If you've got a couple of extra pickaxes, we'll help.'

'I always have extras, thanks,' said Gavan.

He drove to the first waterhole, and he and the three older boys got out. Gavan showed them what to do, and in a short time they had broken the ice around the edge of the waterhole.

'Are there pickaxes at Cairns?' asked Nimal, after the last waterhole. When Gavan nodded, he continued, 'We'll look after de-icing the waterholes around the area – can we load pickaxes on the ski-doos?'

'Definitely, and that would be wonderful, laddie,' said Gavan. 'But we don't want you working on your holiday.'

'No problemo – it's the least we can do,' said Rohan.

'Thank you,' said Gavan gratefully.

Three minutes later they entered the driveway to Cairns. Set in extensive, snow-covered grounds, the castle was spectacular.

'It's right out of a fairy tale,' said Anu.

'Indeed, it is,' said Gavan, stopping under a high, arched porch. 'When we needed the stables and old carriage houses to be turned into sheds and garages, we asked the architects to keep the old design. I'll let Brian tell you about the ruins which you see over there.'

They climbed out of the ATV, and the dogs immediately ran off to investigate the interesting new smells.

'Is that a boundary wall?' asked Umedh, pointing to the high wall, topped by wiring, which ran behind the castle.

'Yes, and it runs right around KWCC; however, Cairns is the only building which lies close to the boundary.'

'What's on the other side?' asked Nimal.

'Heavy forest,' said Gavan.

'Are these grounds used for anything in particular?' asked Amy.

'It's a camping ground in the summer, and lots of university students who are eager conservationists stay here – sometimes for a month at a time.'

'That's great,' said Rohan. 'I'm so glad we're allowed to stay here on our own.'

'We were assured that you were well behaved,' teased Gavan, 'but I have doubts about Mich and Gina – and, of course, Brian's the worst of the lot. But Burns is only a twenty-minute ski-doo ride from here, so if they misbehave, let us know, and we'll deal with them.'

'I know what *you* were like as a lad, Gav,' retorted Brian, winking at the others. 'His mom told me lots of stories about him – he always fell into *any* water around – whether it was a waterhole, bathtub, stream, ocean or lake, and . . .' He trailed off as the others laughed, and Gavan threatened to extinguish him.

'I've known you since you were born and can tell them thousands of tales about *you*, laddie. Luag's my mother's youngest brother,' explained Gavan.

'So that explains the resemblance,' said Amy, looking at them. 'I almost expected you to call Luag *Dad*.'

'We're like Jay and Umedh – Luag's not much older than I am,' said Gavan, carrying Brian into the building, the others following with the baggage.

'Hunter! Tumbler! Come along or you'll be locked out,' called Nimal.

The excited dogs rushed up and scampered into a large lounge, where the others were gathered.

'We'll put your baggage in the dorms, and then I'll show you how the ski-doos work and which ones you can use,' said Gavan. 'On this floor we have a dining room, the eat-in kitchen which can hold fifteen, a library, four dorms with attached bathrooms, several bedrooms, offices, conference rooms and various other rooms. Upstairs, we have more dorms, bedrooms and conference rooms. In the cellar (which used to be a dungeon) we have a well-equipped gym – all floors are accessible by elevator. The sheds house the ATVs, ski-doos, sleds, snow removal equipment, various tools, et cetera. It can get pretty cold in the winter, so we're fortunate to be able to access the sheds without having to go outside.'

Brian grabbed his crutches, and they followed Gavan out of the room, turning left into a short corridor which ended with a door on either side.

'This one's for the lassies,' said Gavan, entering a room with eight beds, four of which were already made up.

'Oh, it's so pretty!' exclaimed Gina, as she and Mich ran into the room which was painted in shades of green and had murals of wildlife on two walls.

'It'll be fun to sleep here,' said Mich.

They placed their luggage in the room and followed Gavan into the boys' dormitory, which was identical, although it was painted in shades of cream and brown.

The boys left their luggage near the beds, and Gavan led them through the house, pointing out other rooms, until they came to a huge wooden door.

'The remotes to open the doors are generally with the person in charge of the group,' he said, pulling out a key ring with several keys and remote control switches on it and unlocking the door. 'There's an extra set in the kitchen; which of you will be responsible for this lot?'

'I will,' said Rohan with a grin, as the others looked at him expectantly.

'Here you are, lad,' said Gavan. 'The keys to all the doors are on this key ring. We only lock the front door if nobody's going to be using the building, but we always lock the shed doors.' He led the way through the door and into the sheds.

'Man, look at those machines,' said Nimal, gazing at the different models and sizes of snowmobiles and other ATVs.

'We have a variety for different uses,' said Gavan. 'Let's go into the next section – that's where we've put the ski-doos for your use.'

There were several ski-doos, including the brand-new models.

'Brian, which machine do you fancy?' asked Gavan.

'The green and brown one, please, Gav – it's beautiful,' said Brian.

'Good choice, mate. Umedh, we have a small, fully equipped workshop through the door on your left – and it's well heated.'

'I can't wait to try it out once Umedh fixes it,' said Brian ecstatically, as the older boys pushed the machine into the workshop.

'And that's my first project,' said Umedh.

'Now, clean out your lugs, lads and lassies,' said Gavan, opening the door of the shed.

'Do *lugs* mean ears?' asked Gina.

'Aye, lassie,' grinned Gavan.

He showed them how to use the machines, and they learnt quickly, skimming around the grounds gleefully. There were machines, identical to Brian's, for Gina and Mich. Anu and Amy had slightly larger ski-doos, which could seat an extra person, while the three older boys had even larger machines which could take two extra passengers. Once they had mastered their machines, Gavan showed the boys how to drive the nine-passenger snow trac. Each boy took a turn on his own, and Gavan was pleased to see how easily each one handled the vehicle.

'This is great,' said Rohan, parking the snow trac in the shed, and climbing out. 'It's perfect if we all want to go out together, without using the ski-doos, and there's room for the wheelchair, food, luggage and the dogs.'

'Yes, and it's particularly useful if there's a blizzard,' said Gavan. 'Brian, don't forget to warn them about frostbite – we don't want Gina and Mich to lose their noses.'

'What'll happen to my nose?' asked Gina.

'If it gets frozen, it may fall off,' teased Brian. 'Well, not really,' he added hastily, as Gina anxiously felt her nose to see if it was about to fall off. 'Only, it's a good idea to wear a balaclava if it's freezing cold.'

'What's a . . . baka . . . bela . . . I mean, what you said?' asked Gina.

'It's a cover for your head, face and neck, Gina – and it's generally knitted and soft,' explained Mich. 'It's called a *bala-clava*, and Amy and I had to wear them once when we went to Alaska. It keeps your face warm and cosy.'

'Oh, good – I don't want my nose to fall off,' said Gina, quite relieved.

'And we've got lots of balaclavas, gloves, mittens, extra sweaters, coats and boots,' said Gavan. 'Just dress warmly, and you won't get frostbite.'

'What about the dogs, Gavan?' asked Nimal.

'We have several carriers which are like bubbles, completely enclosed, to protect an animal from the wind and cold, with a few small holes at the top, for air. These can be strapped onto the ski-doos and are perfectly safe. We've taken Tumbler, and some of the animals from the petting zoo, in them. I'm sure Hunter will enjoy going in one – you can check them out later.'

'Cool,' said Anu. 'I had this vision of Hunter wearing snowshoes or trying to ski – like Snoopy does in some of the comic strips. Though Hunter's such a smart chap that I'm sure he'd quickly learn how to use those, too.'

Hunter sat down in front of her, waved one paw, and barked.

'He agrees,' said Anu, hugging the dog. 'And, yes, Tumbler, I'm positive you can teach Hunter how to ride a ski-doo,' she laughed, as Tumbler bounced over for his share of hugs.

'Right. I've got to get back to Burns, and I'm sure you lot must be hungry,' said Gavan. 'We'll go out through the shed doors, since you're coated and booted.'

Rohan closed the door of the shed with the remote control, and they returned to Gavan's ATV.

'I nearly forgot,' said Gavan, as he climbed into the ATV, 'the walkie-talkies are in the lounge, Brian, in the cupboard under the TV. Any questions?'

'None, thanks, Gavan, and I'm sure Brian can answer any which crop up,' said Rohan.

'Thanks for everything, Gavan,' said the JEACs.

'Have fun,' said Gavan, and drove off; the others waved till he was out of sight and then went inside.

'Food?' said Amy.

'Yes!' shouted the group hungrily, and they made their way to the cosy kitchen.

Amy found a note from Ceana saying that their first meal was on the cooker, and between her and Anu, they quickly dished it out, while Gina and Mich fed the dogs. The boys set the table, and soon everyone was tucking into a delicious stew with warm rolls and butter.

Brian, who had lost his shyness, joined in the joking and teasing and, in a lull in the conversation, said, 'Please tell me about yourselves. You know about me, and I'm sure Jay told you how I lost my legs. Also, I'd like to hear about the JEACs.'

'I don't know if you can handle the gory details, Brian,' said Amy, 'but it's a fair question, so we'll start with the youngest – and that's you, Mich – age, height, hobbies, what you want to be when you grow up, and how many JEACs you recruited last term at school, hon.'

Mich looked a little shy, but said quickly. 'I'm Amy's sister and I'm ten; I'm four foot ten and a half inches tall; I love drawing cartoons and want to work with Disney when I grow up. I like gym, swimming, winter sports, singing and reading. It's great being a JEAC, and last term I recruited eight girls. I'm not too good at school work,' she added humbly, 'but I'm trying a little harder than when I was a kid.'

'Excellent, Mich,' said Anu, nodding encouragingly at the girl who was the shyest of the group. 'And her cartoons are *brilliant*, Brian. You'll see some when we sing our JEACs' theme song, along with the slide show. Gina?'

'I'm Rohan, Nimal and Anu's sister,' said Gina. 'I'm also ten; not so good at studies either, but I *love* reading. I'm four foot eight inches tall; I adore music and singing. I also like gym and swimming, and am longing to learn how to skate, ski and snowshoe. I recruited twelve girls, and two of my male cousins want me to tell them about our group when we return home. When I grow up, I want to play music and compose tunes and songs.'

'As you know, she already composes her own tunes and words,' added Nimal. 'She and Mich are a great team, and we old fogies just obey their orders – we don't have any choice because, as you can tell, they're a bossy pair.'

'Now, girls,' said Rohan, laughingly restraining them when they grabbed bread rolls and threatened to throw them at Nimal. 'At least *pretend* that you have some manners – Brian must be appalled.'

'I'm not,' grinned Brian, who loved the friendly badinage that went on among the group. 'I'm only surprised that Nimal isn't hiding under the table.'

'The only reason I'm not running for my life is because they love their food too much to throw it at me,' grinned Nimal.

'You're begging for it, yaar,' muttered Umedh. 'Beware retribution after the meal.'

Gina and Mich were whispering to each other. They chuckled and then looked angelically at Nimal.

'Peace, infants,' said Nimal, holding up his hand and making the peace sign.

The youngsters just smiled. Nimal shot a terrified look at them and urged Anu to speak quickly.

'I'm fourteen, and five foot four inches tall; I adore reading and writing; I'm okay at school work and, when I grow up, I'm going to be an author. I love being a JEAC, and last term I recruited eight girls.'

'Actually, Brian, she's already an author,' said Amy, smiling affectionately at her friend. 'Her first book, *Peacock Feathers*, will be published next year. It's the true story of an adventure the Patels had.'

'She's also working on her second book, *The Dolphin Heptad*,' continued Umedh. 'That's about another adventure the Patels and Larkins had when they went to Brisbane, Australia.'

'There was a group of seven dolphins at the Aquatic Fantasia Conservation and Dolphin Bay, which Uncle Jack – Amy and Mich's uncle – started last year,' added Nimal.

'You're so lucky to have had two adventures,' said Brian. 'I would love to be part of an adventure and have Anu write about it.'

'Actually, so far we've had three adventures,' said Rohan. 'Our last one was in Sri Lanka, and Umedh joined us for the relocation of the elephants, but Anu hasn't had time to write that story yet. Have you even thought about it, Anu?'

'Well . . .' said Anu, embarrassed at being the focus of attention, 'I've thought of a title – it's called *An Elephant Never Forgets* – but there's not enough time for my writing.'

'True, sis,' said Rohan. 'And are you going to write a story about whether snow leopards can roar or not?'

'I don't know,' said Anu, chuckling so infectiously that it set the others off. 'The story's just beginning – and Brian, you'll be in it, too.'

'I can't wait,' grinned Brian. 'Please may I have an autographed set of your books, Anu?'

'Absolutely. Nimal, you're on,' said Anu.

'I'll be fifteen in January; I'm five foot nine and a half inches tall, and Rohan, Anu and Gina, when I think of it, are *actually* my cousins – our fathers are brothers, and I've lived with them my whole life, since my parents travel a lot.'

'I keep forgetting you're our *cousin*, Nimal,' said Gina; Rohan and Anu nodded in agreement.

'Thanks, kiddo,' said Nimal, grinning affectionately at her. He continued, 'As you know, I have a passion for animals. I'm going to be a conservationist, working mainly with dolphins and other endangered species, and although I'm not an academic, I'm doing my best to get good grades so that I qualify for university and further studies. I'm eager to try out winter sports, and last term I recruited fifteen boys.'

'I warn you, Brian,' said Amy, 'when it comes to getting into trouble at school or, in fact, anywhere he goes, and specializing in playing the most unbelievable tricks, there's no one to beat Nimal. But the spell he weaves on any animal, making them long to cuddle in his arms, is out of this world.'

'I know. How I *wish* I could make animals calm down and come to me, the way you did with Gràinne, Nimal,' said Brian. 'And, yes, Amy, he has a very naughty look in his eyes – I wish you'd tell me about some of the tricks you've played, Nimal.'

'I'm a saint,' said Nimal, innocently. 'Ask my teachers – they'll assure you that I'm quite, er . . . unusual.'

'You mean absolutely incorrigible, reprehensible and impossible, not to mention, "If he would *only* put as much time into *behaving properly* in the classroom as he does in *causing trouble*",' quoted Rohan, cheerfully. 'At least, that's what his last report card said.'

'Oh, what tricks have you played in school?' begged Brian.

'We'll tell you all about them, Brian,' laughed Anu. 'Just give us time – they're innumerable, and it would take hours – perhaps one evening, as we sit around a fire for warmth, because, I assure you, some of them will make your blood run cold.'

Everyone burst out laughing as Nimal pretended to look indignant and retorted quickly, 'Let's move on to the old folk now, before Anu's imagination runs away with her, and we have a fifth book in the making.'

'Okay, Nimal; I'll be my usual, kind self and protect you from harassment,' smiled Amy.

'May I remind you, my *kind* Amy, in case your senility has affected your memory, that *you* were the one who started the horrible rumours about me just now?'

'Did I, indeed? It must be old age,' said Amy smoothly. 'Brian, I'm sixteen, and five foot five inches tall. I'm not brill at academic studies but, like Nimal, I'm studying harder than I was a year ago – in fact, I just finished major exams and am awaiting results. I'm crazy about conservation and want to become a psychologist – perhaps specializing in dolphin therapy. I love water and winter sports and recruited five girls last term.'

'She forgot to mention that she won the ski-jump and skiing competitions this year,' added Rohan. 'Inter-school competitions, at that.'

Amy blushed but gave Rohan a warm look, while Nimal and Umedh winked at each other. 'Now you, Umedh,' she said.

'I'm a couple of days older than Amy,' said Umedh, 'five foot, ten and a half inches tall and, thank goodness, I am not related to the Patels – I could handle having Anu and Gina in my family, but the boys . . .' he shook his head mockingly. 'I enjoy studying and want to do computer engineering; like Amy, I'm awaiting exam results. Since I also love inventing things, hopefully I'll be able to work with conservation centres – not only programming for their special needs, but also inventing things to assist in the protection and conservation of endangered species. I recruited four chaps.'

'Amazing,' said Brian. He added, 'If you don't mind my asking, Umedh, is it difficult for you to do things with only one eye?'

'Of course I don't mind – I was born with only my left eye, so I've had plenty of time to get used to it. It doesn't stop me from doing anything I want to, and over the years I've learnt how to deal with the challenge of having limited viewing ability.'

'Don't people laugh at you, or pity you?' asked Brian.

'Sometimes,' said Umedh, with empathy. 'You know, I believe people like that are generally ignorant or embarrassed, and I don't let them affect me. Only I can decide how I feel, and I find that when I don't let my disability bother *me*, it doesn't bother others. My friends learn how to work around my closed eye, and don't show me things on my right side, while pictures of me are taken only from the left.'

'True, and he always manages to look at least slightly handsome when you take his picture from the correct side,' Rohan teased.

'He's *very* handsome, no matter which side you take his picture from,' said Gina immediately, frowning at her brother.

'Amy showed some girl friends a picture of him, and they all want to meet him,' added Mich.

'Thank you, angels,' said Umedh. 'What would I do without you to stand up for me when Rohan and Nimal insult me constantly? You see, Brian? I have two beautiful girls who think I'm okay.'

'You're more than just okay, Umedh,' said Anu, warmly. 'You're a great buddy and, frankly, I can't imagine our group without you.'

Brian caught Nimal winking slyly at Amy, and was surprised that none of the older ones made any jokes. However, before he could inquire further, Umedh laughed and said, 'You're making me blush, Anu, but muchas gracias. Now, Rohan, you're the oldest, and getting older by the second.'

'Thanks, yaar,' grinned Rohan. 'I'm a whole four days older than Umedh, six feet tall, and I'm going to be a detective – I love solving mysteries. Like Amy and Umedh, I'm awaiting the results of my exams. I recruited only three new JEACs last term – studies and karate were demanding.'

'He forgot to mention that he's absolutely *brill* at his studies – much better than the rest of us,' said Amy. She added, as Rohan turned red, 'Well, yaar, you never give yourself any credit, and we're so proud that you've won the academic medal at your school for the past six years – and that's a record.'

Rohan quickly changed the topic saying, 'Right, enough about us. Brian, what are *you* interested in doing when you grow up?'

'I want to be a zoo architect and travel around the world, working with zoos and breeding programmes, especially designing housing for endangered species,' said Brian. He looked a bit hesitant and added slowly, 'I've *always* wanted to do that, ever since I read some of Gerald Durrell's books on zoos and the importance of the right habitat for breeding programmes, but I don't know if it's possible now.'

'Why not – it's a specialized field,' said Anu.

The others agreed vociferously, and Brian, encouraged by their support, said, 'I used to carry a sketch book around, and whenever I got an idea as to how habitats could be improved, I would immediately put it down in a drawing. But now, because I'm either in a wheelchair or on crutches, it's not been possible,' said Brian.

'I'm positive Umedh can design something to help you use your sketch book whether you're in a wheelchair or on crutches,' said Rohan. 'What do you say, yaar?'

'No problemo. Off the top of my head, I would think something to do with a foldable tripod and a flat top, where the crutches are concerned, and a foldable table top for the wheelchair should do the trick,' said Umedh, smiling at Brian. 'I'll think it through.'

'You're all so kind,' said Brian, looking rather overwhelmed.

'I don't know about that, Brian,' said Anu quickly. 'When it comes to Nimal, I doubt you'll think he's *kind* when he's played a few tricks on you. Some years ago, we were playing outside – the three of us, Gina was an infant – and it was an extremely hot summer. I was beginning to turn red from the heat and told the boys that I needed to cool off – Mum had warned us about sunstroke. Nimal decided to be helpful and, when questioned after the event, assured everyone that he was *just being kind* and trying to make me feel cool when he pushed me into a muddy waterhole.'

The JEACs shouted with laughter, and Brian said, wiping away tears of mirth, 'Was it a long time ago?'

'He was six,' said Anu, 'and I'm a few months younger than him – but the waterhole was deep and I was only just learning to swim. Fortunately, Peter, a good friend of ours, was passing by and fished me out.'

'Then what happened,' asked Brian.

'I bawled my head off – more from fright than injury, though I'd swallowed a couple of mouthfuls of muddy water before Peter saved me. Rohan and Nimal couldn't see what the fuss was about. "He was only trying to make her feel less hot, Mum," explained Rohan, taking Nimal's side as usual.'

'Please don't be *kind* to me, Nimal,' teased Amy.

'I can do without your kindness, too, Nimal,' laughed Brian.

He attempted to stop laughing but failed as Nimal said cheerfully, 'I was just a kid at that time – I'm much better now.'

'I'm *so* glad I met you,' said Brian. 'I haven't laughed so much in months. You're a talented group, too.'

'We're just regular people, Brian,' said Anu. 'I guess, other than the fact that we're book-a-holics and JEACs, we each have a special talent – and, fortunately, our faults keep us humble. We believe that *everyone* has a talent – whether it's drawing, sports, academics, kindness, sensitivity to others, or being able to keep a room tidy.' The others laughed, and Anu continued with a grin, 'That's my greatest failing – any room I use takes on the appearance of a disaster zone. I start off well, and then . . . pure chaos.'

When they stopped chuckling at her droll expression of sorrow, Rohan turned to Brian and said, 'Please tell us about the snow leopards and why you dislike Beiste so much.'

'Hang on a second,' said Amy. 'Doesn't anyone want dessert?'

'Yes,' chorused everyone, and bustled around.

'Now that we've got heaping plates of delicious apple crumble and ice cream, tell us what happened, Brian,' said Rohan.

'What did Jay say?' asked Brian.

'That you were the best person to ask for details. We know . . .' Rohan ticked off the points on his fingers.

'Three weeks ago, on the morning after the event to celebrate the birth of four more snow leopards, the three older cubs and their parents were missing;

'The cops couldn't find any clues – hundreds of people had been milling around;

'Ten days ago, Craig, at the Edinburgh airport, became suspicious, and Huang, whose suitcase contained the pelts and bones of a male snow leopard and cub, was arrested on his way to China; he only admitted to purchasing the pelts from someone in Hackney;

'Airport officials, Craig and Brenda, kept a lookout for more animal skins, and the next day, Rizana, on her way to India, was caught with the remaining pelts and bones from the female and two cubs;

'The police tricked her into believing Huang had betrayed her, and she admitted that a man named Zulfikar had given her the packed bag – she didn't know much more, but the cops are making inquiries about Zulfikar; and that's it,' concluded Rohan.

'Okay, I'll fill you in, but a lot of it's guess-work,' said Brian.

The others nodded, and Rohan pulled out a notebook.

'Breeding snow leopards in captivity was a major achievement,' began Brian, 'and, since we didn't do anything when the first litter were born, we wanted to celebrate with the conservation community at large, at the birth of the second litter. A home movie of the birthing, good food, a couple of talks by Dad and Taran, and trips to see the cubs and their mother were planned. The focus was on the new cubs, so nobody paid much attention to the older cubs, even though they were only nine months old. By the way, jump in with questions as I go along – it'll help me to give you all the facts.'

'Thanks,' said Rohan. 'Quick question – where were the older cubs housed?'

'If you go past Gràinne's enclosure, down the path for about twenty minutes, and turn left, that's where the older cubs and their mother were housed. The father was in the next enclosure – a little further along.'

'Okay, carry on,' said Rohan, making a note.

'The celebration was at Ruthven from 6 p.m. to past midnight. The animals had been fed, so there was no reason to check on the older cubs. The newborns were fed their milk, and people were fascinated at the way they had learnt to drink out of the bottles. There were people everywhere, but Ruthven is fairly far away from Burns, so it was only staff or volunteers, in ATVs, who took visitors back and forth. All the staff attended the event.

'A small incident occurred, and I'm mentioning it because after everything happened, I wondered if it was connected. I was at Ruthven with my friends Cormag and Eadan, on a small balcony, when I saw Beiste, Clyde, and a woman I didn't know, talking in the rose garden – I was surprised, and gasped. The chaps wanted to know why I was shocked, and I explained that everyone at KWCC knew that Beiste and Clyde (one of the rangers) avoided each other, so it was really weird seeing them together.'

'How long have Beiste and Clyde been at KWCC?' asked Amy.

'Beiste's been here just over a year, and Clyde arrived a few months later.'

'Did they know each other previously?' asked Nimal.

'Not to our knowledge,' said Brian. 'Anyway, we were curious, so when they began moving out of the garden, since there were trees which would block our view, Eadan shinned down a drainpipe, to keep an eye on them. Cormag and I rushed downstairs and out through a side entrance, but by the time we reached the rose garden, nobody was in sight.'

'Where was Eadan?' asked Nimal.

'He turned up a bit later, looking disappointed. He said that Clyde went towards Knox. He followed Beiste and the woman, who went towards the helipads and took the path to Burns, but they stopped and began to talk. Eadan, slipping between the trees, crept as close as possible and heard Beiste say, "But Moire, suppose we're caught?" and the woman said, "Stop worrying – Xian and Soofi have planned everything . . ." She stopped when some others came up the path from Burns. They returned to Ruthven and went inside.'

'What next?' asked Anu.

'It didn't make sense, and Eadan wasn't sure if he'd heard the names correctly; we went back inside and looked for Beiste and Moire.

Beiste was talking to Dad, and we heard him say he'd relieve Gav for a few hours – he went off and we didn't see him again that evening; Moire wasn't around. We searched the rooms, and figured she must have left KWCC.'

'But how could she leave?' asked Gina. 'I thought you had to take a helicopter.'

'True, Gina,' said Brian, 'but the choppers were picking up and dropping people off every half hour – she could easily have left.'

'What next?' asked Umedh.

'Nothing else unusual occurred, so we concluded it was a weird coincidence and returned to enjoy the party, and by midnight everyone had left. The next morning Gav rushed into Burns, shouting that the older cubs and their parents were missing. Dad, Taran, Doilidh, Beiste and I were there, and we gaped at Gav, before rushing off to the enclosures – but there was no trace of them. Everyone assisted in the search, and the police were called in.'

'What about fingerprints on the gates,' asked Rohan.

'Only staff fingerprints. The police stayed for a week, speaking to everyone and checking everything. Inspector Jeffries finally concluded that we'd have to wait for further developments, and suggested we keep our eyes open. Our rangers searched diligently – absolutely nothing was discovered.'

'They must have been removed that same night,' said Umedh.

'Agreed,' said Rohan. 'Choppers were going back and forth all evening, so what was to prevent crooks taking off in a chopper *with* the snow leopards? Nobody would have wondered why a chopper was leaving.'

'Golly! We didn't think of that,' said Brian, excitedly.

'What did you do next?' asked Amy.

'I wasn't happy sitting around and waiting, so I called Cormag – he wants to be a detective, too, Rohan – and updated him. I asked if they could come over on Friday, for the weekend, which was a common occurrence.'

'Carry on,' said Rohan.

'On Friday evening I met the chaps at Ruthven and gave them details. They were furious, agreed that there was something bizarre going on, and we puzzled over it most of the night – we didn't think of crooks taking our snow leopards in a chopper that very evening. The next morning Cormag suggested that the snow leopards must have been tranquillized or killed *before* they were taken out of their enclosures, since none of them were tame. It made sense and we concluded that they were *tranquillized* since the police found no traces of blood in the enclosures. So we decided to search for tranquillizer darts and a gun.'

'Good thinking, yaar,' said Rohan.

'We went to the enclosures at Burns. There wasn't any snow on the ground, and Cormag suggested that darts and a gun would most likely be stuffed down a rabbit hole or a hole in a tree. Since we agreed that crooks would keep off the main trails, we searched the smaller ones, and examined every trail leading to the Burns helipad – no luck. Cormag suggested we check other trails; ten minutes along a trail leading to Cairns, he gave a low whistle – and a few seconds later, joined Eadan and me. He was carrying a bag which he emptied onto my lap – and out fell six *used* tranquillizer darts and two pairs of transparent gloves – the darts were not the kind we use.'

'Gosh!' gasped Mich and Gina.

'Cormag warned us not to touch anything – in case of fingerprints.'

'Good man,' said Rohan.

'Using his handkerchief, he put everything back into the bag, and hid it in the pocket of my wheelchair. We checked the area thoroughly – going right up to Cairns, looking for tranquillizer guns, but found nothing more. It was nearly 2:30 p.m. so we returned to Ruthven, locked the door to our room, and emptied the bag once more. Cormag got out his fingerprinting kit, which he had brought along, and set to work – but we found nothing.'

'They used the gloves,' commented Nimal.

'True,' said Brian. 'After further discussion, we decided to speak to Dan, who called the police. The inspector examined our find and asked us what seemed like a million questions; taking turns, we told him everything. He asked Dan to check that none of our darts were missing – none were. Finally, the inspector took our bag and, since it was time for Cormag and Eadan to go home, offered to drop them off. And that was that. I haven't spoken to the chaps since then because they're studying for exams; and then there was the excitement about arresting Huang and Rizana.'

'Did you tell anyone about the incident at the celebration?' said Rohan.

'Beiste, Clyde and Moire?' Rohan nodded. 'No, we were so upset and angry that we clean forgot about them.'

Rohan said quietly, 'Brian, could this be connected with that trio?'

'But Clyde and Beiste are *staff* . . .' Brian trailed off, looking shocked.

'Sorry, yaar,' apologized Rohan, 'but in light of your tale, it's evident that the incidents which occurred before the disappearance of the snow leopards are a bit weird. May I tell you what I think?'

'Please,' said Brian. 'I barely come in contact with Clyde, and I dislike Beiste, but I can't imagine anyone living here being so cruel.'

'We understand, Brian,' said Nimal. 'Rohan?'

'Right, and JEACs, jump in with questions and ideas. Brian, firstly, the fact that Clyde and Beiste – we'll code name them *CAB* in case others are around when we mention them – were hanging out together aroused your curiosity sufficiently for you and your mates to keep an eye on them.'

'And Eadan overheard the name "Soofi",' said Anu. 'Could it possibly have been *Zulfi* – short for Zulfikar?'

'Good point, sis,' said Rohan. 'We'll check with Eadan.'

'I'll call him on the eighteenth – the day after tomorrow; their exams are over that morning,' said Brian.

'Point two: CAB and Moire disappeared from the party and weren't seen again that night. Choppers were taking off frequently – could they not have tranquillized the snow leopards, loaded them onto a chopper, and flown off?'

The others gasped in shock.

'What! With hundreds of people milling around?' said Amy.

'The crowds were at Ruthven; since the new cubs were the focus – nobody would have approached the other enclosures at Burns. CAB and Moire could have used other trails, tranquillized the snow leopards, taken them to the Burns helipad and loaded them into an animal chopper. They could have hidden the darts later on.'

'How could three people carry two adult snow leopards and three cubs?' asked Mich.

'By putting them into cages on a gurney,' said Nimal. 'Two people could lift an adult snow leopard, and one man could easily carry three cubs.'

'Did you see any gurney tracks on any of the trails?' asked Umedh.

'We didn't think of that,' admitted Brian.

'No problemo. You found darts – but no tranquillizer gun and, I assume, CAB have guns,' said Rohan.

'True,' said Brian. 'But . . . they couldn't have flown the chopper at Burns. Osgar, he's the pilot and one of our rangers, said he would put the chopper into the shed since we wouldn't need it, and I'm sure he keeps the keys.'

'Brian, would you trust Osgar?' asked Anu.

'With my life,' said Brian immediately. 'He's been with KWCC forever – all the animals, including Tumbler, love him, and Tumbler can't stand Beiste. Osgar would *never* harm any creature.'

'That rules him out – animal instinct is rarely wrong,' said Anu. 'But then, the crooks' chopper must have landed somewhere near Burns, and it could have been an animal chopper so that the gurneys could be wheeled in.'

'It would be easy enough, with choppers coming and going,' said Rohan. 'And, if I'm not mistaken, you can't see Burns from Ruthven, and the helipad is off the main trail between Ruthven and Burns, right, Brian?'

'Yes – but neither Beiste nor Clyde knows how to fly a chopper.'

'Xian and Zulfikar's roles are unknown; they could be leaders, or standing by to fly over when called, to collect the snow leopards and Moire,' said Rohan. 'CAB couldn't afford to be missing from KWCC that night.'

'That makes sense,' said Umedh. 'And when they reached their destination, they killed the poor snow leopards.'

'But . . . that's terrible,' said Amy. 'It's so . . . *calculating*.'

'If we're right about CAB, this plot was either set up prior to their arrival at KWCC, or they were bribed *after* they'd started here,' said Rohan.

He looked at the others, who were digesting the information, and continued, 'Most of this is pure conjecture – we need facts and proof. Let's do something outside while there's still daylight. Over dinner we'll discuss ideas as to how we can keep an eye on CAB, talk to some of the others who know them, et cetera. So, what shall we do?'

'Let's go tobogganing, please, Rohan,' begged Mich and Gina.

'Sounds like fun, but I'm going to look at the ski-doo,' said Umedh, 'and, Brian, it'll be helpful if you were around.'

'Of course, Umedh,' said Brian. 'Nimal, please take Tumbler with you – he loves tobogganing.'

'Okay,' said Nimal, picking up Tumbler. 'I'll put Hunter and him in a toboggan with me – that should be exciting. Let's go, people.'

'Amy – I'll help Umedh,' said Rohan, as they all headed for the sheds.

She nodded her approval.

CHAPTER 6

The Ingenious Mr. Q!

'Thanks, yaar – two heads are better than one – let's take a dekko,' said Umedh, as the three of them entered the workshop.

He studied the machine carefully, referred to the manual, and asked Brian several questions about his mobility. Brian gave details, giving Umedh and Rohan a clear understanding of his disability. Then Rohan and Brian watched silently while Umedh spent the next few minutes in intense contemplation of the ski-doo, after which he plundered the storage room, next to the workshop, returning with a bucket seat, a cushion and various other items. After further examination of the machine, Umedh looked at Brian and grinned.

'Piece of cake,' he said, and Brian beamed.

Rohan assisted as requested, and in a short time the original seat was replaced by the bucket seat and cushion, while a strap was used as a seat belt. Two pieces of fibre glass were fitted to the sides, and one side opened like a door; Velcro straps were fixed inside the ski-doo, to hold Brian's crutches securely.

Brian, watching in stunned silence, could hardly believe it when Umedh finally pronounced himself satisfied.

'Fortunately, I only had to adjust the hardware,' said Umedh. 'Brian, may I put you in the seat?' Brian nodded, and Umedh placed him in the machine. Rohan had already strapped the crutches into place.

Brian settled into the bucket seat easily, fastened his seat belt, and tried to thank Umedh. But his voice failed, and he could only look up at the boy, eyes filled with a gratitude too deep for words.

Umedh and Rohan high-fived him, and asked him if anything needed to be adjusted.

'We'll test it outside,' said Umedh, 'but let's first ensure you're comfortable and can get in and out on your own.'

'I'm sure I can, Umedh,' said Brian, finding his voice as he reached for his crutches. Smiling proudly, he climbed out of the ski-doo.

'You're a *genius*, yaar,' said Rohan, punching his friend in the arm.

'No two ways about it, Umedh,' said Brian. 'You're a marvel, and you spent less than an hour and a half on it.'

'Enough! My head's beginning to swell,' grinned Umedh. Brian's radiant face was thanks enough.

'Let's test it,' said Rohan.

Umedh and Rohan pushed the ski-doo outside. Brian climbed on, started the machine, and with Umedh and Rohan on either side, began moving slowly.

'Do you feel you have complete control of the machine, and are you comfortable?' asked Umedh, as Brian came to a halt after a few metres.

'It's awesome!' said Brian. 'I'm perfectly balanced, and I'm going to speed up a little. I'll be okay – I promise I won't do anything foolish; but you should move back or you'll get covered in snow.'

The boys nodded, and Brian started up again, going slowly at first and gradually speeding up until he was zooming around the grounds, yelling with excitement. Rohan and Umedh cheered him on, and after he had circled the grounds twice, he came to a neat halt near the porch, his face glowing with joy.

As the older boys watched with deep satisfaction, Brian pulled out his crutches, emerged carefully from the machine, and hopped over to them.

Their yells had brought the other JEACs and dogs to the top of the hill, and when they saw Brian in the ski-doo, they raced down.

'Wow! Let's see you ride, Brian,' said Nimal, picking up Tumbler, who was trying to jump into the ski-doo, and putting him safely into the bubble.

Brian got into the ski-doo again, started the machine and sped off, while Hunter raced beside him. The others cheered, and Anu took some great pictures. When Brian came to a halt, the others gathered around, asking him what Umedh had done, and his face glowed as he explained everything.

Led by Brian, Umedh was given a hearty cheer. As they trooped towards the sheds to put away the toboggans, Rohan's watch alarm beeped.

'I set it for 5 p.m. because we need to de-ice the waterholes,' said Rohan.

'Do we take a snow trac?' asked Amy.

'Well, since Brian's comfortable in the ski-doo and knows his way around, why don't we ride?'

'Brilliant!' agreed everyone, going into the shed.

They loaded the ski-doos with the required tools; Hunter was strapped into the bubble on Nimal's ski-doo and Tumbler rode with Brian.

'All set?' said Rohan.

'Ready and raring to go, yaar,' said Nimal, revving up his ski-doo. Hunter and Tumbler barked excitedly.

They quickly de-iced the waterholes and returned to Cairns. The ski-doos were parked and cleaned before the JEACs made their way back to the house.

'I don't know about any of you,' began Nimal, 'but I'm st. . .'

'*Starving!*' yelled Brian, Mich and Gina in unison.

Nimal looked at them in surprise. 'Really? I was going to say that I was star-*ting* to get a feel of KWCC and where things were,' he said mildly, 'but mes amis, if you're hungry, I guess we'd better feed you.'

'We know you meant *starving*, Nimal. Don't try and pull the wool over our eyes,' said Gina.

Amy chuckled, 'Come on – let's see what's for dinner.' She and Anu led the way to the kitchen.

'How does roast chicken, potatoes, veggies and rolls, sound, folks?' asked Amy. 'It'll only take 45 minutes – and there's pudding for dessert.'

'Wonderful, Amy. What do you want us to do?' said Rohan.

'Anu and I can manage, thanks,' said Amy, who loved cooking. 'Mich and Gina, please lay the table; the rest of you can disappear and return at seven – you can do the dishes afterwards.'

'Certainly, ma'am,' said Nimal, bowing obsequiously, until his nose touched his knees. 'And if you decide that you can't bear to be parted from, er . . . shall we say . . . *some* of us, for too long, please join us.'

'Buzz off, wretch,' said Amy.

'Come away, man, before she throws something at you,' said Umedh, propelling him out of the door.

'We'll be in the lounge,' said Rohan, following with Brian who had settled into his wheelchair. 'Call Burns, Brian, and see if they want us to do anything else; I'll call Ruthven, just in case the APs are wondering how we're doing.'

Brian spoke with Gavan who answered the phone.

'There must be a reason you didn't tell him about your ski-doo,' said Rohan, when Brian hung up without asking to speak to his father.

Brian grinned. 'Absolutely! Could we ride our ski-doos there first thing in the morning and surprise them?'

Laughingly, the boys agreed.

'I won't say anything when I speak to Ruthven,' promised Rohan, dialling the number. 'Hi, Dan. We're fine, thanks. We've been busy talking, tobogganing, de-icing waterholes, and getting to know Brian.' He listened for a moment and then said, 'We'd love to have breakfast with you. Also, could I speak to the mater for a moment? Thanks – see you tomorrow.'

After speaking to his mother, he hung up and said, 'Right, what shall we do now?'

'Please tell me about the JEACs,' said Brian.

'Sure, and we'll teach you the theme song, now that Mich and Gina are here to help with the singing. Girls, do you have the words and cartoons handy?' said Rohan.

'We'll get copies and the DVD,' said Gina, who had bounced into the lounge with Mich. They dashed off to their dormitories.

'Such energy,' sighed Nimal. 'Oh, to be young again.'

'Puir laddie, 'tis old ye are the noo, and it's all of fourrrteen thou art,' teased Brian in the dialect used in certain parts of the country.

'I say, that's great, Brian,' said Umedh, grinning, while the others burst out laughing. 'Does "the noo" mean at *the moment*?'

'More or less,' grinned Brian.

'Can you imagine what the boys in school, or even the teachers, would say, if I spoke to them like that?' said Nimal. 'Could you teach me some of that dialect, Brian?'

'Sure – but only if you promise to tell me their reactions,' said Brian.

'Deal,' said Nimal, high-fiving him.

Gina and Mich returned, and Umedh set up the equipment.

'Before we play the theme song, JEACs, let's tell Brian about our group,' said Rohan. 'Nimal, you begin.'

'A year and a half ago,' said Nimal, 'Anu suggested we should start a group for young people who were keen on environmental and conservation issues. So we called ourselves the *Junior Environmentalists and Conservationists*, the JEACs for short, and our main goal is to save our planet. Gina, you're next.'

'We want to protect wildlife, especially endangered species, and help others understand the harm caused by, for example, the people who killed the snow leopards. We talk about recycling, composting, and other energy savers, and practise it at home, too. Mich?'

'We try and create awareness about these issues and involve everyone,' said Mich. 'Early this year, several kids from other schools heard about us and wanted to start groups. Three more groups have now been formed and they've donated funds to various conservation centres as well as the Calgary zoo.'

Umedh continued. 'We educate ourselves and create awareness amongst our peers about ecological issues: the effects of deforestation and destruction of habitats for wildlife, and how this endangers them. Our website has articles contributed by people all over the world, and also has links to conservation centres and zoos globally.'

'We plan to be JEACs until we're twenty-one, and then we'll join a group of peers,' said Rohan. 'Our website has our global mission statement and goals, newsletters, letters from other JEACs in different parts of the world who have formed their own branches, games, a section with the songs Gina has composed and the cartoons drawn by Mich.'

'You said you'd each recruited people,' said Brian. 'How's it done? Do you raise money? Is there a fee to join?'

'It's free,' said Umedh. 'In poorer countries, lots of kids who would love to join because they're crazy about animals don't get pocket money, so those of us who can afford it pay enough to cover for those who can't – we want *everyone* to join. Also, parents and others often make donations to cover the cost of badges, pamphlets, and maintaining our website; anyone who wants to can make a donation.'

'And we do lots of fundraising,' added Nimal.

'What happens to the money raised, and to the donations?' asked Brian.

'Each group of JEACs is connected with zoos and conservation centres in their area. Twice a year they decide who gets the funds,' explained Rohan. 'Where the fundraisers are concerned, since they're held for a specific cause – say you need money to obtain more snow leopards for breeding in captivity – then, naturally, the money goes to that cause.'

'Awesome,' said Brian, enthusiastically.

'Let's teach you the song,' said Gina.

They gave Brian a song sheet, and soon they were all singing lustily. Brian picked it up quickly and loved the cartoons drawn by Mich.

'Dinner's ready,' called Amy, as they finished singing the song for the third time.

The dogs made it to the kitchen first, and the JEACs tucked into the food hungrily.

'Getting back to the snow leopards, I think we have a problem *within* KWCC,' said Rohan.

'You mean CAB?' asked Brian.

'Yes.'

'But since five snow leopards have been killed, surely nothing else can happen, can it?' said Amy.

'I don't know, Amy,' said Rohan. 'But we can't take a chance. The police don't know what happened, and they haven't nailed the crooks. Why were darts hidden in KWCC? It would be helpful to discover whether CAB *are* connected with Zulfikar, if that was, in fact, the name Beiste and Moire mentioned; also we don't know who Xian is.'

'Why do you think something else could happen?' asked Umedh.

'Instinct and questions, yaar. If CAB truly do know each other, why are they pretending they don't? Also, if they're involved, and they don't intend to do anything else, why are they still here – and that makes me wonder if they are, in fact, innocent.'

'Hmmm . . . so what do we do next?' asked Anu.

'We keep our ears open,' said Rohan. 'Get to know CAB, get other staff opinions of them, and try to keep an eye on them.'

'Hang around them?' asked Nimal.

'Yes – and since everyone will be involved in the fundraiser, it shouldn't be problematic,' said Rohan.

'Okay, yaar,' said Umedh. 'Let's split up – some of us keep an eye on Beiste and some on Clyde.'

'But what should we look for?' asked Mich.

'For example, Mich and Gina,' said Rohan, 'if you go to the petting zoo and get friendly with the staff there, when you talk about the animals, one of them may mention Clyde.'

The girls nodded eagerly.

'What about the rest of us?' asked Umedh.

'We'll attend that staff meeting,' said Rohan. 'Dan said everybody will be there and details for the twentieth will be finalized. We'll get everyone's schedule – listen carefully to anything which involves CAB – then make plans.'

'Sound idea,' said Nimal. 'I hate the idea of more snow leopards, or other animals, being killed. Also, let's get Hunter's reaction to Beiste.'

Everyone agreed.

'What shall we do until bedtime – it's nearly nine?' said Rohan, as they cleared up.

'Mich and Gina were yawning a while ago. We had an early start, so I think we should pack it in,' said Amy.

By 10 p.m. everyone was fast asleep.

CHAPTER 7

Meetings and KWCC Staff

Rohan rose at six on the seventeenth, woke the boys, and then knocked on the girls' dormitory door. Half an hour later, the JEACs gathered in the kitchen for a cup of hot chocolate.

'What's our programme this morning, Rohan?' asked Anu, putting down food for the dogs.

'Waterholes first, Burns next, so Brian can surprise everyone – and then on to Ruthven.'

'And here are your JEACs' badges,' said Amy, handing them out.

'Thanks, Amy – these are great. How do we get badges for new members?' said Brian, as everybody pinned them on.

'Aunty Janet, Amy and Mich's mum, brought a stock to leave with Jay, and we have a few more which we'll give your buddies,' said Anu.

'Super, thanks,' said Brian.

Shortly thereafter, they were zooming along on their ski-doos, heading for the first waterhole. Once the last one was de-iced, they formed a plan as to how Brian could surprise everyone at Burns and Ruthven.

'It'll be great. Simply G-R-E-A-T!' chanted Mich and Gina, who were so excited for Brian that they couldn't keep still.

Mich looked at Gina and said, 'Sing, Gee,' and Gina burst into song:

'Brian, Brian, watch him on the ski-ii-doo.
Brian, Brian, he can do what we-ee do.

Umedh is a super chap, fixed the ski-doo just like that,
And it's easy for us all to see – see – see – tha-a-a-t . . .

Brian, Brian, won't be left behind again.
Brian, Brian, racing over hill and plain,
And we'll surely follow him, learning how to zoom and skim;
One day we may go as fast as he does – aaand;

Brian, Brian, we are thrilled for you-oo-oo,
Brian, Brian, now it's time we flew-oo-oo
Gavan and your happy dad, will be oh, so very glad,
That they're sure to join us as we sing – to you-oo.

Brian, Brian, you are really awfully cool.
Brian, Brian, what will boys say at your school?
It's so grand that we have met, and we never will forget,
That we're proud to have you as our friend – friend – friend –
friend,
Fre-eh-eh-eh-en-nd!'

Brian gaped at her as she finished her song, and said, 'Did you make that up last night?'

Gina shook her head.

'But . . . gosh – that's some talent!'

'It's a gift,' said Gina, unconsciously imitating her parents and siblings.

'Yes – remember the one she made up yesterday?' said Mich, who was proud of her friend's talent. 'Gina, teach us the words.'

Brian grinned broadly and said, 'None of the chaps at school have ever had a song made up about *them*, right on the spot, too – they'll be *so* impressed.'

'Let's learn the words, kiddo,' said Rohan, to cover Gina's embarrassment.

They learnt the song quickly, and decided to sing it for the adults after Brian had surprised them.

They set off for Burns, and Brian and Rohan stopped just before they reached the clearing near the building. The others parked close to the porch and banged on the door, calling loudly for Luag.

'What's the hullabaloo about?' grinned Gavan, opening the door and poking his head out. 'Where's Brian?'

'With Rohan,' said Nimal casually. 'Are Luag, Dolly and Taran around, and, of course, Beiste?'

'Beiste'll be here shortly – he's feeding the animals,' said Gavan, 'but the others are finishing breakfast. Aren't you coming in? Did Rohan and Brian go straight on to Ruthven?'

'Actually, we've something important to show you – outside. Could you call the others, please?' said Amy.

'Sure, lassie,' said Gavan. He called the others, saying they were wanted immediately, and winked at Gina and Mich, who were dancing around excitedly.

As soon as the adults were on the porch, Brian rode his ski-doo into the clearing, yelling loudly to his father. The adults watched in amazement as the boy skimmed around for a few minutes, and then stopped in front of his father, whose face was so full of joy that it brought tears to the eyes of the girls.

Rohan joined them as Luag hugged his son. The others crowded around the boy, too, and Luag hugged Umedh, saying, 'God bless you, laddie.'

'I can get out by myself, too,' said Brian, who had been showing them everything.

He lifted Tumbler out of the bubble, took his crutches from the ski-doo, and stepped out of the vehicle confidently. As he did so, the JEACs burst into song, and Brian, flushed with joy, stood beside his father as they sang *his* song.

The adults applauded and began to ask the JEACs so many questions that Luag persuaded everyone to go inside for a few minutes. Sitting around the kitchen table, steaming mugs of cocoa in their hands, the JEACs encouraged Brian to do the explaining.

'And look at my JEACs' badge, Dad,' said Brian, unzipping his coat and displaying it proudly. 'I'm a JEAC, too, and I know Eadan and

Cormag will join up at once. I've learnt the theme song – Gina wrote the words and tune, and Mich drew the cartoons – it's super.'

'And Jay and I are hoping you'll sing it for everyone this morning, after the meeting,' said Doilidh.

'No problemo,' chorused the JEACs.

Mich and Gina began to sing Brian's song again, as the adults admired the badges, and the others joined in. As they were finishing it, Beiste walked into the kitchen, heard the end of the song, and asked what the excitement was about.

Taran told him, and Beiste said to Brian, 'Good. Now you can join in a few things and won't feel sorry for yourself.'

Mich and Gina glared at him. But Anu said quickly, 'Good morning, Beiste. Have you met Hunter, our dog?'

Beiste shook his head apprehensively.

'Hunter – come out and *shake*,' said Anu, looking under the table.

Hunter emerged and Anu pointed at Beiste. Hunter looked at the man and then sat down in front of Anu – his back to Beiste. He didn't growl or bark – simply ignored the man. Anu looked at Nimal, who joined her and tried to persuade Hunter to *shake*, but the dog, though he licked Nimal and Anu apologetically, would not obey.

Tumbler, bouncing out to join Hunter, saw Beiste and immediately began to growl and bark. Nimal grabbed him and calmed him down.

'I don't seem to get along with dogs,' said Beiste, laughing nervously.

'I wonder why?' said Rohan, politely. He changed the topic of conversation, and said, 'Come on, JEACs, we'll miss brekker at Ruthven if we don't move.'

'Do the Ruthven crowd know about your ski-doo, lad?' asked Luag.

'No – I wanted to surprise everyone,' said Brian, grinning at his father. 'Let's go, JEACs.'

He led the way, hopping along quickly on his crutches, and Doilidh, smiling mistily, said, 'Bless him, and you! He's gained so much confidence since you JEACs came along; that's the best Christmas gift we could receive.'

Luag watched his son settle confidently into the ski-doo.

'Okay, JEACs – Brian and Nimal lead the way,' said Rohan, starting his vehicle.

Waving to the adults, the JEACs set off. Upon reaching the edge of the forest at Ruthven, they saw several ATVs already parked on the grounds, so they pulled over to talk.

'How do we surprise everyone at once?' said Nimal.

'Call and tell them to look out of the windows,' suggested Amy.

'Good thinking,' said Rohan, pulling out the mobile telephone.

'Call Jay – she'll use the intercom,' said Brian excitedly.

'Hi, Jay,' said Rohan, seconds later. 'Would you ask everyone to look out over the front grounds in three minutes, please – we have a surprise for you. Thanks. And perhaps someone should have a camera handy.'

He rang off and said, 'She's making an announcement.'

'How shall we do it this time?' asked Mich excitedly.

'Rohan, get in front of Brian – it'll block him from view,' said Anu. 'We'll form a line and fan out with Mich, Amy and Nimal on Rohan's left; Gina, Umedh and I on his right. When we see Jay and the others, everyone, except for Rohan and Brian, start moving slowly. Brian, when we're halfway there, zoom out from behind Rohan and race towards the castle – passing between Gina and Mich, and Rohan, catch us up – Brian should reach the porch first, and as he gets out of his machine, we'll sing his song.'

'Brainwave, Anu,' said Umedh, as everyone moved into position. 'I can see heads looking out of the windows already.'

'And some of them are coming onto the porch,' said Rohan. 'Anu, we're awaiting your signal.'

'Start up your ski-doos – one – two – three – *go!*'

The formation fanned out, making its way to the castle. Unexpectedly, Brian sped out from behind Rohan. It worked beautifully, and everyone was astounded to see Brian riding his own machine. The people at the windows rushed down to join the group on the porch. Brian got off his machine and the JEACs burst into song; once it was finished, everyone cheered and crowded around Brian, hugging the boy and clapping him on the back as they examined the ski-doo with interest.

'Umedh fixed it,' said Brian, looking at him with shining eyes.

Jay hugged Umedh, tears of joy pouring down her face. 'I *knew* you'd figure out something,' she sobbed.

'Well, it's better than the seat I made for the swing, years ago,' grinned Umedh, offering Jay his handkerchief. 'Remember?'

'Could I forget?' said Jay, her tears turning to laughter. 'He was six, and his mother had said she would love to have a go on the swing which Umedh and I played on, but the cushion kept falling off. Umedh, who was inventing things even then, fixed a bucket seat on to the rope for her. She didn't want to hurt his feelings by saying she didn't think it was safe – a few of his inventions hadn't been completely successful – so I offered to test it. It worked brilliantly, for a few seconds, and then tipped me out – right into a thorny bush.'

Everyone roared with laughter, and Umedh, relieved that Jay had stopped crying, said with a grin, 'I couldn't understand why she couldn't sit down properly for a week. By the way, did anyone take pictures just now?'

'I captured it on the video cam,' said Saroj. 'Has Luag seen you ride, Brian?'

'We went there first,' said Brian, 'but we did it differently, so Dad, Gav and the others will be glad to see the video – thanks, Saroj.'

'Come on in, everyone – let's eat,' invited Dan.

They crowded into the castle and over a scrumptious meal the JEACs met other Centre staff.

'I like your badges,' said Drostan, examining Gina's. 'I have scores of nephews, nieces and cousins who would love to join up. How can they do that?'

'We're working on a plan, Drostan,' said Jay. 'Nilini and Saroj want to recruit children in Scotland, England and Ireland. We'll keep you posted.'

'Okay, folks, time to move,' said Dan, rising from the table, along with other staff members. 'Dilki will give you details, JEACs.'

'Aunty Dilki, I've been hearing choppers ever since we sat down to brekker. Were they bringing volunteers?' asked Umedh.

'Yes. Twenty fundraising committee members, who will stay until the event's over; thirty more volunteers will arrive early morning on the nineteenth. All of them will leave on the evening of the twenty-first, after everything's been put away. This will allow the KWCC staff to do their regular work as well.'

'That's great! What do you want us to do today, Aunty?' asked Nimal.

'Sing the theme song at the end of the meeting. Once we break up into small groups, you'll meet the volunteers handling the young people's programmes, and they'll brief you on your role.'

'What else can we do, Mum?' asked Rohan.

'The last agenda item is to draw up schedules. The first is for the next three days, including today; the second is for the day of the fundraiser; the third has the shifts for coverage at Burns, starting at 6 p.m. on the nineteenth and going right through to 10 p.m. on the twenty-first. Assist wherever you like, but we have plenty of volunteers and Jay and Dan want you to enjoy yourselves. You can also participate in some of the events on the twentieth. Any more questions?'

'Not at the moment, thanks, Aunty Dilki/Mum,' said the JEACs.

'Good – see you in the conference room shortly.'

She hurried off, and the JEACs looked at one another.

'Great,' said Rohan. 'I have some suggestions as to how we can combine detective work with assisting for the fundraiser.' The others nodded and he continued, 'Once we know CAB's schedules, we'll plan our own. Brian says Clyde lives in one of the other buildings, but eats most of his meals at Knox; Ailean, one of the vets at Knox, is friendly with him.

'Mich and Gina, spend time at the petting zoo with Ailean's wife, Mòrag, and the other staff; ask questions about the animals and slip in a few questions about Clyde. If you do meet Clyde, be polite – but careful. We not sure if he's a crook, but don't go off with him for any reason *whatsoever* – okay?'

'Sure, Rohan,' said the girls.

'Shall I tackle Beiste?' asked Nimal.

'I think Amy and I should tackle him,' said Anu. 'We'll use his smarminess to our benefit.'

'But . . .' began Umedh and Rohan.

'Don't worry about us,' said Anu. She smiled at the boys, who were frowning, and said, 'Come on, guys – we *need* to find out what he's up to. What do you say, Amy?'

Amy grinned, and said, 'Absolutely, hon, we'll deal with him.' She turned to Rohan and chanted, 'I promise not to slug him – unless he goes o'er the top, and *then* I'll get him quickly, with a good *karate chop!* See, I can rhyme, too.'

The group burst out laughing.

'Okay. And we will play it by ear – assist as needed,' said Rohan.

'Sound idea – let's move. It's time for the meeting,' said Umedh.

They went to the second floor and joined the others.

'Sit at the back,' said Rohan. 'Any sign of Clyde, Brian?'

'Not yet,' said Brian, who was seated in the aisle, in his wheelchair.

The meeting began and everybody participated enthusiastically. As they began filling in the schedule for the next few days, a couple of men entered the room and sat four rows ahead of the JEACs.

'Clyde's the chap with the beard and moustache,' whispered Brian. 'The other one's Ailean.'

Rohan nodded and quietly passed the information along the row.

Drostan and Nilini put up a huge flip chart listing the tasks for the next three days, and Jay wrote down names as people volunteered. The chart filled up quickly.

Each time Clyde or Beiste volunteered for anything, Rohan made a note. 'Will we have access to the schedules?' he whispered.

'Yes – everyone receives a copy of each,' replied Brian, as the schedule for the day of the fundraiser, was filled.

Finally, the most important schedule, to ensure the protection of the snow leopards and other animals at Burns, was brought forward: two-hour time slots from the evening of the nineteenth, right through to 10 p.m. on the day after the fundraiser, which would be the twenty-first of December.

The slots were filled up – the staff being asked, when possible, to handle night shifts. A few shifts were moved around, and Jay promised that all schedules would be ready by noon.

'I couldn't get every detail,' said Rohan, softly to Brian, 'but CAB both have shifts on the evening and night of the nineteenth, paired with Taog and other rangers; on the twentieth they're paired with Uisdean and

Uallas for some evening and night shifts, two of which go right through until 3 a.m. on the morning of the twenty-first.'

Nimal, seated on Rohan's other side, whispered, 'There's one shift on the twentieth, where Beiste's on duty at Burns, but Clyde's patrolling KWCC, around Cairns and Burns.'

'Taog and Ailean are also patrolling at that time, but they're far from Burns,' said Brian.

'And that's it for the business section of our meeting,' said Jay. 'Thanks, everyone – we'll have further meetings as required. And now, I have a special treat for you.'

The JEACs, along with the dogs, assembled on the stage, and Jay introduced them. She said that their theme song was composed by Gina and Mich, and signalled Saroj who started the slide show.

While Mich's drawings ran on the screen, the JEACs sang, accompanied on the piano by Janet Larkin. Hunter and Tumbler joined in with barks whenever they felt like it. Janet, a trained musician, had worked with them painstakingly, both over the harmony and the clarity of the words, and she was proud of their performance. Everybody applauded enthusiastically.

'Take a short break, folks, before we reconvene in small groups at 11:15,' said Jay, after thanking the JEACs.

The meeting broke up, and volunteers and staff surrounded the JEACs, eager to meet them and to congratulate Brian on his ability to ride the ski-doo.

'JEACs, I've heard so much about you,' said Ailean. He was a charming man, a couple of inches taller than Rohan, and extremely muscular. 'These are my colleagues – Clyde and Taog.'

The men shook hands with the JEACs, congratulating them on their performance. Clyde, slightly taller than Nimal, looked strong, and was exceptionally reserved. Taog, six and a half feet tall and very broad, looked morose, and was even more silent than Clyde, but when he smiled at Gina and Mich, bending almost double to speak to them, and told them that they had done a great job with the song and the cartoons, his entire face lit up. Umedh and Nimal, standing beside Clyde, tried to engage him in conversation about his work, but although he answered politely enough, he was brief.

'We're impressed with everything we've heard about your group,' said Ailean. 'You must come to Knox and have a meal with us. My wife, Mòrag, insisted that I fix a time with you – she couldn't make it to this meeting.'

'We'd love to visit, Ailean,' said Amy. 'It's most kind of Mòrag and you, but we hear you have a baby, and we'd hate to be a bother. How about tea? We could ask Ceana and Drostan for some goodies.'

'That's very considerate – an excellent idea,' said Ailean. 'When can you come?'

'What about today – if it's not too short notice?' said Rohan. 'Will you be joining us, Clyde, Taog?'

Taog nodded.

'I'm . . . I don't . . .' hesitated Clyde, but Ailean overrode him, insisting that he join them, and Clyde agreed, albeit reluctantly.

'That's grand – 4 p.m.?' said Ailean.

Taog nodded again, smiled at the JEACs and moved away.

'Do you have a daughter or a son, Ailean?' asked Anu.

'A wee lassie,' said Ailean. 'Her name's Gormal.'

'And Gormal means "deep blue eyes",' said Janet, joining the group. 'She really does have eyes of the deepest blue – we saw her yesterday. She's a darling. Amy, Anu, I want a word with you, please.'

They moved away; Gina and Mich ran to get Hunter and Tumbler, who were being spoilt by some of the staff, and Brian was still speaking to some volunteers. Ailean and Clyde left for their meeting, and Rohan, Umedh and Nimal waited for the others.

'Did Clyde say anything much? How did you react to him?' asked Rohan in a low voice.

'A man of few words, and Taog has even less to say,' said Nimal, softly. 'But unlike Taog, Clyde's smile doesn't reach his eyes. I felt as if he was simmering – like a volcano about to erupt.'

Umedh looked astonished. 'That's *exactly* what I thought, yaar – he's dangerous.'

'We'll discuss it later, after tea,' muttered Rohan, as the others came up.

'And here's Brian with our volunteers,' said Janet.

At the meeting, the volunteers, all of whom were teachers, quickly outlined their plans for the JEACs' presentation.

'We'll each host a session,' explained Latharna, 'and ask you to relate experiences with endangered species or why you think conservation and environmental issues are important; and then we'll invite group participation.'

'Please wear your badges,' added another teacher. 'We'd like to start a JEACs' group on the twentieth.' He smiled and added, 'I looked at your website and my son, who's eight, loves it and wants to join immediately. I see that you're already a member, Brian.'

'Yes, and it's superb,' said Brian.

'We'd also like you to sing the theme song, and teach it to the groups, and we'll give out your pamphlets,' said the third teacher. 'A pro-conservation band, called *Go, Go, Greeners*, will accompany you at the sessions. They're a group of youngsters, in their early twenties, whose parents are eager volunteers, and they were keen on volunteering their services at the event.'

'What time does the fundraiser begin?' asked Anu.

'At ten,' said Latharna, 'and the first group of visitors will arrive before nine.'

After tossing around a few more ideas, Janet wrapped up the meeting, and the adults went off to other meetings.

'It's 11:30,' said Rohan, looking at his watch. 'Brian, is there a small room we can use for half an hour?'

'I'll ask Saroj,' said Brian, and zoomed off to speak to her. He signalled the JEACs, who joined him. 'We can use a small meeting room upstairs – it's free till one,' said Brian, leading the way.

They crowded into the room and looked at Rohan expectantly.

'Clyde's dangerous,' said Rohan. 'Both Umedh and Nimal got the same impression, and I think one of us guys should keep an eye on him – no offence, girls.'

'None taken,' said Amy and Anu.

'He gave me the creeps,' added Anu.

'His smile didn't reach his eyes,' said Amy, 'and, although Taog *looks* morose, he has a whole different *aura*, and the nicest smile.'

'He's a great chap,' said Brian. 'He rarely says anything, but he's so caring. You should see him with Gormal and the other kids around the place – he's so gentle and kind. All the animals at the petting zoo, as well as Tumbler, love him.'

'*We* liked him,' said Gina and Mich.

'We all agree that Taog's a good chap,' laughed Rohan. 'But back to Clyde – Brian, it'll look weird if you hang around him, so Umedh, Nimal and I will take turns, and we'll pair up with you for other tasks.'

'No problemo,' said Brian.

'Mich and Gina,' said Rohan, 'in addition to spending time at the petting zoo, make friends with the staff at Ruthven, especially Ceana, Drostan, Nilini and Saroj – keep your ears open.'

'Okay,' promised the girls.

'We'll report back as soon as we discover anything,' said Mich.

'Good,' said Rohan, smiling at their serious faces. 'Every evening, by 5:30 or 6, we need to return to Cairns to check in and make further plans.'

'It's nearly lunchtime,' said Anu. 'Let's have an early meal; after tea with Ailean and Mòrag, we'll return to Cairns, study the schedules, and discuss next steps.'

'Good idea,' said Amy, and the others nodded.

'What should we do till 3:30?' asked Brian. 'It'll take us half an hour to get to Knox from here.'

'Hang around here – helping in the kitchen and office and talking to as many people as possible,' said Rohan promptly.

'Won't we be in their way?' asked Mich.

'No, hon – especially if you and Gina offer to help with the tea for Knox,' said Anu. 'Ceana said she would make a cake, sandwiches and biscuits.'

'Goodie,' the girls said happily.

'At lunch, spread out – try to sit with different people. Nimal, Brian – try and get Hunter and Tumbler's reactions to Clyde. Let's go, JEACs.'

In the dining room they met several new and interesting staff and volunteers. Half an hour later, Nilini and Saroj came in with the schedules.

Nilini gave Rohan a copy of each and said, 'If things change, we phone the people involved, and update it immediately on the computer – so that we don't waste paper.'

'Thanks, Nilini,' said Rohan.

The staff and volunteers ate quickly and left their plates on the trolleys beside the door on their way out. Rohan and Umedh wheeled the first two loaded trolleys into the kitchen.

'Thanks, chaps,' said Drostan gratefully. 'Leave them here and we'll deal with them.'

'We're here to help, Drostan,' said Umedh, he and Rohan rolling up their sleeves. 'Just direct us.'

'That's very kind,' said Ceana, as Amy and Nimal came in with two more loaded trolleys, Anu, Brian, Gina and Mich following with used cutlery in bins, 'but I'm sure there must be more interesting things for you to do.'

'You mean more interesting than watching the three older guys trying to wash dishes and not break them?' asked Amy.

'Hey!' said Nimal. 'Not at *all* PC, Amy.' He beamed at Ceana. 'I'm *the* best dishwasher in the world. Trust me – watching me work will make your life one long, sweet, dream.'

'Of course it will – of the *nightmare* type,' said Anu, smoothly. 'A grade A+ klutz is our Nimal, but he is excellent at drying unbreakable stainless steel cutlery – and only drops them a couple of times.'

'Och, laddie,' said Drostan, grimacing at the boy, 'the lassies don't have much faith in you, do they?'

'It's one of . . .' began Nimal, when Gina and Mich chorused, '. . . the saddest stories of his life.'

'With such vociferous, boisterous kids around,' moaned Nimal, 'it's no wonder I'm the strong, silent type.'

The resulting peal of hilarity made the dogs bark excitedly.

'Ouch, I've got a stitch in my side,' groaned Brian, holding his ribs and trying to sober up.

Drostan grinned at the JEACs as he gave Hunter and Tumbler two huge bowls of food, and said, 'Right, then. Keeping in mind what Anu says, thanks for your offer, which we will gladly accept. We usually have two dishwashers – but one's out of order and won't be fixed until tomorrow.'

They divided up the tasks. Saroj and Nilini joined them, and Drostan, who was a fun leader, soon had the whole crowd '. . . singin' in the kitchen, banging on the pots and pans.' By 2:15, the kitchen was spotless, as was the dining room.

'Thanks a bunch,' said Drostan.

'Yes, many, many thanks,' added Ceana. 'Now please relax till tea time, or we'll feel guilty about making you work on your holiday.'

'Work?' said Nimal, looking astonished. 'I understood we were participating in a musical comedy.'

'Buzz off, wretch,' said Drostan.

'Ceana, please may we help you make sandwiches and cakes?' begged Gina.

'Sure thing, lassies,' said Ceana. 'What will the rest of you do?'

'May we assist in the office?' asked Anu, turning to Saroj and Nilini.

'Super, thanks. We have tons of work,' Saroj said gratefully. 'Boys, we need to haul out electronic equipment from storage.'

'Lead on,' said the older JEACs.

'Come back by 3:15. We'll have everything ready – along with wide-awake dogs,' said Drostan, nodding over at Hunter and Tumbler who were fast asleep after their huge meal.

'Will do, Drostan, thanks,' said Rohan, following the others.

The JEACs met the librarian, Friseal, a young man with a great sense of humour, who soon had them in fits of laughter.

Another man entered the office. 'This is U. . .' began Saroj, but trailed off with a wink at Brian, as Umedh greeted the man warmly.

'We met at lunch,' said Umedh.

Brian shook with silent laughter as the man grinned at Umedh, shook hands with him and the others and said, 'Actually, we haven't met before, Umedh – I wasn't at lunch.'

'But . . . Brian, tell me I'm not losing it. You're Uisdean Ashby, right? We had lunch together – just a little while ago,' reiterated Umedh.

'You must have met my brother – I'm Uallas.'

'Are you kidding me?' protested Umedh.

'He's not, Umedh – Uallas is our computer expert,' chuckled Brian, and the other KWCC folk nodded, laughing at Umedh's astonishment.

'Gosh, you're *absolutely* identical,' said Umedh. 'Uisdean was also wearing a red shirt at lunch. Was it planned?'

Laughingly Uallas denied it.

'We specialize in twins at KWCC,' said Nilini. 'There's Saroj and myself, Taog has a twin sister, and Gavan has a twin brother and sister, too.'

'But only Uisdean and Uallas are identical twins,' said Saroj.

'I'm looking forward to meeting Uisdean,' said Nimal. 'I can imagine what fun you must have, playing tricks on everyone.'

'We do have a wee bit of fun – now and then,' confessed Uallas.

'Now and then?' exclaimed Saroj in mock irritation. 'They're incorrigible! Why, just the other day . . .'

'Peace, Saroj,' begged Uallas. 'We really need to get to work. I've had several chats with your father, Nimal – and can't wait to meet with him, and you, Umedh, to discuss the programming for KWCC.'

'Is Uisdean also a computer expert?' demanded Umedh.

'Doesn't know the difference between a CPU and a keyboard. He's learning a little, now that he has to use a computer, but when he starts talking about remote delivery systems – that's Greek to me,' admitted Uallas.

They set to work, the girls and Brian helping in the office, while the boys, Friseal and Uallas organized the required equipment. It was fun and time sped by.

By 3:30 they were on their ski-doos, following Brian to Knox. The dogs were safe in their bubbles, while an enormous quantity of delicious food had been packed carefully and placed in the carriers.

The JEACs were thrilled to see deer, ptarmigan, mountain hare and even a couple of wildcats at various points along the trail, and immediately stopped their ski-doos until the creatures had vanished into the forest.

They zoomed up a steep hill, which was flat at the top, and found themselves 30 metres away from sheds, with the castle just beyond.

Nimal released Hunter, who jumped out of the bubble. 'Need a hand, Brian?' he asked, noticing that the boy looked pale.

'If you could release Tumbler – thanks,' said Brian, frowning slightly as he switched off his machine.

Nimal caught Rohan and Umedh's eyes for a split second and raised an eyebrow.

'Take it easy on the ski-doo today, yaar,' said Umedh, setting up the wheelchair quickly – it was in the carrier on his ski-oo. 'Our muscles need to be broken in gently – mine are jolly sore already.'

'And mine,' groaned Amy and Anu in unison.

'I feel ancient,' said Anu. 'All that tobogganing last afternoon added to it.'

'I've not used some of my muscles for a long time,' said Brian, brightening up. 'The wheelchair will be easier than my crutches at the moment.'

'We'll use Deep Heat tonight,' promised Rohan.

Nimal lifted Brian out of the ski-doo and put him in the wheelchair just as the front door opened.

'Welcome to Knox, JEACs,' beamed Ailean.

The JEACs unloaded everything and followed him into the castle, where they were ushered into a large room.

'Make yourselves comfortable – the others will join us shortly,' said Ailean, patting Hunter and Tumbler who were fawning over him. 'Hunter's a clever chap, and so well trained. He came to me when he first arrived, and Mòrag fell in love with him instantly. He seemed to know when Gormal was sleeping and kept absolutely quiet at that time.'

'Is Clyde joining us?' asked Rohan.

'He'll be here in ten minutes,' said Ailean. 'Since Quentin (our zookeeper and vet), Sally (his assistant), and two other rangers want to meet you as well, it's going to be a large crowd.'

'Please may we visit the animals in the petting zoo after tea?' begged Gina.

'Absolutely,' said Ailean, 'and here are Mòrag and Gormal.'

The JEACs rose politely. Mòrag handed Gormal to Ailean and welcomed the JEACs warmly. 'I'm happy to meet you. Thank you so much for taking the time to come and visit. I've heard wonderful things about you. Brian, lad, I'm thrilled that you can ride a ski-doo again.' She hugged the boy affectionately, and Brian grinned.

Mòrag had deep blue eyes, golden hair, and the top of her head just reached her husband's shoulder. The JEACs took to her immediately; she winked at them and nodded towards Ailean. The JEACs grinned and went over to where he was seated on the sofa, rocking his daughter and whispering to her dotingly.

'He's quite potty over her,' said Mòrag in a pseudo whisper. 'I come last in the family now.'

'She's like a doll,' whispered Gina.

'She's looking at me – and her eyes are sooo blue,' said Mich, softly.

The girls were entranced with the baby, who was a happy little soul with a riot of golden curls and long eyelashes.

'Would you like to hold her?' asked Mòrag.

'Could we?' said Amy and Anu at once.

'Of course,' said Mòrag. Ailean passed Gormal to Amy, and everyone crowded around to admire the baby, taking turns to hold her.

'Baby worship of the best kind,' said a deep voice as two people entered the room.

'You must be the JEACs, and that has to be Nimal, left as usual, holding the baby.' As the JEACs burst out laughing and Mòrag took Gormal from Nimal so that the boy could stand up, the man continued, 'I'm Quentin, the chap in charge of the zoo, and this is Sally.'

'Where's Clyde?' asked Ailean, as more rangers joined them a few minutes later and further introductions were made.

'Coming,' said Taog. He smiled at the JEACs and assisted in opening the packages of food.

'Shall we begin without him?' asked Mòrag, looking at her husband.

'I guess so, since the JEACs shouldn't start back to Cairns too late,' said Ailean. 'I'll wait for him.'

Everyone helped themselves and settled down; the dogs were given huge bowls of food, which they finished quickly. Hunter lay between Nimal and Brian, and Tumbler fell asleep, his head resting on Hunter's paws.

A knock on the door heralded Clyde's arrival, and Ailean ushered him into the room. The noisy chatter ceased, as everyone paused to say hello. Ailean and Clyde helped themselves to food and coffee and made their way to a couple of empty seats, past Quentin, Nimal, Brian and the dogs.

When Clyde, who had not noticed the dogs, passed Hunter, the dog lifted his head and growled deep in his throat. Tumbler woke up at once and yelped.

'Hush, Hunter, quiet!' said Nimal softly, placing a hand on the dog's head and grabbing Tumbler, while checking to see if Clyde had heard the growl. But the noise level in the room was loud, and neither Clyde nor Ailean heard anything as they settled down in their seats and began speaking to Sally and Taog.

Quentin, observing the excited look that passed between Brian and Nimal, drew his chair closer to them, patted Hunter, who licked his hand, and said in a low voice, 'Hunter doesn't seem to like Clyde, does he?' Nimal looked at Quentin sharply, and the man continued, 'I'm not surprised. None of the animals like him – for that matter, he doesn't appear to want to make friends with them either. I've often wondered why someone like that lives and works here.'

'Do *you* like him?' asked Nimal.

'He's a colleague,' began Quentin, but when he saw that both boys were looking at him straightforwardly, he shrugged and said bluntly, 'To be frank – no, I don't, and goodness knows I've tried. I feel very uncomfortable around him – he's *untrustworthy.*'

'That's *exactly* how we feel,' said Nimal quietly. 'But why does Ailean like him so much?'

'Ailean's an extraordinarily compassionate man,' explained Quentin. 'He believes Clyde just needs a good vacation – let's see when he returns.'

'Is he going away?' asked Brian.

'He leaves for India on the morning of the twenty-first – right after his shift.'

Ailean called out, 'Hurry up with your tea, folks. Clyde says there's a blizzard warning for tonight from around eight or so, but it could start earlier. We'd better finish with the zoo and send the JEACs back safely – it's nearly five.'

Some of the others had to leave, and Clyde went with them. Sally offered to look after Gormal and the dogs, so everyone else went to the petting zoo.

The JEACs had a wonderful time visiting the enclosures, petting and feeding the little creatures. There were wildcats, mountain hare, otters, foxes, wild goat, red deer, badgers, voles, and even, to their especial delight, three baby reindeer. All the babies wanted to cuddle with Nimal, though they were friendly with everyone else, too.

'You'd better come and live here, Nimal,' smiled Quentin, preventing the baby wildcats from following Nimal as he left their enclosure.

'I've never seen them react like that before,' marvelled Mòrag, watching the baby badgers bounce into the boy's lap in the next enclosure. 'They're always friendly, but they're *crazy* about Nimal.'

'You should have seen him with Gràinne,' said Brian. 'That was awesome!'

They reluctantly left the petting zoo. Gina and Mich had to be dragged away from the enchanting baby reindeer.

'Would you like to spend a whole day here?' asked Mòrag, smiling at them.

'Oooh, that would be superfantabulous,' chanted Mich and Gina, looking at Anu and Amy for permission.

'Sure thing, girls,' said Amy. 'What about tomorrow – weather permitting, of course?'

'They'll help you with feeding and cleaning,' added Anu. 'We can drop them off early in the morning and pick them up in the evening.'

'Good idea,' said Rohan. 'Some of us will bring them over – I think it's about 45 minutes from here to Cairns. What time would be convenient, Mòrag?'

'We're up at four to prepare the first batch of food, so the girls can come any time after that,' said Mòrag.

'Let's get rid of them around 5 a.m.,' teased Nimal, adding hastily when Gina and Mich advanced on him threateningly, 'I mean, naturally, it would be my *deep and intense pleasure* to bring them over.'

'I'll come, too,' said Brian with a grin. 'At the rate you're going, mate, I wouldn't be surprised if they murdered you and left your body somewhere on the trail.'

'Yikes! I'll depend on your protection, yaar,' said Nimal.

They collected Hunter and Tumbler, and said goodbye to Sally and Gormal.

As they thanked Ailean and Mòrag for everything and mounted their ski-doos, Taog said, as he shook hands with Nimal, 'You have a very special gift, young man – use it well.' Looking around at the other JEACs, he added, 'At KWCC we are heartbroken at the loss of the snow leopards. The world needs more people like you JEACs to be passionate about the protection of wildlife – they were, after all, left to our care. Keep up the good work.'

Recovering from their astonishment at hearing Taog make such a long speech, the JEACs responded, 'We'll do our best, sir.'

'My nieces and nephews will be attending the fundraiser, and they'd love to join your group,' said Taog. 'I am delighted to meet you.' He shook hands with all of them, tipped his hat, and went off after giving Hunter and Tumbler a last pat.

'I've never heard him say so much,' said Ailean, thoughtfully.

'Let's go,' said Umedh. 'We have to de-ice the waterholes and get back before the blizzard hits.'

'Someone's mobile phone is ringing,' said Amy.

'Mine,' said Rohan, answering it. 'Hello? Hi, Gavan. Yes, we had a super time, thanks.' He listened for a few seconds, said 'Right, mate, thanks. We'll do them tomorrow morning,' and hung up. Turning to the others he said, 'Our waterholes have already been de-iced – Gavan heard the blizzard warning – let's move, folks.'

'Thanks a ton for everything. See you soon,' called the JEACs as they rode off, following Brian and Umedh.

CHAPTER 8

Happenings in the Early Hours

'We made it home in 40 minutes – thanks to Brian who knows the trails so well, despite the fact that it's pitch dark,' said Rohan as he parked his ski-doo.

'Oooh, it's snowing – humongous flakes,' exclaimed Gina, who was first out of the shed when the ski-doos were cleaned.

'It's heavy and wet – and it's only 6:30,' said Anu.

They went to the porch and watched the snow falling thickly onto the ground, while Gina and Mich danced about with the dogs, trying to catch the flakes. When the wind started howling, the JEACs hurried inside and watched as the weather rapidly worsened, and the snow was swirling around under total white-out conditions.

Soon everyone, except Rohan, was lazing around the fireplace, drinking hot chocolate and chatting about the animals at the petting zoo. The dogs were curled up next to Gina and Mich, fast asleep.

Rohan sat down at a small desk, pulled out the schedules, and began to jot down points. Once he was done, he joined the group around the fireplace.

'What's our plan of action, yaar?' asked Nimal eagerly.

'Here's tomorrow's plan,' said Rohan. 'Mich and Gina – you'll be dropped off by Nimal and Brian, and should leave here around 4:30 – did you groan, Nimal?'

'Did not,' said Nimal indignantly. 'You know me. Up with the lark – good night, all. I'll go to sleep immediately.'

The others laughed; Gina threw a cushion at him which he caught and promptly returned.

'Gina, Mich, remember to talk with Mòrag and find out what she thinks of CAB. Also, Quentin's a nice chap, so when you're around him, try and get him talking, too. Perhaps . . . yes, Brian? You don't need to raise your hand, yaar.'

Brian grinned sheepishly, nodded, and said, 'Rohan, Quentin spoke to Nimal and me about Clyde – Nimal, you tell them.'

'We both will,' said Nimal encouragingly, and they told the others about the incident with the dogs.

'So . . . Quentin, Hunter and Tumbler don't like Clyde, nor do the other animals and, to add to that, Clyde doesn't seem to be interested in making friends with either the animals or the humans,' said Anu thoughtfully. 'Explain *why* he works at KWCC?'

'It doesn't make sense,' said Umedh.

'But no conservation centre would hire someone who didn't have a good background in the field,' said Nimal.

'True, but you can always fudge a résumé and give false references,' said Amy.

'And I wouldn't put that past him,' said Rohan. 'I could be prejudiced, but the fact that he's going away, *the very day after the fundraiser* – to *India* – sounds bizarre,' said Rohan. 'Rizana was arrested on her way to India – in my mind, things are adding up against him. What do you think?'

There was a brief silence, and then Amy said, 'I liked Taog a lot, even before his speech. However, I simply didn't take to Clyde – though I tried not to be too prejudiced, and both Taog and Clyde are silent men.'

'I agree, Amy,' said Anu. 'You don't feel uncomfortable in Taog's presence – in fact, you *like* it when he's around. He's sort of . . . soothing, and makes you feel safe.'

The others smiled at her imagery, but understood, and Nimal added, 'Neither the dogs nor the other animals like Clyde, and that says a lot. Brian, what do you think? You've known him longest.'

'Actually, I really don't know him or anything about him, other than what Ailean says,' said Brian. 'The staff are polite to him, but none of them, except for Ailean, try to befriend him.'

'Let's carry on with our plans,' said Anu. 'What should Brian and Nimal do once they've dropped off the girls? And what about the dogs?'

'Go on to Ruthven and take the dogs. Brian, help in the office – talk to Saroj, Nilini, Uallas and Friseal, in particular – they probably have the most contact with both men – and find out what you can about how CAB were hired, what they're like, et cetera.'

'Won't they think it strange for me to ask those questions now, all of a sudden?' said Brian.

'Not if you start by saying that you find it weird that neither Hunter nor Tumbler like them,' said Anu.

'That's a great idea, thanks,' said Brian.

'Nimal, Clyde's scheduled to help set up various booths in the grounds,' said Rohan. 'Hang around the kitchen till breakfast time, find out how Drostan and Ceana react to our suspects, and then offer to help in the set-up of the booths.'

'Aye, aye, Captain,' said Nimal.

'The four of us will de-ice the waterholes, and then leave Anu and Amy at Burns, to check on Beiste. Umedh and I will carry on to Ruthven and assist in setting up, too – but we'll each work with a different group,' said Rohan.

'Do we have to stick around Beiste the whole day?' asked Anu, wrinkling her nose.

'Until noon will be sufficient, and then join us for lunch at Ruthven,' said Rohan.

'What about our reports, Rohan?' asked Gina. 'We could join you for lunch, too.'

'But I thought you wanted to spend the whole day at Knox, honey,' said Amy.

'Yes, but *protecting* animals is more important.'

'We can spend the day there another time,' added Mich.

'Sure we want your reports,' said Rohan. 'One of us will pick you up around noon.'

'That's great, Rohan, if you don't mind,' said Gina politely. She and Mich were learning, from friends at school, that few older siblings were as caring as theirs, and Anu and Amy were encouraging them to appreciate this and not take it for granted.

'It'll be a pleasure, kiddo,' said Rohan, tweaking her nose affectionately.

'Thank you, Rohan. I'll set my watch alarm now, so that we're ready in time,' said Mich.

'Good idea, Mich,' said Gina. 'Set it for 11:45 tomorrow.'

'After a quick lunch and meeting,' continued Rohan, 'Nimal, Umedh and I will continue to assist, joining groups with Clyde or Beiste, and try to observe their interaction with others. Brian, Mich and Gina, keep the dogs with you, and help the volunteers with decorating the booths. I believe some of that group are involved in scheduling the helicopters, and it would be good to get details as to how that works.'

'And what's our task?' asked Amy.

'Brenda's on the list of volunteers,' said Rohan.

'I don't . . .' frowned Anu, and then her face brightened. 'Oh, the volunteer at the airport.'

'Spot on, sis,' said Rohan. 'She's one of the greeters, welcoming people when they arrive at the fundraiser. Since we didn't meet her, I figured she arrived last afternoon while we were at Knox.'

'We'll get details about what happened at the airport,' said Amy.

'Also, try and discover how they plan to ensure nobody crooked is allowed in.'

'Do you really think something else is going to happen, Rohan?' asked Amy, and everyone looked at him anxiously.

'I don't want to be a scaremonger, but there's some weird stuff going on. Let's keep our ideas in the group, and our eyes wide open.'

Everyone agreed, and since it was nearly eight and the storm was still bad, they decided to have a light meal, play a board game or two and then have an early night.

'Deep Heat's calling me,' groaned Nimal, as he rose from the floor.

'There's some in the medicine cabinet in the study,' said Brian.

Umedh found the Deep Heat, and everyone used it gratefully.

Somewhat diffidently, Brian said, 'Nimal, would you mind taking me tomorrow? I don't want to overdo it and be laid up for the rest of your stay.'

'Smart thinking, yaar – we can't do without you,' said Nimal. 'I'll drive a snowcat tomorrow, and take you, Gina, Mich and the dogs. I'm glad you realize I'm not always a klutz.'

'Brian, don't do it,' shrieked Mich and Gina.

'He'll bump into a tree, the snowcat will come apart, and you'll all exit, rapidly, in multiple directions,' added Amy.

Amidst much laughter and teasing, the JEACs ate and then settled down to a game. But they were tired and sleepy, and shortly after nine they all went to bed.

*****

Rohan woke with a start and sat up in bed. What was that noise? He looked at his watch – it was nearly 2 a.m. on the eighteenth. He went to the window which had been left slightly ajar. Hunter jumped off Nimal's bed, growling under his breath until Rohan placed a hand on his head.

'What's up, yaar?' said Umedh softly, joining Rohan.

'Don't know,' said Rohan. 'I thought it was the storm, but it's dead calm outside, and the sky's clear.'

The sound increased gradually, waking Brian and Nimal, and Nimal joined the others at the window.

'It's a chopper – coming in this direction,' said Umedh. 'Do you think something's happened?'

'They'd call us – and if they were taking animals to town, this is the wrong direction,' said Brian, looking puzzled.

'I'm going out,' said Rohan.

'Us, too,' said Nimal and Umedh.

'Hunter, Tumbler – stay!' said Nimal.

Hunter looked mournfully up at Nimal, but obeyed, while Tumbler snuggled down beside Brian.

'Don't turn on the lights,' said Rohan hastily, as Umedh reached for the light switch. 'Just a thought,' he continued, as the others stared at him.

The boys hurriedly pulled on jeans and sweaters, and as he placed a couple of thick sweaters within the boy's reach, Rohan said, 'Brian, can you make your way to the lounge – without turning the lights on?'

'Of course,' said Brian, pulling on a sweater and using his crutches to get into his wheelchair. 'I'll have some hot chocolate ready – you'll need it when you return.'

'It's getting louder, chaps,' said Rohan, slipping a torch into his pocket. 'Let's go.'

They hurried out of the dormitory. Pulling on coats and boots, they left the building, closing the door behind them.

Outside was a fairyland! The snow lay in deep drifts along the walls where it had been blown, and everything was covered in pure white.

'Talk softly, keep together, and don't use your torches,' muttered Rohan.

'The sound's louder,' whispered Nimal, 'and it's on the other side of the wall.'

They made their way through the trees and stopped opposite the window of their dormitory. The pile of rocks and stones, which were the ruins of the previous castle, was further away, while the forest, which began a few metres away from the building, was extremely dense, and extended to the boundary wall, a hundred metres behind.

Hidden just inside the tree line, the boys listened intently.

'Where's it coming from? It's not coming *over* KWCC,' said Rohan.

'Look – a light flashed among the ruins,' said Umedh excitedly.

'And there it is again,' whispered Nimal, as they saw a light flash up into the sky and arc towards the boundary wall. 'Let's get closer to those rocks.'

'Hold it,' said Rohan urgently. 'The chopper's descending.' Two minutes later, the engine cut off and there was silence.

'It's landed on the other side of the wall,' said Umedh. 'I'm sure those lights were signalling it.'

'Let's go,' said Rohan softly, moving deeper into the forest, the others at his heels, and within a few minutes they were opposite the pile of rocks.

The ruins covered an area of some 1,200 square metres. Three or four columns were still standing, some of them broken in half, while the rest was a pile of rocks and stones.

The boys kept their eyes peeled, but there was nothing unusual to be seen. No more lights flashed, there was no sound from the helicopter and there was nobody in sight.

'Brrr, it's freezing,' whispered Nimal, 35 minutes later.

'Let's wait another . . .' Rohan broke off.

They heard the helicopter start up and move away, the sound getting fainter, until they could not hear it anymore.

'Let's see if the signaller comes out of hiding,' whispered Umedh.

They waited expectantly, but saw nothing.

'Let's get back,' muttered Rohan, finally, 'but go quietly and stay alert.'

Soon they were pulling off their coats and boots in the warmth of the castle and making their way to the lounge, where Hunter welcomed them joyfully. He did not bark, but whined softly.

Thick curtains were drawn across the windows, electric heaters were turned on, along with a couple of lamps, and the lounge was warm and cosy. The boys sank onto the carpet, thankfully toasting themselves in front of the heaters.

'You've been out for nearly an hour – you must be frozen,' said Brian, joining them quickly. 'Tumbler yapped as we left the dorm and woke Amy and Anu. I updated them; they're preparing hot chocolate and sandwiches.'

'Excellent thinking, Brian – drawing the curtains and turning on heaters instead of a lighting a fire,' said Rohan.

'I didn't want anyone to see smoke coming out of the chimney at this hour,' said Brian.

'Are Mich and Gina still asleep?' asked Nimal.

'Yes, but Anu said she'd wake them when you returned,' said Brian. 'I'll go and tell her.'

He whizzed out at top speed. Within ten minutes everyone was sipping hot drinks and eating sandwiches. Mich and Gina, thrilled to have what felt like a midnight feast, were surprisingly wide-awake for 3 a.m.

'What happened?' asked Brian eagerly.

The boys updated everyone.

'Crooks – obviously,' said Amy.

'Brian, these walls are pretty solid and soundproof, right?' asked Rohan.

'Absolutely. I figure that if our window was *closed* we'd never have heard the chopper; the Burns crowd wouldn't hear it either.'

'And it would be assumed that during a snowstorm, our windows would be shut – especially since many of us are used to warmer weather,' said Rohan. 'But the chopper landed *outside* the boundary wall, somewhere in line with the ruins, and lights flashed from *inside* KWCC.'

'If, for instance, the crooks were meeting with CAB,' said Nimal, 'how and where did they meet?'

'The secret passage!' yelled Brian excitedly. The others stared at him. 'There used to be a secret passage from the cellar to the forest outside the boundary.'

'Where? Is it still there? Can you show us?' shouted the others.

'One at a time, JEACs – give Brian a chance to explain,' said Anu, speaking over the hubbub.

They quietened down, and Brian said, 'I learnt about it a year ago. Robert MacCale, KWCC's patron, was here for meetings. Cormag and Eadan spent the weekend with me, and we met Mr. MacCale at lunch. He's super, and wanted us to sit at the table with him and some of the others from Burns.

'Over lunch, he asked us what we liked best about KWCC. We told him we loved the animals, riding the ski-doos, helping around the Centre; and then Cormag, who had finished one of the Enid Blyton adventure stories that day, added that it was superb to live in these old castles, and that the only thing missing was a secret passage.

'Mr. MacCale laughed and said that *of course* there used to be a secret passage in Cairns before that section collapsed. It began through a secret entrance in the cellar, went under the forest and the boundary wall, and came out on the other side. We were thrilled and asked if we could explore it immediately. But Mr. MacCale didn't know where it was, though he said there was probably a book in the library which would have information. He told us to wait until the ruins were examined, to ensure they were safe – and Mum made us promise that we wouldn't sneak off. We were returning to school after lunch, so there wasn't even time to check the library.'

'So, when did you check it out?' breathed Mich and Gina.

'Never.'

The others groaned in disappointment. 'Why not?' asked Rohan.

'Because, while we were at school, some of the staff checked the ruins, discovered it was still dangerous, and nobody was allowed to play there,' said Brian. 'In fact, one of the chaps triggered a landslide when he climbed up a pile of rocks, and was injured – that's when they put up danger signs.'

'Blow! What a shame,' said Nimal. 'Didn't you ever check it out?'

'Yes, some years ago, and there was no landslide,' said Brian. 'But since we didn't know about a secret passage, we thought it was just a pile of rocks, and didn't bother.'

'And I guess, shortly after you heard about the passage, you were in the accident, and had other things on your mind,' said Anu.

Brian nodded, 'Yes – I haven't thought about it until this minute.'

'Brian, who checked the ruins?' asked Rohan. 'Did Dan delegate someone?

'Beiste offered, and John, who was also at the table, offered, too,' said Brian. 'John left KWCC some months ago; Beiste's the one who fell and was injured.'

'Why Beiste?' said Rohan. 'Was he particularly free at that time?'

'No – but Beiste was new, and eager to help, and he and John lived closest to Cairns,' explained Brian.

'Beiste's name keeps popping up,' said Rohan, thoughtfully. 'Nimal, if you don't mind, I'll switch tasks with you because I need you at this end – wish I could be in two places at the same time. Brian and I will find out about the secret passage. We'll drop the girls off and go to the library; hopefully, Friseal will be around to assist us with the old books.'

'Great idea, yaar,' said Nimal. 'What's my job?'

'Find footprints and draw them – you're an excellent artist and tracker,' said Rohan. He glanced at his watch. 'It's nearly four, and we should leave in half an hour. Umedh, Amy and Anu, join Nimal. Examine the ruins and surrounding area – look for footprints and anything else. I'm almost positive those danger signs are just for show. Staff and volunteers will be starting work shortly, and outsiders, if any, will be in hiding. Try and discover where the light flashed from. Set your watch alarm, Umedh, and start de-icing the waterholes by six at the latest. JEACs, this is our secret – keep mum. And Umedh, lock the front door.'

In great excitement, the JEACs rushed off, each of them wishing they could be in more than one place at a time.

Rohan, Brian, Gina and Mich, along with Hunter and Tumbler, set off for Knox in a snowcat, while the others headed for the ruins.

CHAPTER 9

Investigative Work

'Split up – we'll cover more ground,' said Umedh, as they reached their destination.

Umedh went to the far end of the ruins, close to the tree line; Anu and Amy walked around the ruins, in opposite directions. Nimal climbed up some of the rubble and examined the columns. At the third one, he quickly called the others.

'It looks as if someone was stamping up and down in the snow, but there are some clear prints,' he said, sketching rapidly.

'Footprints galore,' exclaimed Amy, shining her torch on them, while Anu took pictures.

'Actually, there are *two* sets of prints,' said Nimal, 'and if the lights were flashed from here, it's not surprising we didn't see anybody – they were hidden by this column.'

'Agreed, yaar; so there were two people,' said Umedh, following the prints. 'Both sets go first in one direction and then in another. There's a bit of a muddle here, where they've stopped and returned along the same path – that's bizarre.'

'Pacing to keep warm,' said Amy. 'And I found more prints around the bottom of the ruins – they were going up that mound of rocks towards the pile of dead branches, near the danger sign. Let's follow that, Umedh, while these two finish here.'

They walked parallel to the footprints, testing each snow-covered rock and stone, before climbing up; fortunately, it was not slippery, and they reached the top of the mound safely.

'Why would anyone climb up this mound to look at branches?' said Amy.

'Yeah, it's weird,' said Umedh, flashing his torch around. 'Look, they descend beyond the branches – come on.'

They called the others and followed the descending prints, which led them towards the tree line.

'There's another set, coming *from* the forest, parallel to this lot,' said Anu, who had been shining her torch in an arc. 'Over there, three metres to the right – Nimal, see where it goes.'

Nimal quickly followed the footsteps and returned to say, 'They lead to the tracks going up the mound.'

'Nimal and I'll check this one leading to the trees, and you two check the other,' said Amy.

Although the prints entered and left the forest at different points, there was a section a few metres inside the forest where it was obvious that they had merged once more onto a path.

'And this path goes through the woods,' said Nimal, who had been examining the ground carefully. 'Come on.'

The trail led away from Cairns and up a small hill.

'It ends here,' said Umedh, 'and there are ski marks, going down.'

'Blow,' said Nimal. 'Should we try and follow them?'

'I'm positive it'll lead to Clyde's lodging, yaar,' said Umedh, pulling out a map and tracing the route.

'You're right, Umedh,' said Amy. 'What next?'

'I'm curious as to why people would walk all the way up to those branches and then walk down the other side,' said Umedh. 'If they wanted to stay warm, they needn't have clambered over tons of rubble; also, if they wanted a good view of the area, they could have climbed up the higher mounds, near the pillars, for instance. The branches are on the lowest heap of rocks – it's illogical. Let's go back.'

They returned to the branches and examined the pile carefully.

Nimal suddenly squatted next to one of the branches and said in a low voice, 'Look! There's no snow on that branch, and see what it's covering.' The others followed his pointing finger. Under the branch was a large piece of black tarpaulin.

'I believe we've found the secret passage,' said Umedh thoughtfully. 'This tarpaulin probably covers the entrance to the cellar, and the passage must begin somewhere in there.'

'Makes sense, yaar,' said Nimal. 'The building is razed to ground level. If the door and part of the floor collapsed, there would be a hole into the cellar. We should . . .' he broke off as Umedh's watch alarm went off.

'Blow – it's 5:45 already, and we've got to de-ice the waterholes,' said Umedh.

'Bother,' said the others, as they scrambled down reluctantly and made their way to the sheds.

'Should we call the others or report in person?' said Nimal.

'The latter. If they've found a map, that'll be even better, and we can explore it together. You know they'd want to be here, too,' said Anu, starting her ski-doo.

They raced off, de-iced the waterholes and, in a short time, were on their way to Burns.

*****

Rohan and Brian dropped the girls at Knox, declined the offer of a hot drink, and reached Ruthven in time for the first breakfast.

'You're early birds,' said Drostan, patting Hunter and Tumbler who were prancing around him and Ceana. 'Are you looking for the worm?'

'Sure – and we're willing to split it, too,' laughed Rohan, 'though we'd much rather have bacon, eggs and some of that delicious-smelling coffee.'

Ceana smiled as she gave the dogs two huge bowls of food, and said, 'Why don't you join us in the kitchen. Where are the others?'

'We dropped Gina and Mich at Knox – they're spending the morning there and I'll pick them up around lunchtime. The others will do the waterholes on their way to Burns for breakfast, after which Umedh and Nimal will come here, and we three will assist in setting up booths, while Brian helps in the office,' said Rohan casually.

'What about Amy and Anu?' said Drostan.

'They'll help with chores at Burns and join us for lunch,' said Brian, imitating Rohan's casual tone.

Friseal joined them and Rohan brought the topic round to the library.

'We've got a marvellous collection,' said Friseal enthusiastically.

'Do you have old books about this piece of land?' asked Rohan.

'Why, yes – come on, I'll show you some of them.'

Thanking Ceana and Drostan for breakfast, the three of them made their way to the huge library.

'In here,' said Friseal, ushering them into a small room and closing the door. There were three book cases, floor to ceiling, along one wall of the room. 'We have to monitor the temperature because some of the books are so old that they might disintegrate in warmer temperatures. This unit contains books about the KWCC land,' he added, pointing to one of the book cases.

'Do you have a book on Cairns before it became a ruin?' asked Rohan.

'Of course,' said Friseal, reaching down a book from the topmost shelf and placing it carefully on the table. 'Cairns was damaged during one of the early wars.'

'Have you read the book?' asked Rohan.

'Not cover to cover, but about a year ago, one of the staff asked me about it, and I found the book for him.'

'Who was it?' asked Brian.

'Beiste – which surprised me – he'd never visited the library before, nor has he visited it since. He said he was curious to see what the Cairns castle looked like so that he could describe it to a friend who was crazy about ancient castles. He wanted to make copies of some of the pages which showed diagrams of the castle and the grounds, but I told him that he would have to draw them – the heat of a copier could destroy the book.' Friseal sounded extremely indignant.

'We promise we won't damage the book,' said Rohan quickly. 'If we need any drawings, Brian will do them.'

'I trust you boys,' said Friseal. 'Once you've finished, leave it on the table for me.'

He got them paper, pencils and an eraser, and went out.

'What a stroke of luck – it's saved us hours,' said Rohan, turning the pages carefully. 'Not a shock that it was Beiste who wanted to see the book, was it?'

'Nope,' said Brian. 'Here's a whole section with maps and plans.'

They studied the drawings carefully and soon found the one they wanted.

'A Plan of the Underground Passage referred to on page 410,' said Rohan, reading the heading. He turned to page 410 and they bent over the page.

'This is it,' said Brian excitedly. 'It starts in the cellar, goes under the building and forest and is about 320 metres long. Would that make sense, Rohan?'

'I think so, yaar. The distance under the building is about fifteen to twenty metres; then to the boundary wall would be approximately 200 or 225 metres, so another 75 metres would take it under and beyond the wall.'

'Perfect,' said Brian. 'I'll make a copy.'

Rohan watched in admiration as Brian, effortlessly, drew the plan, not once using an eraser.

'Man, you're brill,' said Rohan. 'Make a couple of other drawings, so that we don't have to lie to Friseal.'

Brian copied three more pictures, one of them a portrait of the complete castle.

Rohan's watch beeped – it was 7:50.

'Time to go, yaar,' said Rohan, closing the book gently. 'Slip the map of the passage under your blanket, and place the other three drawings on top, in case Friseal wants to see them.'

As they reached Friseal's desk, his telephone rang. He picked it up, placed his hand over the mouthpiece and asked them if they'd found what they were looking for. They nodded, thanked him, told him they had left the book on the table, and went out.

'When should we call your mates?' asked Rohan.

'They'll be home by noon. I say – could they join us?'

'Absolutely – they're part of this adventure.'

'I'll call their parents immediately and arrange things,' said Brian.

They reached the office and, delighted with their success, high-fived each other before Brian went in and Rohan joined the rest of the volunteers who were starting work on the booths.

*****

Mich and Gina were having a blast. After a hot drink, they followed Sally and Quentin to the petting zoo, going first to the panda enclosure to gaze at the baby panda rapturously, while Sally put food into the enclosure.

'Let's feed the red deer,' said Sally, opening the door to their pen. 'Last night we had to move the mother, because she was sick.'

The three fawns came rushing over to greet Sally and the girls, nosing them eagerly for milk.

'Sit down and they'll cuddle up. Although they can lap the milk, they still prefer feeding bottles.'

They sat down, each selecting a fawn, and soon the little creatures were feeding hungrily.

'They're so cute and I love feeding them,' said Gina, and Mich agreed.

'I know,' said Sally. 'They're such harmless, friendly little things – I wish people weren't rough with them.'

'But . . . surely nobody could even *think* of hurting them – you wouldn't let them,' said Mich, shocked at the thought.

'We try not to,' said Sally. 'But that's why I don't like Clyde.'

Mich and Gina looked at each other quickly, and Gina said, trying to sound casual, 'Why, Sally?'

'A week ago we needed assistance with feeding the babies, and only Clyde was free. We split the rounds; I finished first and came to see if he needed a hand. As I came up, he smacked the fawns and pushed them away when they tried to get at the milk. He didn't see me; I wanted to yell at him, but since he's senior to me, I bit my tongue.'

Sally's voice rose with indignation while the girls wiped away tears of anger.

'What did you do?' whispered Gina.

'I called out that I was done and he pretended to pet the fawns, who were now lapping up the milk, saying, "They're such impatient creatures, aren't they?" I said nothing and he came out of the enclosure.'

'What a horrid man,' said Mich.

'He is,' agreed Sally. 'I don't know why he works here – he obviously doesn't love the animals.'

'Did you tell the others?' said Gina.

'Yes, and they were upset, too. Anyway, let's forget about him, girls – we have lots to do.'

They spent the next hour happily feeding the babies, and then returned to a huge breakfast and the added fun of feeding Gormal.

After the meal the girls assisted with various chores. Ailean, when he heard that they were going to Ruthven for lunch, offered them a ride since he had to go there for a meeting, and promised to inform Rohan accordingly.

'Thanks, Ailean,' said Gina and Mich gratefully, and were happy when Mòrag said they could stay for an entire day once the fundraiser was over.

*****

Umedh, Amy, Anu and Nimal reached Burns just as some of the staff were sitting down to breakfast.

'Have you eaten?' asked Doilidh.

'No, but Nimal and I need to get to Ruthven by eight to help with the booths,' said Umedh.

'Lots of time for a meal,' said Luag.

So they sat down to a hearty breakfast, explaining, briefly, where the others were.

'Since we're not going to Ruthven until lunchtime, we thought we'd help out here,' offered Amy.

'That would be grand,' said Doilidh. 'Gavan's going to Ruthven around ten, and Beiste after lunch.'

'We're yours to command,' said Anu. 'Aren't Gavan and Taran joining us?'

'They've already eaten,' said Beiste, 'and they're finalizing the schedule for security around the animals during the fundraiser.'

'Let us know if we can help, Luag,' said Nimal.

'Okay, thanks.'

The boys finished their meal and set off for Ruthven, and Luag went to his office. The girls, Beiste and Doilidh began preparing food for the animals.

'Doilidh,' said Luag, entering the kitchen, 'my computer's playing up – could you give me a hand, please?'

'Okay,' said Doilidh. 'Ladies, don't cut yourselves.'

'I'll look after them, Doilidh,' said Beiste, with a smirk, and Doilidh winked at the girls before following Luag.

Amy, remembering their goal, smiled and said in a sugary voice, 'Thanks, Beiste – that's kind of you.'

Anu bit her lip and bent over the carrots she was slicing so that her hair covered her face, hiding a grin.

'So, Beiste,' continued Amy, fluttering her eyelashes, 'what do *you* like doing when you're on holiday?'

Beiste was flattered – not many people were interested in him. 'All kinds of things, Amy, I'm a man of varied hobbies. I like to travel, and I dabble in archaeology – you know, I diggy, dig, dig,' he said, laughing idiotically.

'Which countries have you visited?' asked Anu.

'Most European countries; and a couple of years ago, a friend and I went on a trip to China, India and Nepal.'

'Which parts of Nepal did you visit?' said Amy.

'Kathmandu first, where we met some hunters – er – they were my mate's pals,' stammered Beiste. He laughed weakly and added, 'I tried to convince them that they shouldn't kill animals, but they're not into wildlife conservation like us.'

The girls pretended they had not noticed his confusion, and Amy said, brightly, 'I'd love to travel around the world, wouldn't you, Anu?'

'Definitely. Beiste, I've finished the carrots; what's next?'

'Apples, please – I'll wash them,' said Beiste, glad to change the topic.

His mobile telephone rang as he put the apples in a bowl. He looked at the number, excused himself and stepped out of the kitchen to answer it.

Amy nudged Anu, who followed him and heard him hiss into the telephone, 'I told you *not* to call me. What's up?' He saw Anu, and added quickly, 'Sorry, Jim – have to run. I'll call you at nine, bye.' He rang off and said to Anu, 'Did you want something?'

'The bathroom, please,' said Anu politely.

He directed her and re-entered the kitchen. When Anu returned, they finished preparing the rest of the food, and Beiste thanked them profusely.

'Now, what will you ladies do?' asked Beiste. 'It's 8:45 and Doilidh should be back soon. I have to do some rounds.'

'May we join you?' asked Anu, smiling sweetly. 'We'd love to see the animals again, and you could tell us more about them.'

'Yes, please, Beiste,' cooed Amy.

Flattered by their apparent eagerness for his company, he agreed. 'Okay – the wildcats are first.'

They reached the enclosure and when Beiste threw in some meat, the wildcats rushed over and started feeding. The girls admired them and asked Beiste many questions.

He answered patiently, though not quite accurately, and said, looking at his watch, 'I have to make a quick call – er – about a dig I'm going on. You go ahead and see the otters – they're behind those trees in the enclosure next to the stream – I'll join you shortly.'

'Sure,' said Amy, and she and Anu walked on through the trees.

'Amy, carry on while I nip back and try to overhear him,' whispered Anu, urgently.

Amy nodded. Slipping silently through the trees, Anu soon heard Beiste's voice, raised in anger. She hid in some bushes and listened hard.

'Stop panicking, Moire. I keep telling you *not* to bug me during the day – there are always people around. *I'll call you* – understand?' He listened and then continued, 'Of *course* everything's under control. Xian called last evening, and said he'd spoken to you; I told him there wouldn't be any outsiders allowed this time.' Another pause, and then Beiste said,

'I've got to go – someone's trying to call me – stick to the instructions, and get cracking on that passage.'

He rang off, dialled another number, and said, 'Gavan? You called?'

Anu ran back and joined Amy, but before she could say anything, Beiste came towards them, still talking to Gavan.

'Sorry about that, ladies,' said Beiste as he rang off. 'Gavan's leaving for Ruthven shortly and had to check something.'

'Do you mind my asking where your dig is?' asked Amy.

'Er . . . we're going to a site they've discovered in . . . er . . . Spain.'

'Sounds fun – when does it start?' said Anu.

'On the twenty-first – I mean, I've got a 5 a.m. flight on the twenty-first and Osgar's promised to take me to the airport.'

'The day after the fundraiser – but what about the Christmas hols?' said Amy.

'We're a dedicated group,' said Beiste, with a silly laugh. 'It's only a week, and we'll probably – I mean, *definitely*, spend Christmas in Spain, and then I'll be back.'

'Exciting,' said Anu, turning her head and winking at Amy.

'Gee, Anu,' said Amy, promptly, 'we forgot to call the APs – may we call from the house, Beiste?'

'Sure,' said Beiste. 'I'd offer you my mobile, but the battery's dying.'

They thanked him effusively. He assured them that the pleasure was all his, and heaved a sigh of relief as they ran off.

As they neared the building, the girls stopped and Anu quickly updated Amy.

'Gosh – Moire, again, *and a passage* – I'm positive it's the one at Cairns,' said Amy, excitedly.

'Absolutely, and I hope the boys have information on it. I wonder what Beiste meant by "get cracking on that passage".'

'Search me. And Beiste's also going away *immediately* after the fundraiser,' said Amy. 'Come on – let's find Doilidh and get her reaction to that beast.'

'Wait, there's Gavan – let's see if we can get his opinion of Beiste.'

Gavan turned at Anu's call. 'Hello, ladies,' he said.

'Are you going to Ruthven, Gavan?' asked Anu.

'That's right.'

'I think Beiste said he was going over after lunch, didn't he, Amy?'

'He did.' She wrinkled her nose and continued, 'I hate to admit it, Gavan, but that guy . . . there's something about him . . .'

She trailed off and Gavan said, 'He's not, shall we say, too appealing?' The girls nodded, and he continued, 'Unfortunately, not everyone's as charming as *moi*.'

The girls chuckled and Anu said, 'Do *you* like him, Gavan, or is it just us girls?'

Gavan hesitated and then said frankly, 'I don't – but he's a colleague, so I try and get along with him; we have nothing in common, but we're working for the same cause.'

He turned the conversation to the fundraiser, amusing the girls with an anecdote from a past event, and then went off on his ski-doo.

'He's a nice chap, isn't he?' said Anu, as they waved goodbye.

'Sure is,' said Amy, opening the door.

Doilidh greeted them with mugs of hot chocolate, which they took to the lounge. 'What were you doing outside?' asked Doilidh.

'Feeding the wildcats, but then Beiste had to make a call about the dig he's going on,' said Amy, 'so Anu and I watched the otters.'

'Dig? I thought he was going on holiday,' said Doilidh.

'No, it's a dig – in Spain,' said Anu.

'Probably another fairy tale – my dad's an archaeologist, and when Beiste first mentioned he liked archaeology, I asked him a few questions; I received the impression that he didn't know a lot and was just conning.'

'Interesting – are you friendly with him, Dolly?' asked Amy.

'We're polite,' said Doilidh, with a rueful laugh, 'but I avoid him when possible, and he *never* talks about archaeology when I'm around.'

'You don't like him, do you?' said Anu.

'What conclusions you jump to, love,' said Doilidh, smiling wickedly. 'He's a colleague; I keep hoping that he'll get a fabulously well-paid job, somewhere at the opposite end of the world. Now, if you've finished your drinks, we'll prepare more food, after which you'll need to leave for Ruthven.'

The girls laughed but didn't question her further – they got the picture.

CHAPTER 10

Double, Double Toil and Trouble!

The JEACs didn't have an opportunity to exchange news over lunch since the dining room was packed.

'Phew! Putting up booths is hot work,' said Nimal, flopping into a chair beside Brian and mopping his brow with a large handkerchief.

'Sure is, mate,' said Uisdean, as he and Uallas joined the group, 'which is why we do this type of work in minus 15°C temperatures.'

'It feels more like plus 40°C, and it's almost too hot to eat much,' said Nimal, heaping stew onto his plate.

'Poor laddie,' grinned Uallas, passing him more dishes. 'I feel for you.'

'Where are Rohan and Umedh?' asked Amy.

'They were finishing off another booth and should be here soon,' said Nimal. 'Where are the kiddies and the dogs?'

'The dogs are in the kitchen, being spoilt by Ceana and Drostan,' said Brian, 'and the girls are having a little nap.'

'Hi, folks,' said Rohan, as he and Umedh joined them. 'Brian, did you speak to your buddies?'

'I spoke to their maters, and the boys will get here around 2 p.m. today,' said Brian.

'Are Eadan and Cormag coming over?' asked Uallas.

'Yes – and they'll stay at Cairns with us,' said Brian, excitedly.

'Superfantabulous,' said Anu. 'I'm looking forward to meeting them.'

'Watch out for Eadan,' said Uallas. 'Nice lad, but a holy terror. A mate of mine, who's a master at their school, claims that his hair is pure white because of Eadan.'

'Sounds like someone I know,' said Umedh, looking slyly at Nimal. 'What does he do?'

'Plays hair-raising tricks,' said Uallas, and he and Brian had the others in fits of laughter at their stories.

'Can't wait to meet him,' said Nimal.

'After that meeting, Uallas, tell your pal to put in his order for a wig – *all* his hair will be raised – right off his scalp, just like Nimal's form master last year,' said Rohan.

'It's not my fault . . .' began Nimal as the others burst out laughing, but just then Dan entered the room.

'It's 12:45 – and we have more booths to put up,' he announced.

Uallas and Uisdean went off immediately, and Dan came over to speak to the JEACs.

'Thanks for your hard work, boys – we're getting along well. I just heard that six more volunteers are arriving at 2 o'clock, along with Cormag and Eadan, so we'll have plenty of assistance. You're welcome to stay here, or you can go back to Cairns and have some fun.'

'Okay, Dan – we'll take the boys back to Cairns when they arrive,' said Rohan.

'How can we help tomorrow?' asked Amy.

'Jay will give you the low-down,' said Dan, as his wife joined them.

He hurried off. 'Hello, JEACs minus two,' said Jay. 'The youngsters are bushed; you need an early evening today and *no work* tomorrow. More volunteers arrive tomorrow morning – and we'll be fine. Take it easy – have fun in the snow, and don't forget, you have to be here by 8 a.m. for the fundraiser, the day after tomorrow.'

'Will do, Jay,' said Rohan, and the others nodded.

'I'm glad Cormag and Eadan are joining you; you'd better ask Drostan and Ceana for extra food – the amount of food those two lads consume would make a boa constrictor jealous.' She smiled and hurried away.

The three older boys left to assist with setting up a stage, while Amy, Anu and Brian helped in the office; a little later, Brenda joined them. She was delighted to meet Amy and Anu, and they were soon discussing the snow leopard situation. She was fanatical about security and told them about the stringent measures that had been put in place to prevent any crooks from entering KWCC.

'You've certainly covered all contingencies,' said Anu, admiringly, 'and we'll keep our eyes open, too.'

'Excellent,' said Brenda. 'And look out for my nephews, please – they'll want to join the JEACs.'

'Sure, Brenda,' promised Brian.

'Thanks. I have to make a number of calls before our meeting – it was great meeting you, girls, and I hope to meet the others soon.'

'Good to meet you, too, Brenda,' said the girls, and since the staff were preparing for a meeting, the JEACs said goodbye and left. It was nearly 2 o'clock.

Mich and Gina were in the kitchen, fawning over Hunter and Tumbler.

'I think I hear a helicopter arriving,' said Mich, running to the window. 'Yes – it's landing.'

'Cormag and Eadan,' yelled Brian, looking at his watch. 'Come on.'

'You three go ahead,' said Anu. 'Amy and I'll collect the food and join you.'

Brian, Gina and Mich sped to the main entrance of Ruthven.

'I didn't know they were coming today,' panted Gina.

'Last-minute decision,' said Brian.

They reached the door as it burst open, and two exuberant boys bounced in.

'Hey, mate, long time no see,' yelled Eadan, shaking hands with Brian.

'Great to see you, buddy,' cried Cormag, high-fiving him.

'The three amigos – together again!' shouted Brian, thrilled to see his friends.

Mich and Gina giggled. Neither boy had noticed them, and Brian was busy asking his friends how they had fared in their examinations.

'Forget school – if I scrape through, it'll be a miracle!' roared Eadan. 'I'm thrilled to be here.'

The boys laughed, and Brian said, 'I bet *you'll* top the form, as always, Cormag.'

Cormag grinned and said, 'Och, now, I guess I'll pass okay, mate. And how are you? You look amazingly fit. What have you been up to?'

'Having a blast, and I want you to meet some very special folk,' said Brian excitedly. 'Gosh – I forgot.'

He turned his wheelchair, and Cormag and Eadan noticed the girls.

'Sorry, Gina and Mich,' apologized Brian. 'These are my buddies; chaps – Mich and Gina – they're JEACs – and they and their families and Jay's nephew are here for Christmas. We have tons to tell you.'

Eadan bounced over to shake hands – he had three older sisters. Cormag, the eldest of four brothers, was a little shy, though he smiled and shook hands, too. Gina and Mich responded politely, and the group stood there for a couple of minutes, not quite sure what to do or say next. Fortunately, Anu and Amy, along with the dogs, joined them almost immediately, smiling warmly at the newcomers.

'Here we are – bag and baggage,' said Amy. 'Now, who's who?'

Brian made the introductions, and soon everyone was laughing and relaxed. Hunter was introduced to the boys, and they adored him.

Anu, her back to the door, glanced at her watch and said, 'And now we just have to wait for those boys – they're *always* late – they're probably . . .'

'Are you calling us unpunctual, sis?' growled a deep voice in her ear, as her brother laid his cold cheek against her warm one.

Anu jumped in shock; recovering quickly, she punched Rohan on the arm. 'Oooh! Your cheek's freezing. Of course I didn't mean *you*, bro,' she offered sweetly. 'I was . . . er . . . you know . . .' she trailed off and said hastily, 'Have you met Cordan and Eamag? I mean . . .'

Amidst gales of laughter, which brought some of the office staff into the hallway to ask what the joke was, the boys introduced themselves.

'We'd better take off,' said Rohan, looking at his watch. 'The ski-doos and snowcat are lined up outside. Cormag and Eadan, for today, Umedh and Nimal will take you.'

They nodded, and Umedh added, 'There are ski-doos for you at Cairns.'

'What about Brian?' asked Cormag.

'He, Mich and Gina are in the snowcat with me,' said Rohan. He winked at Brian and glanced briefly at the other JEACs – they understood, immediately, that they were to keep mum about Brian's abilities on the ski-doo.

'I'll come with you, Nimal,' said Eadan, who had instinctively taken to the boy.

'Naturally,' said Nimal. 'We have lots to discuss.'

'*Double, double toil and trouble!*' muttered Anu, pretending to stir a cauldron.

'Hopefully,' said Amy, sotto voce, 'they'll be so busy yapping that they'll miss the route and end up in China.'

'I heard that, darling Amy,' said Nimal wickedly. 'You do enjoy having icy feet in bed, right?'

'Nimal,' shrieked Amy, 'If you *dare* to put an ice block . . . I'll . . . well, you'd better watch out!'

Nimal hugged her affectionately, and said, 'I'd *never* do anything mean to you, Amy – I love you too much. And,' he added, sotto voce, 'I'm petrified of subsequent measures Rohan will take to avenge you.'

'*Goodbye*, JEACs,' laughed Nilini, as she and Friseal handed out coats and boots.

The ATVs made it back in record time. A huge amount of hot chocolate was prepared, cookies, cakes and dog treats were put out, and the group settled down in the lounge, eager to share their discoveries.

CHAPTER 11

The Sco-Js

'Right – it's 3 p.m. and I'm eager to hear what was discovered this morning at Cairns,' said Rohan. 'Since we need everybody's report, and Cormag and Eadan must be brought up to speed, let's do that first. Do you want me to give them the low-down, Brian?'

'Yes, please.'

'Okay, chaps – jump in with questions,' said Rohan, 'and JEACs, as always, feel free to interject with extra info.'

Eadan raised his hand immediately and said with a grin, 'Excuse me, please, sir, but what does *JEACs* mean?'

'Good question, son,' said Nimal paternally.

Anu explained quickly, and both boys joined up at once.

Next, Rohan laid out the scenario concisely, up to the point where the JEACs had parted that morning.

'Wow!' breathed Cormag and Eadan.

'Things *have* been developing,' said Cormag. 'Thanks, awfully, for including us. It's so exciting.'

'Yeah, we're thrilled to be here,' added Eadan.

'You Sco-Js were . . .' began Rohan. He trailed off as everyone yelled, '*You whats?*' Rohan chuckled, 'I meant the Scottish JEACs – and abbreviated it.'

'We love it,' laughed the Sco-Js.

'To continue, you Sco-Js were involved first, and we'll see this through together. After all, we're JEACs, and anything that threatens our beloved animals must be dealt with.'

'Three cheers for the JEACs!' yelled Eadan, exuberantly, and the roof rang with their cheers.

'Okay – starting with the youngest, we'll only report on CAB for now,' said Rohan. 'Mich and Gina, begin. Cormag, I hear you want to be a detective, so feel free to make notes – I always do.'

'Thanks,' said Cormag, pulling out his notebook.

The girls reported the incident with Clyde and the baby deer, which upset everyone.

'Another black mark against him,' growled Nimal.

'Brian, you're next,' said Rohan, 'at least, are you the youngest of you three chaps?'

'A couple of months younger than Cormag; Eadan's the oldest.'

'Fire away, yaar,' said Umedh.

'I spoke with Saroj, Nilini and a couple of others. I also spoke with Osgar, who came in to make some calls. In brief, not *one* of them likes either Clyde or Beiste.'

'Anything specific, Brian?' asked Rohan.

'No. But Osgar said, "Beast, by name and nature, is what that one is", and that Clyde was untrustworthy – though he had no facts and was going on instinct.'

'Thanks, Brian. Cormag?' said Rohan.

'Only one thing which struck me, a couple of days ago – Clyde was carrying a tranquillizer *pistol* that night – it's another point against him. The impact of a pistol-shot dart is very hard on an animal and is never used here, so why would he need one?'

'Excellent point,' said Rohan making a note. 'Eadan, do you recall the conversation you heard between Moire and Beiste, where Moire mentioned the name *Soofi*?' Eadan nodded. 'Since then, we've heard the name *Zulfikar* – could it have been *Zulfi* you heard?'

Eadan closed his eyes, thinking hard, and then said firmly, 'It *was* Zulfi – given the situation, it couldn't have been anything else.'

'Makes sense,' agreed Cormag and Brian.

'Great,' said Rohan. 'Anu, Amy – Burns?'

Amy and Anu reported their findings, and also gave details of their conversation with Brenda.

The three older boys had each joined a different group, so Nimal reported first.

'Nothing much,' said Nimal. 'But neither of the Ashby twins likes our suspects.'

'Umedh?' said Rohan.

'Same as Nimal,' said Umedh. 'My group had Clyde, and when he went off to get something, another chap in the group said caustically, "You'd never guess that that chap was pro-conservation", and Gavan nodded in agreement.'

'I was in the same group as Beiste,' reported Rohan. 'Nobody said a word against him, but they heaved a collective sigh of relief when he left to assist another group, and the atmosphere lightened up instantly.

'Anything else?' The others shook their heads. 'So, given the feedback, it appears that most negative things point to CAB,' concluded Rohan.

'You mean – because they're both going away immediately after the fundraiser,' began Anu slowly. Her brother nodded, and she continued, 'They're both scheduled on evening and night shifts on the nineteenth and twentieth, right into the early hours of the morning of the twenty-first; they pretend that they don't know each other well, but the Sco-Js saw them together the night the snow leopards disappeared; they appear to be misfits; the animals don't like them and they seem to have no real love for animals; none of us like them and most of the staff we've spoken to appear to tolerate them; and the police still haven't solved the mystery of how the snow leopards were taken away and killed. There are too many suspicious facts.'

The group agreed.

'A quick stretch, refills of hot chocolate, and then we'll report on findings at the library and the ruins,' said Rohan. 'Meet in the kitchen.'

In less than five minutes, everyone was seated around the dining table.

'Library?' said Anu eagerly.

'First – we found a book and a map of the *secret passage*,' said Rohan. The others cheered, and he continued. 'Brian made drawings and blew one up to three times its size on the copier. Secondly – Brian?'

'Beiste knows about it, and if our assumptions are correct, so does Clyde. We think Beiste found it and pretended that the ruins were unsafe so that nobody else would discover its whereabouts,' said Brian.

'Here are the drawings,' said Rohan, laying them on the table.

As the JEACs pored over the drawings, Rohan and Brian told them about their conversation with Friseal.

'The passage begins here,' said Rohan, using a chopstick as a pointer. 'There's a hidden entrance to it from the cellars of the old castle. It slopes down gradually and goes under the castle, the woods and the boundary wall – you can see it's really deep under the wall; once past the boundary wall, it rises again and comes out somewhere in the forest.'

'Brian, these are awesome – you've even given us the scale,' said Nimal. 'From a rough calculation, the passage emerges approximately 75 to 80 metres on the other side of the boundary wall. Does that sound right?'

'Yes,' agreed Brian and Rohan.

'It appears to start around here,' said Umedh, pointing at the map, 'and I think the four of us can show you exactly where it is – time for our report?'

'Fire away, yaar,' said Rohan eagerly.

Using the map as a reference, Amy, Anu, Nimal and Umedh quickly updated the others on their discoveries.

'So, if we're correct, it looks like CAB are the inside crooks – perhaps Beiste, who was here first, was sent by the group, and then Clyde arrived; Moire, Zulfikar, Huang, Xian and Rizana are part of the same outfit, but only two of them have been caught, and there could be more. This could turn out to be an international gang of illegal animal pelt traders,' said Rohan thoughtfully. 'Based on our findings, I believe there's more trouble ahead: we overheard a phone call with Moire and mention of a passage and Xian's name; it's possible, based on the chopper, flashing lights around Cairns, and our discovery of the entrance to the passage at this end, that the crooks had a meeting in the early hours of this morning.'

He paused. 'I'm almost positive that our snow leopards are in danger – at the time of the fundraiser – and that CAB will not return to KWCC.'

'We *have* to save the animals,' said Nimal passionately. 'We need a plan of action.'

'Actually, we need several plans, yaar,' said Rohan. 'But the first step is to check out the passage . . .'

'Let's go,' yelled Eadan.

'Hold it, yaar,' laughed Umedh. 'We must be cautious – it could be dangerous.'

'Do you think crooks are *living* in the passage or cellar?' asked Amy, looking worried and casting an anxious glance at Mich and Gina.

'Unlikely – it's far too cold. From what we've learnt, it's not a place in which one could hide for a day or two. The cellar was huge, but most of it collapsed, so I would imagine there's only a small section of the cellar left, and it must have the entrance to the passage,' said Rohan reassuringly. 'I think what Umedh means is that we need to make sure none of the crooks, including CAB, are around.' Umedh nodded. 'After all, while we were at Ruthven, the crooks might have been dropped off by helicopter, entered KWCC through the passage and met with CAB – and we'd be none the wiser.'

'How can we check?' asked Anu.

'Call Friseal about CAB, Rohan,' said Brian 'He'll know their schedules for the next few hours.'

Rohan nodded, and signalling Nimal and Umedh, they left the kitchen, returning some minutes later, each carrying a rifle and darts with fluorescent yellow tailpieces.

'Gosh, it's hitting home,' gasped Eadan, as the significance of the guns dawned on them. 'Why *yellow* tailpieces?'

'We used the mildest dosage possible,' said Nimal, as they loaded the darts. 'We just want to knock out the crooks if necessary. The chart on the cabinet door in the clinic indicated yellow tailpieces were for the mildest dosage and red the most potent.'

'That bad, eh?' muttered Amy under her breath.

'CAB will be at Ruthven until ten tonight,' reported Rohan. 'Give Nimal, Umedh, Hunter and me fifteen minutes to check the area around the ruins – Hunter will sniff out strangers in a jiffy. If it's clear, one of us will stay on guard, and the other two will return for the rest of you. Brian, I'm afraid we'll have to leave Tumbler behind – he's too small. Is that okay?'

'Sure, Rohan,' said Brian, realizing that although they wouldn't want to leave him out, he might also have to stay behind, since he would be a handicap to the group. He continued valiantly, saying, 'He's tired, and if we give him some treats and put him in his basket, he'll go to sleep.'

'Great,' said Rohan, and instinctively understanding the boy's thoughts, continued quickly, 'How are your muscles? Can you ride piggyback?'

Brian nodded bemusedly.

'Good! The three of us will take turns carrying you – you're light enough – and Umedh says that if there are no steps into the cellar, we'll figure out how to lower you in and get you out – game?'

Brian grinned and high-fived him.

'Careful, yaar,' said Nimal, in mock concern. 'If your grin becomes any wider it'll meet round the back and take the top of your head off.'

Hilarious laughter eased the tense moment – nobody wanted to leave Brian out of things. They trooped into the hallway.

'It looks like snow again,' said Anu.

'Yes – but it won't start till eight or so,' said Cormag. 'I heard the weather forecast.'

'Excellent – it'll cover our footprints,' said Rohan. 'Keep the door locked.'

'Will do – be careful, okay?' said Amy quietly.

'Sure thing,' said Rohan. 'Cormag, find a length of strong rope.'

The older boys left, Hunter bounding ahead, and Amy closed the door. It was getting dark, even though it was only 4:30, and they soon lost sight of the boys.

'We'll put Tumbler in the dorm – he'll be nice and cosy there,' said Brian, hugging the drowsy puppy.

'I'll do it,' said Eadan, taking the puppy and dashing off, while Cormag went to find some rope.

They put on their winter gear and hung around the entrance, Gina and Mich peering out of a window.

'They're coming,' shrieked Gina, and Cormag opened the door quickly.

'Not a soul around,' said Rohan. 'Nimal and Hunter are on guard at the entrance to the passage.'

Umedh passed his gun to Amy; Rohan lifted Brian onto Umedh's back and said, as they went outside, 'Stick together, JEACs, and speak softly.'

He locked the door and they set off, reaching the ruins quickly. Hunter heard them approach and raced down the mound to greet them. He didn't bark or whine – he knew he had to be quiet.

'On guard, Hunter,' said Rohan, and the dog sat down obediently, his ears pricked up alertly. 'Follow the beam from Nimal's torch – Umedh, I'll help you and Brian.'

A few minutes later, everyone was on top of the mound, examining the branches and the tarpaulin.

'Let's move the branches,' said Cormag.

'Okay,' said Rohan, 'but don't put them too far away. We'll put them back once we're down.'

Umedh lowered Brian onto a large stone. They got busy and, in a short time, had rolled the tarpaulin to one side, uncovering a large hole.

'Hold on a sec,' said Nimal. 'Hunter – here, boy!'

Hunter bounded up the mound and sniffed down the hole, but didn't growl.

'Excellent. Nobody lying in wait for us,' said Nimal.

An ecstatic sigh went round the group. They were about to explore the secret passage at last.

CHAPTER 12

The Secret Passage

Umedh shone his torch into the opening. 'It's not very deep – perhaps four or five metres, and there are steps going down.'

'I'll go in first,' said Rohan.

'Okay – but as a precaution, tie the rope around your waist and we'll tie the other end to this huge stone – it won't budge,' said Umedh, taking the rope from Cormag and knotting it quickly.

Everyone shone their torches into the hole and Rohan descended cautiously.

'The steps are sound. I'm on solid ground, in a section of the cellar which is about ten or eleven metres wide,' said Rohan, softly. 'The rest of the cellar is full of rubble; the damage must have destroyed the secret opening, since the passage is clearly visible. Send Hunter to me, and we'll check the passage a little way before you come down.'

The minutes seemed to drag interminably for the others, as they knelt around the opening; but Rohan returned shortly.

'It looks all right for the next twenty metres and it's about two metres wide,' he reported. 'Hunter's on guard. Girls, you come down first, and then you chaps.'

'Right,' said Umedh, 'and once we've brought Brian down, we'll arrange the tarp halfway over the hole with the branches over it so that, at least from a distance, it'll look as if the entrance hasn't been discovered.'

'Good point,' said Rohan. A few minutes later, everyone had joined him.

'Man, this is really cool,' whispered Eadan, looking around eagerly.

'I'll lead the way. Try not to make a noise – just in case . . .' said Rohan. 'If Hunter growls, stop, and turn off your torches immediately.'

They set off. The passage was quite smooth under the castle, but beyond the building, it was hewn through rocky terrain and became a little uneven. It went in a fairly straight line, and every five or six metres, there were little niches carved out in the sides, about one and a quarter metres above the ground.

'What are these for?' asked Amy, as she passed one.

'Candles – there's a little wax left in this one,' said Anu, shining her torch into it.

After another 70 metres, they came to a halt at a small landslide which narrowed the passage down slightly.

Rohan shone his torch down the passage, and Hunter, who was sniffing ahead, brought something to him.

'What is it, boy?' asked Rohan. Hunter dropped a piece of paper into his hand.

The others crowded round. Rohan examined the paper and his eyes shone as he said, 'It's a phone number with the initials *CAM.*'

Brian gasped and said, 'Ceana Arleen McArdle? What's the number?'

Rohan told him and Brian said, thankfully, 'No, that's not her number.'

'What's *Clyde's* middle and last name?' asked Anu.

Brian thought hard and said, 'I'm drawing a blank at his surname, and I don't know his middle name – everyone goes by first names. Sorry.'

'No worries, yaar,' said Rohan, tucking the piece of paper into a pocket. 'We'll check when we get back.'

'Hunter's digging for something,' said Cormag, flashing his torch on the dog. 'It's the handle of a shovel!'

'Hunter, good boy – sit,' said Rohan. The dog obeyed.

Cormag pulled out the shovel.

'This is new,' said Umedh, as everyone examined the implement.

The JEACs looked at each other in excitement.

'I'll take Hunter down the passage and leave him on guard,' said Rohan. 'It looks as if this landslide was cleared fairly recently.'

The others switched off their torches and waited silently. Within fifteen minutes, they saw a faint flicker of torchlight, and Rohan returned.

'It's a minor landslide – about ten metres along the passage, and the rubble has been cleared all along it. No sign of anyone else, and Hunter is waiting for us twenty metres away. We'll examine this area thoroughly; check for footprints or anything unusual, which will give us a clue as to who was using shovels here recently – I kept to the rocks.'

The JEACs switched on their torches and spread out.

'Where shall we look, Brian?' asked Nimal.

'Just beyond the rocks – where there's a patch of smooth earth,' said Brian.

He shone his torch over Nimal's shoulder when they arrived at the spot. Nimal, who was examining the ground carefully so as to avoid stumbling, stopped suddenly.

'Look at that, Brian,' said Nimal, pointing with one hand, 'A wheel track and a couple of footprints.'

'Can you put me down?' asked Brian.

'Sure thing, yaar,' said Nimal, squatting so that the boy could slide off and sit on a stone near the patch.

They examined the markings carefully; Nimal pulled out his notebook and passed it to Brian, who quickly drew copies of the wheel track and footprints; then they called the others.

'What made the wheel mark?' breathed Mich.

'A gurney,' said Brian. 'Like the ones we use to move animals in.'

'And it's deep – which means something *heavy* was on it – perhaps a cage with animals,' said Umedh.

The JEACs gasped.

'You mean – the snow leopards?' said Amy.

'Definitely,' said Nimal. 'Why else would there be a cart track down *here*?'

'This landslide doesn't look new – it could have been here when the first snow leopards disappeared. The crooks could have cleared the landslide, taken the animals through here, and shoved them into a chopper outside the boundary wall,' said Rohan.

'Let's go on,' said Brian eagerly.

'I'm going to put the shovel back where Hunter found it,' said Rohan. 'We won't leave any clues that we've been here.'

They walked along slowly, examining the ground for further signs of tracks, but since most of the rubble was stone, nothing else was found.

'How far have we gone?' asked Anu, after the passage rose gradually and became level once more.

'Approximately 250 metres or so; we're now on the other side of the boundary wall,' said Umedh.

'We must return before the snow starts,' said Amy, 'and also before CAB finish their shifts.'

'There's plenty of time,' said Nimal. 'It's only 6:10, and the return journey will be quicker since we won't be stopping to check things.'

'Keep moving, JEACs,' said Rohan, leading the way with Hunter.

But they had barely gone another ten metres when they had to stop.

'Another landslide, and this one's blocking most of the passage,' said Rohan, shining his torch over the pile of rubble. 'One of us should crawl over and see how far it goes – without disturbing it. Unfortunately, I'm too big.'

'I'll go,' said Cormag.

The others watched him scramble over the landslide, Hunter ahead of him.

'There's another shovel,' said Cormag, his voice muffled. 'Bring it here, Hunter. Good boy – come on, let's get back to the others.'

They scrambled back and Rohan said, 'It's identical to the other one – was it hidden, too?'

'No, it was just lying on the ground at the end of the landslide. It looks like the landslide was about ten to twelve metres,' said Cormag, 'and they've cleared about five.'

'Let's check it out,' said Eadan eagerly.

'No – if we disturb the rubble, the crooks will know that someone's been here,' said Rohan. 'Cormag, can you return this to where it was?'

'Sure, and since this landslide is all gravel, there aren't any footprints,' said Cormag.

'Good man,' said Umedh, as Cormag scrambled over the landslide again.

'Hunter, sit!' said Rohan, patting the dog, who obeyed, despite wanting to follow Cormag.

Cormag returned shortly, looking excited. 'The shovel's back, and I didn't disturb anything. There are candles in every niche along the landslide, as well as five lanterns, a little gas stove, some cocoa and mugs, a couple of thick blankets, and two more shovels,' he said.

'Gee whizz! I think we can safely assume that the passage is going to be used,' said Amy.

'Also, this landslide is fairly recent,' said Nimal, who had been examining the rocks and the sides of the passage. 'The soil's still moist – it can't be more than a few days old.'

Rohan's watch alarm beeped softly. 'Time to return to the castle,' he said.

Reluctantly they turned, and were back in less than 30 minutes. Rohan, armed with a rifle, went up first, taking Hunter with him. The dog sniffed around but did not growl, so Rohan put him on guard at the bottom of the mound, and climbed back to the opening.

In a few minutes everyone was out of the passage, the tarpaulin and the branches were replaced, and the youngsters returned to the castle.

'Good timing, JEACs,' said Amy. 'It's 7 p.m. and it's beginning to snow.'

'Excellent,' said Umedh, as Rohan unlocked the front door. 'It'll wipe out signs of us having climbed up.' He lowered Brian into his wheelchair.

Rohan locked the door again, and the group thankfully removed their heavy jackets and boots before making their way into the lounge, where Umedh lit the fire. Rohan and Nimal put away the guns and darts.

CHAPTER 13

Securing the Castle

'Time for food,' groaned Eadan. 'I'm simply . . .'

'*Starving!*' shrieked Gina and Mich.

'How did you know I was going to say that?' said Eadan, looking astonished.

'Nimal *always* says that,' said Mich.

'Then I'm in good company,' grinned Eadan. 'What's for eating?'

'Give us fifteen minutes . . .' began Amy.

'Sorry, Amy,' interrupted Rohan, 'but we'll first check the kitchen thoroughly, cupboards and all, and then the rest of us will split up and check the entire building while you prepare dinner.'

'Why?' asked Gina.

'Until this morning, we've never locked the doors of the castle,' said Rohan. 'However, since it's apparent that there are unwanted people roaming around, I think we should ensure none of them are hiding *inside* here.'

'But Hunter would warn us,' said Mich.

'Yes – if they tried to enter while we're here,' said Rohan. 'But they could have come in while we were away, and might be anywhere – in a cupboard, room, or even the sheds – we haven't been near the sheds since we returned from Ruthven this afternoon. And unless Hunter sniffs everywhere, he won't be able to tell.'

'So *that's* why you wanted me to lock the front door when we left this morning and also why you locked it when we went to the passage,' said Umedh, and Rohan nodded. 'Good thinking, man. Let's check the castle – open every room and cupboard; look behind every door and under everything. And make sure every door and window which leads *outside* is locked and bolted. How do you want us to divvy up, yaar?'

'Us, too,' begged Mich and Gina.

'Of course: Mich with Nimal – check the cellar; Gina and Umedh – upstairs; Sco-Js – this floor, starting with the kitchen so that Amy and Anu can work there safely, and get Tumbler from the dorm first; I'll take Hunter and check the sheds and the passage leading to them. Make sure the curtains are drawn in every single room so that nobody can look inside. Let's move, JEACs.'

They sped off, and once the kitchen was declared safe, Amy and Anu began preparing dinner. They could hear the Sco-Js opening door after door on the main floor, and calling to each other, Tumbler yapping excitedly.

'Soup, sausages, mashed potatoes and salad should do the trick,' said Amy, putting a huge container of chicken soup on the cooker. 'And here's a dish of mashed potatoes.'

'So we only need to grill the sausages and make a salad,' said Anu, setting to work. 'And there's a large fruit salad and cake for dessert.'

The door opened, and Brian, followed by an excited Tumbler, zoomed in, went directly to the large bay window, drew back the curtains and examined the window carefully.

'What's up?' said Amy.

'Look,' said Brian. Amy and Anu hurried over – the outside ledge, which should have had smooth, untouched snow on it, was mucked up. 'Someone's checked to see if the window was fastened, and it's the same in every room we've examined – thank goodness all the windows were secured.'

'Golly, Rohan was right,' said Anu. 'What made you look for that, Brian?'

'I was checking the windows to make sure they were locked and then drawing the curtains,' explained Brian, 'while Cormag and Eadan checked in cupboards and under things. I didn't think of looking at the outside ledges, but when we checked the east side of the castle, where snow was in high drifts against the windows, I noticed that someone had mucked up the snow on the window around the latch. Cormag, Eadan and I rechecked all the windows, including our dorm, and found the same thing – in some places we even saw glove prints. But the snow's falling pretty heavily, and the signs will soon be covered.'

'Good work, Brian,' said Amy.

'I have to get back to the others,' said Brian, drawing the curtains and zooming towards the door. 'We have five more rooms to check.'

'Rohan should be told – shall I find him?' said Anu.

'Okay, but I don't like the idea of you going to the sheds on your own, hon.'

Just then Nimal and Mich arrived.

'All okay in the cellar,' said Mich, 'but we found snow disturbed at every window.'

'As if someone were trying to prise it open – has anyone else reported it?' said Nimal.

'The Sco-Js,' said Anu. 'Nimal, find Rohan and check the shed windows as well; Mich, run upstairs and tell Umedh and Gina to check that floor – though I doubt anyone would have got that high without a ladder.'

'Will do,' they said in unison, running off.

Ten minutes later, most of them had returned.

'What news, JEACs?' asked Amy. 'I guess Nimal, Rohan and Hunter are still checking the sheds.'

'Not one of the window ledges upstairs was mucked up,' reported Gina, receiving an encouraging nod from Umedh.

'And every window ledge on this floor is,' said Brian.

'I also checked outside the front door,' said Umedh. 'The porch had our footprints when we came in, but on either side there were footprints leading around the castle. But the snow's rapidly covering everything.'

'Do you want a hand with that salad, Amy?' asked Eadan politely.

'Are you that hungry, mate?' teased Brian.

Eadan grinned, but he and Cormag got busy chopping vegetables, while the others set the table.

'Here come the rest,' said Umedh, hearing an excited bark, and Hunter dashed in ahead of Rohan and Nimal.

'Here's your meal, boys,' said Anu, setting down bowls of food for the dogs.

'Well?' said Amy, as everyone looked at Rohan and Nimal.

'Every single window ledge was disturbed,' said Rohan, 'and there were footprints at the entrances to the sheds.'

'Fortunately, not a single window or door was open,' said Nimal.

'And the same on each floor,' said the others.

'So the castle's secure,' said Rohan. 'Let's make sure it stays that way. We have two sets of keys – one in my pocket and the other here in the kitchen. Brian, who else has keys to Cairns?'

'I'm not sure – Gav would know.'

'I'll ask him,' said Rohan. 'Since dinner's not yet ready, you check that phone number and I'll call Gavan.'

'Dinner in ten, boys,' said Amy.

'We'll be back soon,' promised Rohan, as he and Brian left the room.

Brian took the number from Rohan, wheeled over to the desk and found the list of names. 'I wish I could remember Clyde's . . . hold it, yaar.' He grinned at Rohan who was about to call Gavan. 'I'll pull up the electronic list and search for the number.'

'Brainwave, yaar,' said Rohan, high-fiving him.

Brian turned on the computer while Rohan dialled Gavan's mobile telephone.

'Hi, Gavan,' said Rohan.

'Rohan, can you JEACs do us a huge favour tomorrow morning?' asked Gavan who sounded stressed.

'Sure thing, yaar – what's up?' said Rohan.

'Gràinne's sick, and we're crazy busy – could you de-ice the waterholes between Burns and Ruthven, as well as the ones you're currently doing? There are four of them.'

'No worries, mate,' said Rohan. 'In fact, leave them entirely to us for the next three days – we'd love to help.'

'Thanks, man,' said Gavan gratefully. 'Gràinne now appears to have injured her *right* leg, and today her stomach's been playing up, too. We might need Nimal's assistance again.'

'Just call us, Gavan. By the way, since we often split up, we felt Umedh should keep one set of keys for Cairns, and I, the other. If we need a third set, where would we find it?'

'I have a set – usually on me,' said Gavan, who was obviously under too much pressure to wonder why they needed extra keys. 'The only other set is in the office at Ruthven, but you can have my set if you like.'

'No, thanks,' said Rohan. 'We'll only need it if we're stuck. Hope Gràinne improves soon – call *any time*, and Nimal will zoom over. I'll let you go, since you're busy. Good night.'

He hung up and joined an excited Brian, who was pointing at the computer and waving the piece of paper.

'It's Clyde's mobile phone number – see, his last name is McNevin.'

'Excellent work,' said Rohan. 'Let's tell the others. And good news: only Gavan and the Ruthven office have keys for Cairns – we're safe.'

They returned to the kitchen where soup was being ladled into bowls, and updated the others.

'Brill – as long as the crooks don't try to *break* into the castle,' said Nimal. 'Did Gavan ask why you wanted to know?'

'No – Gràinne's sick, again, and he's stressed. I told them to call if they needed you.'

'Of course – what's the problem?'

Rohan explained as they were eating, and the JEACs were very concerned, hoping the snow leopard would recover quickly.

'What next?' asked Eadan.

'Everything seems to connect the crooks to CAB,' said Rohan, 'and there's lots happening around Cairns.'

'Also, remember, Beiste told Moire to get cracking on that passage,' said Anu. 'I bet he wanted it cleared so that more snow leopards could be wheeled through it to a chopper outside KWCC.'

'Exactly! But we need proof. We'll continue to keep this to ourselves – let's not disrupt the fundraiser, or stress KWCC staff any further,' said Rohan.

'I would love to catch them in the act – but I don't want the snow leopards to be injured,' said Nimal. 'Perhaps we should keep an eye on CAB and the entrance – in shifts – after all, there are ten of us.'

'Agreed,' said Rohan thoughtfully. 'But tonight we need to sleep. We'll split up tomorrow.'

'That makes sense – each group can keep watch over a different area,' said Umedh.

'Yes, three or four points of action,' said Rohan. 'Around Cairns, where we may see some of the crooks, hear the chopper, see Clyde or Beiste coming to meet the crooks – though that's unlikely since they'll be busy preparing for the fundraiser – they'll probably communicate via phone.'

'At Burns – near the snow leopards, and keeping an eye on Beiste,' said Nimal.

'We also need a clear picture of Clyde's movements on the twentieth, and whom he talks to from now on – it's the critical time frame,' said Anu.

'And we should check the trails between Burns and Cairns: firstly, to look for gurney tracks, and secondly, which trails they're likely to use again,' added Umedh.

'How did they manage to get the gurney with the cage and snow leopards up the mound and into the secret passage?' said Cormag.

'It sounds impossible,' said Eadan.

Rohan nodded to Mich and Gina, who were falling asleep at the table, and said, 'Let's each try and figure it out. It's nearly 8:30 – Gina, Mich – why don't you go to bed and we'll wake you early tomorrow.'

Brian, Cormag and Eadan opted for bed, too.

As the teens cleared the dining room, Umedh said, 'The snow leopards could have been in a cage and brought on the gurneys to the bottom of the mound; the cage moved off, and the gurney pushed to the top of the mound and rolled down the steps – the opening's wide enough.'

'But they couldn't carry two grown snow leopards up the mound without taking them out of the cages – and what if the tranquillizer dose wore off,' said Amy.

'They could have given them potent dosages – they wouldn't care if they died from it – then removed them from the cage, and once the cage was in the passage and on the gurney, ropes and pulleys would easily drag the poor things up the slope and drop them into the passage,' said Umedh.

'And since the police didn't know about the secret passage, nobody would have checked the mound for tracks, and snow would have covered any trace of them. It would be easy enough to wheel the gurney through the passage and haul the poor animals out at the other end. I've a nasty feeling they killed them before placing them in the chopper. Nobody would have heard gunshots over the boundary wall, especially if silencers were used,' said Rohan, angrily.

'We must stop them from harming any more animals,' said Nimal.

'Absolutely!' said everyone.

They finished up and went to bed. The youngsters and Tumbler didn't stir as the boys entered their room.

'I guess we have to keep the window closed tonight – we can't risk intruders, even though Hunter would warn us in a jiffy,' whispered Rohan, drawing the curtain back and looking out of the window.

'True. What time are you setting your alarm for?' asked Umedh.

'Five – we need to de-ice nine waterholes,' muttered Rohan, dropping the curtain and changing.

'Wake me, too,' said Nimal, pulling on his pyjamas. 'I got Brian to mark the four other waterholes on my map.' He lay down and was asleep in seconds.

'Three of us should be able to deal with the waterholes, so we'll let the others sleep in. The next couple of days are going to be hectic,' said Umedh.

'Good idea,' said Rohan, climbing into bed. 'But . . .' he stopped.

'You want to know if the chopper comes again – right?' said Umedh, who often read Rohan like a book.

'Bang on,' grinned Rohan. 'I just want to *know*, so we can plan accordingly.'

'Let's go to the lounge at 1:30, and we'll each take an hour's watch. There are plenty of rugs and we can sleep on the sofas when it's not our turn to be up. We'll open a window slightly – people won't expect a window in the *lounge* to be open.'

'Sound idea, yaar, and we'll take Hunter – just in case we fall asleep. This morning the chopper arrived around two, so perhaps we should do 1:30 to 3:30.'

'Agreed.'

They set their watch alarms, placing them under their pillows so they would not disturb the others, and within minutes there was silence in the dormitory.

When the alarms woke the boys, Hunter came up to Rohan's bed and licked his hand. The boys grabbed torches and left the room with Hunter.

'It's stopped snowing,' said Rohan, peering through the curtains and opening a window a smidgen.

Umedh turned on three small heaters, placing a rug for Hunter in front of one, and the dog settled down quietly, while Umedh cuddled down on a sofa and was soon fast asleep.

Rohan lay down on the other sofa, mulling over plans, but it was so cosy that he fell asleep, too.

The boys slept soundly for nearly an hour, and then Hunter, who always slept with one ear on the alert, heard the distant sound of an approaching helicopter. He growled softly and padded over to the window. As the sound grew louder, Hunter went over to Rohan, licked the boy's face and whined. Rohan awoke with a start, heard the helicopter and shook Umedh awake. They rushed over to the window and opened it wider.

'It's from the same direction as yesterday,' muttered Rohan, laying a hand on Hunter to keep him quiet.

'Yes, and it's coming in, not going away,' said Umedh.

A few minutes later the engine shut off.

'At least we know it's back,' said Rohan. 'There's no point in going out again, I guess – it's nearly 2:50.'

'No – if our suspicions are correct, they've only got today and tomorrow to clear the passage.'

'Let's get a couple of hours more sleep – these sofas are comfy and snug with the blankets. I'll set my alarm for five and then wake Nimal.'

'G'night, or rather, 'morning', said Umedh, closing the window. 'We'd better leave a note for the girls before we go out.'

'Okay,' said Rohan yawning widely.

A few minutes later both of them were sound asleep. Hunter put his head down on his paws and went to sleep, too. There was no further sound from the helicopter.

CHAPTER 14

Keeping Their Eyes Peeled

Nimal woke before five, feeling well rested. He looked at the luminous dial of his watch – a quarter to five. Hunter was missing from the foot of his bed. He flashed his torch across Rohan and Umedh's beds – they were empty.

He pulled on jeans and a sweater, crept out of the room and peeped into the kitchen, but it was in darkness. He went towards the lounge, and Hunter, hearing a noise in the hallway as Nimal stumbled into a coat rack, growled softly and went to the door just as Nimal arrived on the other side. Recognizing him instantly, Hunter whined and scratched at the door, which Nimal opened quietly.

Shushing Hunter, the mischief-loving boy took in the scene at a glance and, deciding to be an alarm, made a sound like a car backfiring.

Startled out of a deep sleep, both boys shot upright on their sofas and, by the faint light of the heaters, saw Nimal rolling on the ground covering his head with a blanket to stifle his laughter. Umedh and Rohan looked at each other and simultaneously threw cushions at Nimal, one catching him in the face and the other in his stomach.

'Ooof! Pests!' said Nimal, throwing back the cushions. 'Did you decide to sleep here out of sheer consideration so that your snoring wouldn't disturb us?'

'We don't snore,' said Rohan.

'Hmmm – says you,' said Nimal cheekily. 'What's up? It's nearly five.'

'Umedh will fill you in while I grab our clothes,' said Rohan.

He went off, and Umedh brought Nimal up to speed. Ten minutes later, after leaving a note for the girls, Hunter and the boys were in the shed; they split up, finished the waterholes and returned to the castle within 40 minutes.

'I wonder if the others are up,' said Nimal. 'It's nearly five-forty.'

'Anu and Amy will probably be making hot chocolate,' said Umedh, rubbing his hands together. 'I could use a hot drink.'

They entered the kitchen, Hunter leading the way. Everyone was up and about, and breakfast was nearly ready.

Nimal went up to Gina, who was putting things into the dishwasher, and gave her an exuberant hug, rubbing his cold cheek against her warm one. She squealed and pushed him away indignantly.

The group settled down, eager to discuss plans for the day.

Rohan reported that the helicopter had returned in the early hours of the morning, and also brought the five younger JEACs up to speed about their ideas as to how the snow leopards were taken into the secret passage.

'I wish I'd been up to hear the chopper,' said Cormag, wistfully. 'Did you hear it leave, too?'

'No. It might have left while we were at the waterholes,' said Umedh.

'What's the plan for today?' asked Eadan, eagerly.

'As agreed last night, there are a few main tasks. One of those is to check whom Clyde talks to,' said Rohan

'That sounds impossible . . . unless . . . we can steal his mobile phone and check the numbers,' said Eadan.

'There's something in that,' said Umedh thoughtfully.

'How shall we divvy up the tasks?' asked Cormag. 'I would love to be everywhere.'

'Me, too,' said Rohan. 'Jay said we needn't help officially, but we can assist casually, and nobody will mind an extra hand here and there. So, let's start with Burns and Beiste.'

'He doesn't seem to mind Anu and me, so we're probably best suited for that horrid task. It will be *such* a pleasure,' said Amy.

'Agreed,' said Anu, grimacing.

'Thanks, that makes sense,' said Rohan. 'Nimal, you go to Burns, too – help with Gràinne. Now, Brian – here's a map of the trails. How many are there from Burns to Cairns?'

'Eight. Three are used by snow tracs and ATVs; two are okay for small ski-doos; and three are rarely used – they're pretty overgrown.'

'Mark the three used by the bigger ATVs.'

Brian did so, and added, 'Eadan, Cormag and I can handle this end: we'll keep an eye open for activity around the secret passage, listen for the chopper and check the trails.'

'Absolutely,' agreed Eadan and Cormag.

'Good thinking, chaps,' said Rohan.

'Clyde's going to be the challenge, Rohan,' said Umedh. 'You and I could take turns hanging around him, whether he's assisting at Ruthven or at Knox where he has his meals – but we'd need runners – Gina, Mich, would you be willing to hang out with us?'

'Sure,' said Gina, 'but what would we do?'

'Not sure at the moment, kiddo,' said Rohan, 'but I imagine that if I snaffled Clyde's mobile phone, I'd pass it to Mich, she'd hand it to you, and you'd take it to Umedh, to check the numbers; or it could be the other way around, where Umedh gets the phone and sends it to me.'

'So we'd each be with one of you?' asked Mich.

'That's right,' said Rohan. 'Among the ten of us, we'll use walkie-talkies and mobile phones. Each group should have one mobile phone and a walkie-talkie.'

'But we only have two phones: Brian's and the spare,' said Amy.

'Take my mom's phone from my desk drawer at Burns, Amy – it's always charged,' said Brian.

'Thanks, hon,' said Amy.

Umedh said, 'I checked the walkie-talkies yesterday – and one set has six handsets. Rohan, Nimal and I'll keep one each from the set of six, and you Sco-Js keep the other three; if we come within range of you chaps, we can use those; plus, you'll have one mobile phone and access to the phones here. That leaves the second set of walkie-talkies, which has four handsets.'

'Super,' said Rohan. 'Anu, Nimal, Umedh and I should keep one handset each of the other set, for the same reasons, and if Umedh or I keep the spare mobile phone, we're covered.'

'Hope we won't get them muddled up,' said Amy. 'Are they identical, Umedh?'

'Nope – the set of six have *Cairns* stamped on them, and the set of four have *KWCC*.'

'Okay – everyone report in hourly, unless you discover something that should be passed on immediately,' said Rohan. 'Synchronize your watches – excellent,' he added as they did this.

'Whom do we call?' asked Cormag.

'Either Umedh or myself,' said Rohan. 'If you can't reach us, send a text message and make sure that the other group is updated. We'll call back ASAP.'

'How do we travel around KWCC today?' asked Anu.

'Individual ski-doos,' said Rohan. 'Umedh, Nimal and I will take the larger ones, which can seat at least two others. Hunter's a good watchdog, so he and Tumbler can stay with the Sco-Js, and also, since neither Beiste nor Clyde like dogs, it won't exacerbate the situation.'

'I'll be the dictionary,' said Anu, grinning at the puzzled faces of the younger JEACs. 'Exacerbate means to make a (bad) situation worse.'

'Oooh – I like that word,' said Gina, dreamily. 'It's similar to aggravate, isn't it, Anu?'

'Yes, but aggravate can mean to irritate or annoy a person, too; exacerbate refers to a situation,' said Anu. 'We don't wish to aggravate Beiste *or* exacerbate the situation!'

'Sooner or later it'll be in one of Gina's songs,' muttered Nimal, sotto voce.

Rohan glanced at his watch. 'It's 6:40, JEACs – let's get cracking.'

Fifteen minutes later the JEACs locked the castle securely, took their ski-doos out of the shed, and set forth to deal with their assignments. Cormag and Eadan were thrilled with Brian's ski-doo, and joyfully thumped Umedh on the back. Hunter stayed with the Sco-Js and obeyed them implicitly, while Eadan carried Tumbler.

*****

Nimal, Amy and Anu zoomed over to Burns. As they parked outside, they heard a helicopter take off.

'Nobody around – that's weird,' said Amy, when they had looked in the lounge and office.

'Nimal, check the clinic and we'll look in the kitchen,' said Anu.

The girls saw a half-eaten breakfast on the table and a couple of chairs tumbled on the ground, as if they had been pushed back hurriedly. As they gaped at the scene, a yell from Nimal made them run to the clinic. The door was open; Nimal, standing beside the large sink, looked shocked.

The girls approached the sink and then backed away hurriedly, covering their mouths, and feeling sick to their stomachs. Nobody else was around.

'The snow leopard enclosures,' gasped Nimal.

The JEACs sped to the entrance, pulled on their coats and boots hurriedly, and raced down the path leading to the breeding programme enclosures.

CHAPTER 15

Taking Out the Twins

'What on earth happened?' gasped Anu, who looked rather green. 'All those towels – was it blood?'

'Yes,' said Nimal. 'Don't dwell on it, Anu.'

'And the medical and linen cabinets were open and in a mess,' panted Amy.

'Someone pulled things out hurriedly,' said Nimal.

As they neared the enclosure, they heard voices and saw a group of people, some of whom were kneeling on the ground. The JEACs hurried to join them.

'What's up?' said Nimal. 'Oh, man!' he gasped as the group parted.

The JEACs turned pale when they saw Uisdean on the ground, Luag and Taran bent over him. He was immobile, his clothing was in tatters, and he was covered in blood.

'Uisdean was mauled by Gràinne,' said Doilidh. 'He fainted when Taran bound up his leg.'

'And what happened to Uallas?' gasped Amy, seeing him seated on the ground, a bloody towel wrapped around his left arm.

'We'll explain shortly,' said Gavan, who was kneeling beside Uallas.

'Beiste's fetching a doctor – in the helicopter,' said Doilidh. 'Luag and Taran have done what they can, but we need a doctor to confirm that it's okay to keep Uisdean here.'

'Stubborn lad – the first thing he said when Gavan shot a dart into Gràinne was, "Is she okay?" and the second was, "I'm NOT going to hospital!" Then he fainted,' said Uallas, grinning at the JEACs.

'So that's why the chopper was taking off,' said Nimal. 'How can we help?'

'Dan and Taog will be here shortly, and we'll move Uisdean back to the house – he'll come round soon,' said Luag, standing up. 'The doctor should be here in under an hour and once I've spoken with him, I'll join you, Taran. In the meantime, Taran will tell you three what needs to be done.'

'Of course,' said the JEACs.

'Thank goodness, here are Dan and Taog,' said Taran. 'Thanks for bringing more darts, Taog,' he added, taking the case from him.

In a few seconds the men had lifted Uisdean carefully onto a stretcher, and Dan, Luag, Taog and Uallas went to the house.

'Ladies, please feed the animals – and we'll deal with Gràinne,' said Taran.

'Where is she?' said Nimal.

'Hiding in her cave,' said Taran. 'Early this morning, Gavan, Uallas, Uisdean and I were doing the rounds. We noticed Gràinne's limp appeared worse, and she had brought up her food – again. I was concerned since I had medicated her last afternoon and evening, and expected some improvement.'

'Uallas and Uisdean said they could help. So we put the cubs in the creep, called Beiste at the house, and asked him to bring out a blow pipe with a couple of darts,' said Gavan.

'Which he did,' continued Taran. 'But that man is such a . . . you'd think, given that it's clearly indicated on the charts, he would know the correct dosage for sedating her. Anyway, he brought a loaded blow pipe and shot it into Gràinne.

'She went out in a few minutes and the four of us went inside and waited for Beiste to bring a gurney to the entrance – which took him about fifteen minutes – he's so slow. But as we lifted her to put her inside the cage, she woke up and, though sluggish, began struggling violently.

'A snarling, struggling, frightened snow leopard is impossible to handle, and Uisdean, who was holding her head, got the worst of it – he tripped over a rock and fell, Gràinne on top of him. Uallas immediately tried to pull her off, and got his arm ripped. Gavan and I tried to help them, and I yelled for Beiste to give us the blow pipe.'

'Fortunately Beiste, who had been petrified, came to his senses and passed the blow pipe to me,' said Gavan, 'and I put another dart into Gràinne. She went limp, and we pulled her off Uisdean and left the enclosure immediately to attend to Uisdean and Uallas. I locked the enclosure, called Luag, telling him to hurry here with lots of towels, and called Dan to explain the situ, before trying to help the others.'

'This occurred over 45 minutes ago,' concluded Taran. 'When Luag and Doilidh arrived, we decided that we needed the doctor ASAP; Doilidh and Beiste took back some of the bloody towels; Doilidh called the doctor, sent Beiste to fetch him, and returned with more towels. Now, let's check on Gràinne – she's gone back into her cave.'

'We'll deal with the cubs,' said Doilidh, and went off with the girls.

Gavan and Nimal looked in the back window of the cave; Gràinne snarled, glaring balefully at them.

'I'll talk to her,' said Nimal.

After a few minutes, the boy's voice appeared to have its usual soothing effect on the poor creature; she stopped snarling and began to lick her right front paw, looking up at Nimal now and then. He continued speaking and then said quietly, in the same tone of voice, 'She's getting up and coming to the grate, limping badly. Poor Gràinne, we'll have you healed soon. Is your foot hurting? How did you injure it?'

Gràinne made a tiny purring sound and looked up at him – she really liked this boy; she rubbed her head against the mesh. Nimal moved away and went into the sectioned off area, in front of the cave. Taran took a new dart from the case brought by Taog, loaded his blow pipe, and nodded to Nimal, who called Gràinne again. She limped out, focusing solely on Nimal as she approached the mesh, and rubbed her head against Nimal's hand. She lay down heavily, content to be near the boy.

Taran sedated her quickly, and then the three of them eased her onto the gurney.

'She looks so peaceful,' said Gavan.

'Aye. Let's get her to the clinic.' Taran automatically locked the enclosure behind him.

In the clinic, Taran quickly examined Gràinne's overall condition, connected her to an oxygen mask, and said, 'She's had three shots today, and her body's undergone severe trauma. Once we're done, we'll give her a reversal agent and keep her under observation for the next few hours. If she's okay, we'll put her back in her enclosure this evening.'

'In the meantime, I'll check on the twins, finish my meeting at Ruthven, and bring back the supplies, before I begin my schedule – I'll cover yours, too, Taran,' said Gavan.

'Thanks. I hear the chopper returning,' said Taran. 'Ask Luag to join me as soon as possible, and keep Beiste with you.'

'Right,' said Gavan, hurrying away.

Luag arrived, and he and Nimal watched as Taran checked Gràinne's paw thoroughly.

'Congealed blood,' said Taran, as they bent over the paw. Taran washed it away, and gently probed the area. 'There's a deep hole in her right forepaw, which could only have been caused if she landed on a sharp rock, from a height.'

'But that's impossible,' said Luag. 'There aren't any sharp rocks or objects in the enclosures.'

Nimal looked thoughtful as Taran finished medicating Gràinne, checked her vital organs, and injected a reversal agent. They put her into a cage on a gurney, closing the door and locking it. Luag brought food for Taran before he left to deal with his work. Taran ate hungrily – he'd missed breakfast.

'Her tail twitched,' said Nimal, ten minutes later.

'Start talking to her,' said Taran, pushing a bowl of water into the cage.

Gràinne woke up to Nimal's caressing voice, stood up shakily and drank a little water. She looked at Nimal and lay down again.

Taran signalled Nimal to move away, and the boy backed off, still talking gently, Gràinne watching him until the door closed behind him. Taran turned on the monitor, and they watched Gràinne drink more water and then close her eyes.

'She'll be okay now,' said Taran, heaving a sigh of relief. 'Thanks, lad; she's calm – and that'll go a long way to her speedy recovery. We'll keep her here for a few hours and then put her back in her small enclosure until she's completely healed. We'll also monitor her diet carefully.'

'Good idea,' said Nimal. 'I'll check on the twins and then find the girls. May I have the key so that I can check for sharp objects inside the enclosures?'

'Sure – mainly in the small enclosure, please. We'll have to check the larger one when the snow melts. Return the key to me.'

'Will do, thanks,' said Nimal.

He found Uisdean and Uallas in one of the spare rooms, in excellent spirits, and asked how they were doing. Amy and Anu were there, too.

'We're okay; how's Gràinne?' asked Uisdean.

Nimal updated them, and they were relieved.

'Poor thing, what a traumatic experience for her,' said Uisdean.

'Yes – that Beiste . . . he's . . .' began Uallas.

'Forget it, twin,' interrupted Uisdean.

'How will you manage, Uisdean?' said Nimal.

'We're both staying here for a few hours,' said Uallas, 'but I'll get back to Ruthven this afternoon – I have lots to do for tomorrow, and everything's going to take twice as long.'

'I'm stuck for today,' grumbled Uisdean. 'That doctor's crazy – told me off because I wanted to do my shift here, tomorrow. I figured I'd be fine, zooming around in a wheelchair – nothing wrong with my arms and hands. However, Beiste offered to take my shift – guess he felt bad since he used the wrong dosage.'

'Unfortunately, I have to return to the fundraiser after my shift here, tomorrow afternoon, so I can't do it,' said Uallas.

'Really? What time were you scheduled for, Uisdean?' asked Nimal.

'Just before Beiste – I had a two-hour shift, on my own, tomorrow evening.'

Doilidh bustled in and said, 'JEACs – I've got to prepare more food for this evening. Would you feed the otters and wildcats and then help Gavan and Beiste to bring the supplies into the house? They should return from Ruthven in about 45 minutes.'

'Sure, Dolly – see you later, twins,' chorused the JEACs, and hurried out.

'I'll feed the wildcats, you two feed the otters. We need to check something, so hurry. Meet at Gràinne's enclosure in ten minutes – we're going to examine it thoroughly,' said Nimal, setting off at a run.

'Okay. It's interesting, isn't it – Beiste offering to take Uisdean's shift?' said Anu.

'Does he think that'll make up for his idiotic mistake?' said Amy.

'I'm adding two and two and getting 50,' said Anu thoughtfully. 'He *should* know the correct dosage – was it deliberate?'

'Definitely – taking out the twins, and Uisdean in particular, changes tomorrow's schedule drastically,' said Nimal grimly, as they parted.

They fed the animals quickly and met at the enclosure. 'Gràinne's injury was caused by something sharp entering her paw, and the depth is the result of her landing heavily on it – which means she jumped from a height,' said Nimal, entering the enclosure.

'So we examine the area around the rocks from which she might have jumped?' said Anu.

'Exactimo – but I told Taran I was going to check the smaller enclosure – so I'll start there.'

They split up and began searching carefully.

'Nothing dangerous, so far,' called Nimal a little later.

'I haven't found anything,' said Anu.

'Nor I,' said Amy, 'and I've checked every square inch of this section.

They continued searching.

'Yikes,' yelped Nimal, a few minutes later as he stumbled a couple of metres away from a high rock. He sat down cautiously and began to clear away the snow around him. The girls hurried over to join him, but he said, 'Don't come closer – something sharp jabbed my foot.'

'I'll fetch some brooms,' said Amy.

She returned quickly and they used the brooms to uncover – 'A sharp flint!' exclaimed the JEACs, looking shocked.

'More like a number of sharp flints,' said Nimal, as they swept away more snow and discovered that the flints covered a large area around the base of the rock.

'But . . . why . . . who?' began Amy, furiously. 'This was put here *deliberately.*'

Nimal looked at the rock, which was about three metres high. 'They certainly don't belong in here; every enclosure is planned and constructed carefully. I can imagine Gràinne sitting on that rock; if she leapt in this direction, she'd land right on target. But why would she leap in this direction?'

'If someone were at the gate with food,' said Anu.

'And with the snow this week, the flints could have been planted, and not noticed, unless someone checked carefully. Whoever planted them probably locked Gràinne in her small enclosure while they were in here,' said Amy.

'Agreed,' said Anu.

'Since Taran's going to keep Gràinne in the smaller enclosure and cave for a few days, I'll assure him there's nothing sharp there – and we'll leave these flints as proof. We can't *assume* that Beiste's at fault – but he's got easy access,' said Nimal.

'What if he removes the flints?' said Amy.

'I doubt he'll risk coming in here at the moment,' said Nimal. 'The shifts begin at 6 p.m. today. Let's cover the flints.'

They quickly pushed snow over the flints once more, and tossed a few branches around so that the area didn't look as if it had been cleared.

'Excellent,' said Nimal, picking up the brooms. 'Let's scram before the guys return from Ruthven.'

They locked the enclosure and went over to the ATV shed. Five minutes later, Gavan and Beiste arrived and the JEACs helped them unload the ATV. Beiste, Amy and Anu began to take things into the house, while Nimal and Gavan went to see Taran.

'There's nothing in the cave or smaller enclosure that could have injured Gràinne, Taran,' said Nimal, handing over the key.

'I didn't think so, but thanks for checking,' said Taran.

He began to answer Gavan's questions about Gràinne, and they agreed that she should not be allowed to leap around too much until her paw was completely healed – and only Taran would deal with her over the next week.

'But both of us have to be at Ruthven tomorrow during the day for certain sessions, Taran. And you know we can't miss the breeding programme question and answer session, which is over dinner.'

'I'll keep an eye on her,' offered Nimal, 'and Dolly's around during the day, too.'

'Aren't you JEACs involved at the fundraiser?'

'Yes, but I can miss some sessions. I can also come here in the evening; I don't need to be at the dinner,' said Nimal. 'Just tell me what you need.'

'Thanks, Nimal – that's a relief,' said Taran, gratefully.

Nimal and Gavan joined the others, and took on tasks which would keep them, and Beiste, busy until lunchtime.

'We'll help Beiste, Nimal,' whispered Amy, 'while you update Rohan – here's the phone; update the Sco-Js, too. We called everyone earlier, said things were crazy and that we'd report in when the dust had settled.'

'Okay,' said Nimal quietly, and ran off to make his calls, after which he helped with the preparation of food.

As soon as Beiste stepped out of the room, Nimal said, 'Spoke to both lots and gave them the basics. They haven't any news, and wish they'd been here.'

'Let's meet the Sco-Js at Cairns for lunch, and do some brainstorming,' suggested Amy.

'Sound idea,' said Anu, 'and we'll update the Knox group, too.'

'Okay. Then . . . hi, Beiste, we've finished,' said Amy, as the man walked in. 'What next?'

'You're a speedy lot,' said Beiste, trying to sound jovial and failing miserably – he looked very uncomfortable. 'Taran wants me to assist in the clinic – could you prepare something for lunch?'

'We're going to Cairns, but we'll prepare something for you folks,' said Amy. 'There's a shepherd's pie in the freezer, and we'll make a salad.'

'Thanks a lot,' said Beiste, and hurried off.

'He's in for a lecture,' said Amy. 'I'm not at all sorry for him, and he – oh, dry up, Amy!' She laughed at the grinning duo and said, 'I know. I promised myself I'd be more sympathetic towards people like him, but it's really tough.'

'We can relate, hon,' said Anu, hugging her. 'It's pretty near *impossible* to like him when it appears that he and his friends are harming the animals and hurting our friends.'

'I'd like to punch him out,' added Nimal, 'but as the APs would say, "Don't judge him – you don't know his story".'

'True,' said Amy, ruefully.

'Let's focus on how we can protect the animals – conscious choices, folks,' said Anu, bringing out the shepherd's pie from the freezer. 'This thing . . . er . . . is it cooked?'

'No, hon,' said Amy, 'it has to be baked.'

They burst out laughing and got to work.

CHAPTER 16

Coloured Tailpieces

Over lunch at Cairns, the other JEACs were updated on the situation at Burns.

'We checked the patrolling schedule which begins at six this evening,' said Amy. 'They adjusted many programmes and schedules after the twins were injured. Therefore, tomorrow, during the fundraising dinner and sessions – from 7:30 p.m. until midnight – CAB are the only staff on duty at Burns.'

'Dolly will be there all day and I'll be in and out, too,' said Nimal. 'Dolly, Taran and Gavan don't need to leave until 7:45 p.m. – they're taking ski-doos, and I'll get there before they leave.'

'That's some consolation, yaar,' said Rohan, who, along with the other JEACs at Knox, was on a speakerphone. 'Looks like taking the twins out of the picture had interesting results – nearly five hours with nobody but Nimal and CAB looking after the snow leopards. We'll have to think this through carefully – anything else?'

'Nothing exciting at Cairns,' said Brian. 'I'm glad Gràinne is well protected, but what about Niall, the cubs, and the other two pairs of snow leopards?'

'Niall has a gorgeous coat,' said Umedh. 'We'll have to keep our eyes peeled tomorrow, JEACs.'

'Nimal, may I go to Burns with you?' said Brian eagerly. 'I'll do a few JEACs' sessions in the morning and afternoon.'

'Us, too?' pleaded Cormag and Eadan.

'Super idea, Sco-Js – you'll recognize strangers more easily than any of us, and the more of us around Burns while CAB are on duty, the better,' said Rohan.

'Smashing, thanks, Rohan,' said the Sco-Js excitedly.

'Any luck with Clyde?' asked Anu.

'No. We went to Ruthven and found Clyde there for the morning; he's now at his lodging, packing, since he leaves the day after tomorrow around 7 a.m., after his shift – two hours after Beiste leaves. Clyde's attending a meeting at Knox this afternoon – we're heading over there soon,' said Rohan. 'Good luck, JEACs – keep in touch.'

'Good luck,' chorused everyone, and rang off.

'We'll finish up here and then get back to the trails – we're on our ski-doos,' said Brian.

'Okay, thanks. See you later,' said the others, leaving the Sco-Js to clear up.

When the Sco-Js returned to their post, Brian and Tumbler kept an eye on the entrance to the cellar, while the other two and Hunter made their way to the two trails which still had to be checked.

'Absolutely nothing to be found,' said Cormag disappointedly. 'I guess there's been too much snow after the first incident.'

After updating Amy and learning that everyone planned to return to Cairns by six, Eadan and Cormag rejoined Brian around 4 p.m. It was getting dark, and since Tumbler was exhausted, Cormag bundled him into the castle, fed him and left him in his basket in the kitchen.

The Sco-Js and Hunter were settled snugly in the woods just beyond the rubble. Their hideout, surrounded by thick, evergreen shrubbery, not only hid them and their ski-doos from sight, but also protected them from the chilly wind which was beginning to swirl around Cairns. Night-vision binoculars gave them a clear view of the mound, the branches which covered it and the surrounding area.

'It's started snowing,' said Eadan, at 4:20. 'The forecast said it would be a light fall, ending in a few hours.'

'Good, it'll hide our ski-doo . . .' began Brian, when Hunter growled deep in his throat. The Sco-Js grabbed their binoculars and looked around carefully.

'Sshh, Hunter.' The dog subsided and stared at the mound. 'The branches are moving,' muttered Brian.

Nothing happened for a few minutes and then a head emerged slowly and studied the area. It wore a black balaclava and a white hood, which made it impossible to distinguish any features. Fortunately, the Sco-Js were well hidden and, satisfied that nobody was around, the person, wearing a white ski suit, hauled up skis and emerged. The entrance was covered, and then, within seconds, the figure descended from the mound, pulled on the skis and disappeared into the woods, skiing expertly.

'Whew!' said Eadan. 'No chance of catching up – I'm sure that was a man.'

'Definitely. Also, our balaclavas are green and brown,' said Brian.

'One of the crooks, then, and he certainly knew his way around,' said Cormag thoughtfully.

'Mmmm. It's 4:30 – should we hang around till 5:45 – in case anything else happens?' asked Brian.

'Absolutely,' said the other two.

But nothing else occurred, and they returned to the castle, glad to be back in the warmth of the shed; Cormag and Eadan cleaned the ski-doos.

'I think I hear the others,' said Brian, a little later, and opened the door with the remote. 'Yes – it's Rohan, Umedh and the girls.'

'Hi, Sco-Js,' shrieked Gina and Mich.

'Gavan and the others are behind us – no reports just now,' warned Rohan.

The others arrived, seconds later. Gavan helped them clean their machines and then parked his ski-doo; they entered the main building, removing their winter gear thankfully and gathering in the warm kitchen.

'Hot chocolate?' said Amy.

'*Yes, please!*' chorused everyone.

'We've done the waterholes,' explained Nimal, 'and Gavan's going to brief us about tomorrow's programme.'

'I have to get back ASAP – Uisdean needs help,' said Gavan.

'Go ahead,' said Rohan.

'Jay confirmed that you should be at Ruthven by eight – if you leave by seven, you'll have plenty of time. She's aware that you're assisting with Gràinne, Nimal, so you can go to Burns in-between the sessions and in the evening, when the rest of us have to be at the dinner.'

'Great,' said Rohan. 'Nimal's going to look after Gràinne, and the Sco-Js want to hang around Burns, too; the rest of us will attend the dinner.'

'Okay – Beiste and Clyde are on duty, but I'm sure they'd appreciate more assistance.'

'Perfect,' said Brian. 'How's Gràinne?'

'Much better – her stomach seems to be settling and although she's still limping, we think her paw's a bit better.' After giving them further details, Gavan left.

The JEACs saw him off, returned to the kitchen, and looked eagerly at Rohan.

'Down to business,' said Rohan. 'Mich and Gina – you're first.'

'We went to Knox after lunch, and Clyde came over around 1:30,' began Gina. 'He said he had to run errands for Dan before the 4:45 meeting with Ailean and others. Mich?'

'He didn't arrive at 4:45,' said Mich, 'so the others began without him. They didn't mind us being around, so Gina and I played with Gormal, while Rohan and Umedh sat where they could see the entrance and listened to the discussion. At 5 o'clock, Rohan rose, and I followed him to the front door. Gina?'

'Umedh winked at me and we left the room, too. Rohan, you explain the plan.'

'We'd agreed that Umedh should check Clyde's mobile phone. If the opportunity arose, I would get the phone, pass it to Mich, who would take it to Gina – waiting at the bottom of the stairs. Gina would race upstairs and hand it to Umedh, who would be in a small office.'

'Like a relay,' said Gina excitedly.

'Rohan opened the door,' said Mich, 'and Clyde was on the porch, removing his skis. He was wearing a white ski suit and taking off his balaclava.'

'Gosh!' gasped the Sco-Js.

'He appeared flustered and out of breath,' said Rohan. 'He rushed in, muttering that he'd been delayed, and hurriedly pulled off his ski suit, which I offered to hang up. He asked where the meeting was and dashed into the living room.'

'And . . .?' breathed the others.

'Once the door shut behind him, I examined the ski suit and – eureka! – his phone was in the first pocket I checked – and our relay began.'

'I wrote down the numbers for yesterday and today, and Rohan returned the phone to Clyde's pocket,' said Umedh, waving a piece of paper. 'Five numbers without names – and the numbers are for India, England, two calls to the same number in Scotland; and the last one is an overseas number, which we'll check soon.'

'Fortunately the timing was perfect – it was ten past five,' said Rohan. 'We said goodbye to Mòrag and Gormal, and left while the meeting was still going on.'

'What colour was Clyde's balaclava?' asked Brian eagerly.

'Black,' said Rohan.

'Yesss!' yelled the Sco-Js excitedly.

'Okay, you chaps next,' said Rohan, with a smile.

The Sco-Js quickly told their story.

'It must have been Clyde we saw,' concluded Brian.

'Possibly meeting with the crooks in the passage,' agreed Rohan. 'What time did he leave Cairns?'

'At 4:30,' said Brian, 'and he knows KWCC well. He once told Dad that he could get from Cairns to Knox in half an hour on his skis – so the timing's right, too. Also, the chopper hasn't left yet.'

'Let's check the phone numbers – things are moving,' said Eadan.

'We haven't had an update from our Burns group,' laughed Umedh.

'Oops – sorry, folks,' said Eadan.

'Nothing as exciting as this morning,' said Amy. 'We assisted with the animals and Uisdean; Uallas went back to Ruthven in the afternoon.'

'Amy and I hung around Beiste most of the day, but he did nothing suspicious,' said Anu. 'We think Taran was extremely blunt with him about the darts, and . . . hang on. Nimal, you've been very quiet.'

The boy grinned mischievously, pulled out an envelope from his pocket and offered it to Anu. 'Voilà! I was a good boy, Aunty – and did exactly what you told me to.'

Anu opened it and found two sheets of paper – one with the dosage chart, the other with the colour coding for the tailpieces – she placed them on the table.

Everyone crowded around.

'These charts are used when darts are prepared – every clinic has them taped onto the door of the medical cabinet. I took copies,' said Nimal. 'As we know, doses are based on the weight of the animal. Beiste prepared the darts. The tailpieces, which are interchangeable, are categorized as red for the strongest dose, which is *rarely* used here, and yellow for the mildest; the other colours are in-between, and green is used for a medium dosage – the correct dose for Gràinne.'

'Now, supposing Beiste, instead of using the proper dosage, substituted *water* for a major portion of the drug? It would only knock Gràinne out for about fifteen minutes and she would wake up jolly fast.'

'Wouldn't someone have noticed?' said Cormag.

'No – Beiste brought a loaded blow pipe,' said Nimal. 'Since the drugs are transparent, the substitution of water wouldn't have been discovered. Also, given that Gràinne was darted a second time, if the dosage had been correct, she wouldn't have recovered so rapidly.'

'Did Taran see you take copies of the charts, Nimal?' asked Anu.

'No – he's too busy at the moment.'

'Excellent work, JEACs – anything else?' asked Rohan.

'No,' said everyone.

'Come on, Brian, let's check these numbers,' said Umedh.

'The rest of us will prepare dinner,' said Amy.

Rohan, who had been making notes throughout the conversation, said, 'Do you mind if I think a few things through before joining you? I promise to do the dishes after.'

'No problemo,' said Amy. 'We've got lots of help, and we'll brainstorm as we work. Dinner at 7:20?'

'Thanks, and chaps, once you've checked the phone numbers, call me in the office,' said Rohan.

'Right,' said Umedh.

They split up; Rohan rapidly sorted things out in his mind and had just finished a rough schedule when Umedh and Brian dashed excitedly into the office and hurried him off to the kitchen.

Everyone served themselves quickly and sat down.

'Phone numbers?' said Rohan.

'Right,' said Brian, responding to Umedh's nod, 'the Scottish numbers were calls to Beiste, and the overseas call was to China.'

'The other two calls were to Hackney, East London and Delhi, North India,' said Umedh. 'We don't know whom the calls were to, specifically, but they cover the locations the crooks have been involved in.'

'Excellent evidence for later on,' said Rohan.

'What next?' asked Eadan.

'I have a plan for tonight and tomorrow,' said Rohan. 'It's currently 7:30; I suggest we watch the entrance to the cellar tonight, just to see if there's any movement at this end.'

'Do you think CAB would risk coming here tonight?' asked Cormag. 'They know we're around and that we're nosy.'

'I don't expect CAB, but the crooks will be clearing the passage, and *they* might pop up for fresh air – that would be additional confirmation that we're on the right track.'

'What do you suggest?' asked Nimal.

'Take turns watching the entrance from the Sco-Js' hiding place, in two-hour shifts, starting at 8:30. Gina, Mich, Umedh and I will begin; the Sco-Js next; then Anu, Amy and Nimal – which takes us to 2:30 a.m.; Umedh and I will take the last shift from 2:30 to 4; we'll all sleep till 5:30, de-ice the waterholes and leave by 7 a.m. to reach Ruthven by 8. I figure that by 4 a.m., no crooks will be around since the staff will be starting duties. I'm convinced that the critical period is tomorrow night, while CAB are covering Burns on their own. So you Sco-Js and Nimal should be on your guard while keeping an eye on Gràinne.'

'Good plan,' said Nimal. 'Anu, Amy and I will de-ice the waterholes, so you two can sleep a bit longer.'

'And we'll get breakfast ready for 6:15,' said Gina, while Mich nodded.

'We'll help,' offered the Sco-Js.

'Great team work, JEACs,' said Rohan, smiling around at their eager faces. 'Any further ideas or questions?'

'What about the dogs?' said Mich.

'We'll take them with us in the morning. In the evening we'll put them in the house at Burns,' said Nimal. 'Unfortunately, we can't keep them with us since Gràinne might get upset.'

'Do we have to stay at Ruthven the whole evening?' asked Gina.

'No, but we should stay till 9:30 p.m., keeping in touch with Nimal and the Sco-Js; we can go to Burns after that to help ensure the snow leopards are okay,' said Rohan.

'Right. We'd better move – it's 8:15,' said Umedh.

The group separated. Later on, the Sco-Js saw three people emerge from the secret passage. Wearing ski suits and black balaclavas, they stood at the top of the mound and looked around, pointing and talking quietly for about five minutes; then they went down again, and the entrance was covered once more. Nothing else happened that night.

'I'm sure they were making plans for tomorrow,' said Cormag. He had been busy with a camera.

'I just hope the snow leopards won't get injured,' said Brian angrily.

'I agree, mate,' said Cormag, 'but we must catch all of them *in the act* – we need a concrete case with good evidence and proof before a jury will convict them. Crooks who can afford a clever lawyer often get off on technicalities these days.'

They updated the next team, and also Rohan and Umedh, who were still awake when the others came to bed.

'We're building up a good case,' said Rohan.

CHAPTER 17

The Day of the Fundraiser, and Poor Gràinne

The twentieth of December – the day of the fundraiser – was a clear, cold day. Over breakfast, everyone was updated on the night's happenings. The JEACs, though looking forward to the event, were more concerned with the safety of the snow leopards.

'I called Gavan,' said Nimal, as they took out their ski-doos. 'Gràinne's stomach is completely okay, and her limp's better, too, but they're glad that the Sco-Js and I will be there from 7:30 this evening, since she knows me. If anything happens, I can keep her calm till Taran arrives.'

'I'm sure they don't trust Beiste – especially after yesterday's incident,' said Brian.

'True, yaar,' said Nimal, 'and if they could, they'd stay at Burns. But they're the best people to speak about, and answer questions on, the breeding programme.'

'Will they be at Ruthven during the day?' asked Amy.

'Yes, but Dolly will stay at Burns to keep an eye on Gràinne – she only needs to be at Ruthven tonight.'

'Good, but I doubt the crooks will do anything during the day – the crucial time is from around 8 p.m. until midnight, since at that time everyone, except Clyde, Beiste and you four, will be busy at Ruthven,' said Rohan. 'Let's go, JEACs.'

Rohan led the way, moving fast on his ski-doo, the others keeping up easily.

'Jolly good time – only 45 minutes at a fast pace,' said Rohan to Umedh, as they reached Ruthven.

'We'd cut off another ten or fifteen minutes if we raced,' said Umedh, thoughtfully, 'which means we can reach Burns from Ruthven in twenty minutes or less, at racing speed.'

'We might need it, too,' said Rohan.

Ensuring that their colourful JEACs badges were well displayed, they set about the various tasks assigned to them.

The eleven helicopters donated for the fundraiser, plus the two KWCC ones, transported people in a constant stream.

It was great fun! The JEACs participated in several events, made new friends, and had a superb time. At 4:30 p.m., all of them, including Janet Larkin, Dilki Patel and Jay, attended a brief meeting with the volunteer teachers who had hosted the JEACs' information sessions.

'Latharna's speaking to some parents and will join us momentarily,' said Dilki.

'How did it go?' asked Jay. 'Almost every kid I see is wearing a JEACs' badge.'

'It was incredible!' exclaimed a teacher. 'I checked at the end of our session at 4 p.m., and hundreds of youngsters between the ages of five and eighteen attended the sessions – and joined the JEACs.'

'That's fantastic,' said Janet. 'We'll have to get more badges and pamphlets before we go on tours to zoos and conservation centres in Scotland and the UK. I'll call the suppliers tonight.'

'Yes, please, Janet,' said another teacher. 'And one of our donors offered to meet all costs for badges and pamphlets, both while your group is here, and touring, as well as later on, when the Scottish JEACs require them. She's thrilled that her sons and daughter have joined such a good cause.'

'Guess what?' said Latharna, joining the group. 'Mr. and Mrs. Elphinstone's twin sons, Blàr and Boisil, who were the first to join the

JEACs, raved about the group to their parents. The Elphinstones are KWCC donors.'

'Yeah, we met the twins – they're fourteen – at the sledding contest, and they asked dozens of questions about our badges and the JEACs,' said Nimal.

'We answered those we had time for, and invited them to the first JEACs' session,' laughed Anu.

'Well, at my meeting with their parents, I was asked a lot of questions about the JEACs, and they want to meet you folks after Christmas to discuss some ideas,' said Latharna.

'Sure thing,' said Rohan. 'Do you know what it's about?'

'Mr. Elphinstone is a wealthy businessman, and a generous donor, in particular, to the breeding programme. He's captivated by the vision of the JEACs and wants to start a foundation called *JEACs International Foundation*, which would assist in funding the JEACs to educate others – especially kids who can't afford to visit zoos and conservation centres in Scotland, as well as in India, Africa, Sri Lanka and Bangladesh, to name a few of the poorer countries.'

'Wonderful!' exclaimed Jay.

'We'd be thrilled to assist in any way,' added Dilki.

'Excellent,' said Latharna, beaming at them. 'All of us would love to be part of the meeting. Janet and Dilki, shall I co-ordinate with you, since I know Jay has her hands full at the moment?'

'Sure, Latharna.'

An excited group of JEACs rushed off to watch the fireworks display. After the show, families with young children began to leave KWCC in batches, while more adults arrived for the evening event.

'That was a superfantabulous event,' sighed Gina, as the JEACs raced back to Cairns.

'We'll save time if we park the ski-doos here,' said Rohan, who had led the way to the porch rather than the sheds.

'Good thinking, yaar,' said Umedh, parking beside him. 'We should leave by 7:30 at the latest so that we get there by 8:15 or so.'

'We'll prepare hot drinks, since we're going to Burns and don't need to change,' said Brian, as they hurried into the building.

'Great, thanks,' said the girls, and rushed off.

'Brian, send me a text at 9 p.m., confirming all's well at Burns; we'll stay at Ruthven till 9:30 and then leave – we should join you before ten or a bit earlier, if we move as fast as we did this morning – right?

'Yes, sir!' said Eadan, saluting smartly.

Rohan grinned, clapped him on the shoulder, and went off with Umedh to change.

*****

'I'll get it,' said Nimal, when the telephone rang a few minutes before 6:30. 'Hello? Hi, Gavan.' He listened intently, his face registering concern, and the Sco-Js gathered around him. 'We'll be over ASAP! Bye.'

He rang off and said, 'Let's go, Sco-Js – Gràinne's throwing up again and they want me to help. I'll get Rohan and Umedh and meet you at the front door; grab your coats.'

Nimal raced to the boys' dormitory, where the other two were putting on ties, told them to come to the front door, and ran back, the others at his heels.

'What's up, yaar?' said Rohan.

The Sco-Js were nearly ready and as Nimal pulled on winter gear, he said, 'Gavan called. He was doing a final check, since the staff were supposed to leave for Ruthven at 7:30, when he saw Gràinne throwing up – she'd been given her special diet an hour ago. Taran wants to medicate her before he leaves, so Gavan phoned Dan who's moving the breeding programme session to 8:45, which means the Burns group don't have to leave till eight; Taran needs me to keep Gràinne calm. I figured the four of us might as well race over now.'

'Agreed. Where were CAB?' asked Rohan.

'Don't know – call us when you reach Ruthven, and we'll give you a further update on the situ,' said Nimal, pulling on gloves and hurrying outside. 'We'll take Hunter, but Tumbler's too small.'

'We'll take him,' said Umedh, helping Brian secure his crutches in his ski-doo.

'Thanks,' said Brian.

'Shouldn't take them more than seven or eight minutes to get there at the rate they're going,' said Umedh, as the boys zoomed off.

'Yes. I wonder why Gràinne's throwing up *again*,' said Rohan thoughtfully, as they returned to their dormitory to finish dressing. 'Gavan said she was perfectly okay this morning.'

'Her stomach's probably extra sensitive due to the drugs she's been on recently,' said Umedh, putting on his jacket.

Ten minutes later, they met the girls in the kitchen and quickly updated them.

'Oh, poor Gràinne,' said Anu. 'Was it something she ate . . . that disagreed . . . hang on.' She paused, thinking hard, and then continued, 'She was fed shortly before she threw up, right?'

'Yes,' said Rohan, looking at her intently. 'Carry on, sis.'

'Who fed her? Did she bring up everything? Can the boys try to get a sample for examination?'

'What are you suggesting, Anu?' asked Amy. 'Poison?'

'Yes,' said Anu bluntly. 'This morning, Gavan said that she was fine. So why would she suddenly throw up again this evening? Her diet's carefully monitored and she's eating small portions. Do we know if anyone else fed her?'

'Not yet,' said Rohan. 'I've been thinking along the same lines, but we'll have to wait for an update.'

'That's horrible,' said Gina. 'It must be Beiste.'

'We shouldn't make assumptions, kiddo,' said Amy, 'but I can't help thinking the same.'

'Me, too,' agreed the others.

'Let's get going,' said Rohan. 'I know it's only 7:10, and if we race, we'll reach Ruthven before eight – I don't want to miss a call from the Burns lot while we're in transition – I've got Tumbler.'

They sped off.

'Jolly good run,' said Umedh, 35 minutes later, as they parked their ski-doos and entered through a side door.

Rohan led the way to an empty office. 'We'll call the boys for an update. Also, I think we should have someone keeping watch at Cairns.'

'Good idea – Cormag and Eadan, perhaps?' said Umedh.

'Yes. I wish we didn't have to attend this function,' said Rohan, 'but unfortunately, we can't always do as we please.'

'Too true,' groaned Amy.

Rohan called Brian's mobile telephone.

'Hi, Rohan,' said Brian. 'Nimal and Eadan are with Gràinne and the others, but Hunter, Cormag and I are in my room – we have news. Hang up, and we'll call you back on the speakerphone.'

'Right,' said Rohan. He hung up and said to the others, 'They're going to call on this extension.'

'Hi, Brian and Cormag,' chorused everyone, the minute the boys came on the line.

'Tell us,' said Rohan.

'We got here in under ten minutes and everyone was around Gràinne's enclosure, including CAB,' said Brian. 'Taran had medicated her; Nimal joined him immediately and began to speak to Gràinne.'

'Brian, Eadan and I overheard Uncle Luag questioning Beiste as to why he had given Gràinne the regular food since she was on a special diet and had already been fed,' said Cormag. 'Beiste said he thought she was okay, that she looked hungry when he threw in meat for Niall in the next enclosure and, since he felt sorry for her, he gave her some, too. He said Taran had told him she was perfectly well.'

'Gav glared at Beiste and muttered, under his breath, that Beiste was a moron of the first degree,' said Brian. 'CAB didn't see us, since we were behind them. Clyde poked Beiste in the back and said soothingly to Dad, 'Don't worry, Luag. I'll *personally* ensure she isn't fed again till you return – you're only gone for a few hours, right?'

'Uncle Luag said they'd be back just after midnight, at the latest, and that Nimal would stay around Gràinne's enclosure to keep her calm; he also said that we'd be around,' said Cormag, 'which is when we said "hi", as if we'd just arrived, and they turned and saw us.'

'Beiste looked surprised, and we saw him look at Clyde,' said Brian. 'But Clyde is smooth – he ignored Beiste, smiled at us and said it was good to have so many people looking after the snow leopards. He said he would continue his rounds and return, for further instructions, before the Burns staff had to leave at eight. He went off with Beiste, and Cormag shadowed them,' said Brian.

'As soon as they were out of earshot,' said Cormag, 'Clyde blasted Beiste, asking why he'd fed Gràinne so early; Beiste said he wanted to make sure the stuff took effect and that he had not expected Gav to do a last-minute round when he knew that he, Beiste, was looking after the animals. Clyde grunted and told him to quit being such an idiot and that because of his stupidity he'd caused more complications and further delayed things. They parted, and I returned to the others.'

'Gràinne remained calm because Nimal kept talking to her,' said Brian. 'At eight, Taran told us and CAB that he'd return shortly after midnight, unless there was an emergency. Clyde assured Taran and Dad that he would check on Gràinne at regular intervals and if Nimal felt that she needed attention, he would ring Taran himself. Everyone left a few minutes ago; CAB went off to do their rounds, and we came inside to update you.'

'Phew – nothing concrete in the argument CAB had, but it sounds like they might have poisoned Gràinne – we've been wondering about that,' said Rohan. 'We've got to get going, but we realized that someone should keep watch at Cairns to see if anyone comes out of the cellar.'

'Gosh, yes,' agreed Cormag. 'Eadan and I'll go over – Nimal and Brian should be okay here.'

'Thanks,' said Rohan. 'Take a WT, and at nine, beep the others to let them know all's well at Cairns; then, Brian, send us a text message to let *us* know all's well at Cairns and Burns; we'll leave here at 9:30 at the latest and race over to help keep watch. Stay in touch – we must ensure that *this* fundraiser doesn't end with a disaster!'

'Absolutely!' agreed everyone and they rang off.

'Hurry, JEACs,' said Anu, 'we're supposed to be seated in five. Wish I could be in three places at once.'

'Us, too,' groaned the others, as they hurried out.

Chapter 18

Captured!

Brian and Cormag left Hunter in the house, and went to update Nimal and Eadan, who were outside Gràinne's enclosure, their heads bent over something in Nimal's hand.

'Is that what Gràinne threw up?' asked Cormag, looking at the piece of chewed up meat.

'Yes. I pulled it through the mesh when nobody was looking – we should examine it for poison,' said Nimal.

'That Beiste! I could . . .' stammered Brian, red with rage.

'We'll get him, yaar,' said Nimal, wrapping the piece of meat in his handkerchief and shoving it in his pocket. 'The evidence is mounting. What did the others say?'

'We updated them, and they want us to keep an eye on Cairns, too,' said Cormag.

'Brian and I'll be okay,' said Nimal. 'Just give me ten minutes to bring out a loaded blow pipe and some extra darts.' He dashed off.

Cormag and Eadan were ready to leave when he returned, and Nimal said, 'Keep in touch via the WT and let us know when you're settled in the bushes.'

'Will do,' they assured him, and raced off.

'They're incredibly fast,' said Nimal. He gave Brian a blow pipe and said, with a grin, 'By the way, I found . . .'

'Watch out – here's Clyde,' interrupted Brian.

'Did someone just leave?' asked Clyde, smiling pleasantly.

'Yes – Cormag and Eadan,' said Nimal casually. 'Where's Beiste?'

'Patrolling the other enclosures; did the boys go to Ruthven?'

'I believe . . . oh, look! Gràinne's playing with the cubs,' said Brian, pointing.

'Excellent,' said Nimal, glad to avoid answering Clyde. 'She must be feeling better, don't you think, Clyde?'

'Definitely,' said Clyde. 'Well, I'll continue my rounds – you boys be sure to call me if you need anything.'

'Thanks,' they said, and watched him walk away.

'I wouldn't call him if he were the *only* person left at KWCC,' growled Brian as soon as Clyde was out of sight. 'How shall we keep watch on the other snow leopards, Nimal?'

'I'll do a quick walk around the enclosures every twenty minutes,' said Nimal, 'but we'll keep our WTs on speaker, so we can hear each other – and if those two try anything funny, we'll know immediately. I'll do a round now – see if I can find Beiste; keep that blow pipe handy.'

He went off and Brian moved closer to the enclosure – he was seated in his ski-doo.

*****

'Seven minutes flat,' said Cormag, leaping off his ski-doo and pushing it into heavy shrubbery near their hiding place.

'It's only 8:25,' said Eadan, hiding his machine, too.

They crawled into their lookout and settled down quickly, pulling out their night-vision binoculars.

'The entrance is covered,' said Cormag, looking across at the mound. 'Turn on the WT.'

'Yeah – we'll . . .' began Eadan.

'Not so fast,' growled a voice, grabbing the WT. 'Keep that gun trained on them, Beiste.'

The boys turned and froze, staring at Beiste, while two other men quickly tied their hands behind their backs and dragged them to their feet.

'We *knew* you were a crook,' shouted Cormag.

'And that's Moire,' yelled Eadan, recognizing her as she joined them.

'None of your lip,' snapped Moire. 'Interfering brats – gag them.' The boys were gagged. 'What shall we do with them, Zulfi?'

'Put them in the cellar . . .' He paused to answer his mobile telephone. 'Okay, I'll leave now,' he said, and rang off. 'Hurry up with these brats – Beiste, join us quickly.'

Grabbing Eadan's ski-doo, he sped away, while the boys were forced to climb the mound and descend into the cellar, which Moire uncovered.

Once in the passage, the boys were placed in a corner, next to a gurney, which had not been there before.

'Remove their gags, but tie their feet,' ordered Beiste. 'You JEACs think you're so smart, but we'll see who's smarter.'

'When did *you* get here?' said Cormag.

'And how did you find us so quickly,' asked Eadan.

'I got here shortly after the Burns crowd left for Ruthven,' boasted Beiste. 'My colleagues have cleared this passage, and we'll take the snow leopards through it on that gurney, kill them, put them into the chopper, and take off. We were finalizing our plans in the shrubbery, next to where you hid your ski-doos, and heard you coming.'

Both boys began to yell at him angrily.

'SILENCE!' roared Beiste, firing his gun into the air to intimidate them.

Everyone jumped in fright; and then there was an ominous rumble.

'What was that?' whispered Moire.

The crooks went down the passage, while the boys looked at each other.

'Sounded like a landslide,' whispered Cormag.

'Agreed,' muttered Eadan. 'Hopefully, it's blocked the passage. Sshh, they're returning.'

'You're a moron, Beiste,' Moire was saying as they reached the boys. 'We won't have time to clear that landfall – I'm calling Zulfi.' She climbed up the steps in order to get a signal, dialled a number, updated Zulfi, and then said, impatiently, 'Yes. As I said, it's close to the cellar and it'll take at least three hours to clear a path wide enough for the gurney. Think of something else.'

She listened intently, hung up, and turned to the others.

'We're going to use a KWCC chopper – the pilot's on duty beside it and Clyde will deal with him. We'll put the animals into cages, use a forklift to move the cages and lift them into the chopper; fly back to *our* chopper; kill the animals, and leave. Garbhan, you can fly any chopper, right?'

'I'm not used to machines which move animals – but I'll try.'

'And what about Clyde and me?' asked Beiste. He was rather subdued.

'You'll come with us, obviously, unless you want to stay and face the music.'

'Don't be silly. What about these two?'

'Leave them here – and,' she added maliciously to the boys, 'your buddies are safely tied up, too.' The boys glared at her, as she continued, 'Piece of cake; while Clyde pretended to check on the sick snow leopard with the other brat, Zulfi held up the lame kid at gunpoint and his mate didn't dare do anything. Let's go, guys, we've got to get there fast – loading six fully grown animals and four cubs into a chopper will take a couple of hours at least. It's nearly nine – how long will it take us to get to the other joint, Beiste?'

'Twenty minutes,' said Beiste.

They climbed out of the cellar, not bothering to cover the entrance, and the boys stared at each other, too horrified to speak.

*****

At Burns, Nimal and Brian, tied and gagged, listened helplessly as Clyde and Zulfi reworked their plan.

'Okay, here's a pistol and a case of darts from the clinic – Beiste prepared the darts in advance. Use the darts with the *red* tailpieces – they're under the green ones. Be very careful, since the darts with the green tailpieces have a lower dosage in them and will only tranquillize a snow leopard for a short time – they're just a cover-up in case any of the staff opened the case – we never use the red tailpieces here. I'll take a ski-doo, deal with the pilot, and return,' said Clyde. 'The others should be here by then. There are five more adult cats, in enclosures along this path. Watch out, though – they're all very restless tonight. We'll deal with the cubs last. One dart for each adult should sedate them for several hours – Beiste used the strongest dosage.'

'Right – should I start with this one?' said Zulfi, pointing at Gràinne.

'No, get her mate first – in the next enclosure,' said Clyde. 'Wait till Beiste arrives so he can drive the ATV with the forklift – it can carry two cages at a time. There's a cage outside each enclosure.'

They separated and a few minutes later, Beiste, Garbhan and Moire arrived, and went to assist Zulfi at Niall's enclosure – Clyde had obviously updated them.

'Your buddies are tied up in the passage,' mocked Beiste, when they got to Gràinne's enclosure. Niall lay in a cage on the forklift.

Poor Gràinne was tranquillized, and her cage placed on the forklift, just as Clyde returned.

'Osgar's looked after – so you three get going,' said Clyde. The forklift set off, while Moire and Garbhan took ski-doos. 'We'll put these two in Gràinne's enclosure,' he added nastily, lifting Brian out of his ski-doo, while Zulfi dragged Nimal.

The boys were thrust inside, and Clyde locked the door, throwing the keys on the ground just outside. He laughed mockingly, and the men went off on ski-doos.

Nimal winked at Brian and nodded at a package lying on the ground outside the enclosure. Brian's eyes lit up – the men had left behind their case containing the tranquillizer darts.

CHAPTER 19

Racing Ski-doos

The JEACs at Ruthven were restless. Their dinner lay, untouched, on the table. Seated at the back of the hall, they listened half-heartedly to the speeches and talks which had begun, and checked their watches frequently.

'Ten past nine and nothing from the others,' muttered Rohan.

'Can't we call them?' asked Amy.

'I texted them five minutes ago,' said Umedh. 'No response – I think . . .'

'Let's go,' said Rohan reading his friend's mind.

The JEACs reached Gràinne's enclosure in record time, screeched to a halt and flung themselves off their machines.

'Golly!' gasped Gina and Mich when they saw the boys.

'It's locked,' said Umedh, rattling the gate. Nimal nodded towards the keys on the ground, and in a few minutes the boys were free and Brian was lifted onto his ski-doo.

'What happened?' asked Rohan.

Nimal updated them, and Rohan quickly shot out instructions. 'Gina, Mich – Ruthven, ASAP – alert Drostan – he'll take over; Umedh, Amy, Anu – find Eadan and Cormag, and deal with the crooks' chopper. We three will get Hunter and go to the chopper shed.'

'We'll stay at that end,' said Umedh, mounting his ski-doo, 'just in case.'

'Right, yaar. Brian, are you okay to come with us?'

'Yes,' said Brian abruptly. 'Just give me a blow pipe and that bag of darts.'

Nimal laughed, and everyone looked at him in surprise.

'What . . .?' began Rohan.

'Just before the Sco-Js left, I ran to the clinic to get a blow pipe and darts for Brian,' said Nimal. 'A large case, filled with darts, lay beside the cabinet – which seemed fishy since most of the staff use kitbags and you rarely need a large case. Then I saw red tailpieces, which are never used here, under a layer of green ones, and I knew Beiste must have put a strong dosage in the red ones – he wouldn't care if the snow leopards never woke up. So I put a very diluted dose into the darts with green tailpieces, and then switched the tailpieces. Therefore, Niall and Gràinne are likely to revive pretty soon – and they'll be cross!'

'Gee whizz, Nimal!' exclaimed Amy, as the others burst out laughing. 'You're a genius. Good luck, boys.'

The others raced off. 'Smart move, yaar. Do we have any darts with the correct dosage?' asked Rohan.

'The case in Brian's ski-doo – there are six extras. Since the animals haven't been given reversal agents, those darts should tranquillize them if necessary,' said Nimal. 'Hide Beiste's case under a bush. Also, the crooks will be busy loading the cages into the chopper and probably won't hear us, but let's stop a short distance away and sneak up – we'll push your ski-doo, Brian.'

'Let's go,' said Rohan. 'It should take the kiddies about twenty minutes to reach Ruthven and another five to find Drostan.'

They collected Hunter from the house and sped off – it was a night for racing ski-doos! Five minutes later they stopped, parked their ski-doos and let Hunter out, bidding him not to bark. They pushed Brian's ski-doo towards the half-open door of the helicopter shed.

'The exit hatch is open,' breathed Brian, looking up.

They stopped outside the door, and peered in.

Chaos reigned! Niall, wide awake, was stamping about in his cage – which was still on the forklift; Gràinne was beginning to move a little, and her cage, only halfway on the ramp despite Moire and Garbhan's efforts to push it into the helicopter, rocked unsteadily; Osgar was tied securely in a corner of the shed.

'You fool, Beiste – you've messed up the dosage,' Clyde yelled.

'But . . . you used the darts with the red tailpieces, right, Zulfi?' said Beiste. 'Did you shoot it properly into the rump?'

'Never mind! Get the bag and give them another shot or two,' snapped Clyde.

'Where's the bag?' asked Beiste, looking around.

'Don't know,' said Zulfi. 'I left it beside the enclosure – didn't any of you bring it?'

Obviously, none of them had.

'Beiste, get it – quick,' yelled Clyde. 'Zulfi, work the forklift and put the other cage on the ground; you others, push this one into the chopper before it topples over – she's still groggy.'

Everyone was rushing to obey him, when Beiste, turning towards the door, saw the boys and yelled.

Brian aimed the blow pipe at Beiste, and the cowardly man stopped at once.

'Move and I'll dart you,' shouted Brian, as Nimal, Rohan and Hunter raced inside, knocking down Moire and Garbhan who had not been able to let go of Gràinne's cage quickly enough. Leaving Hunter to guard them, Nimal went for Zulfi who was about to climb into the forklift, while Rohan turned to deal with Clyde.

But although the men had put down their guns to lift the cage, Clyde grabbed a revolver from his waistband and aimed it at Gràinne. 'One more step and I'll kill her; and call that dog off,' said the man, coldly.

The boys hesitated, and were lost. It would take a cold-blooded person, indeed, to allow Gràinne to be killed.

'Hunter, here boy!' shouted Nimal. The dog obeyed, but continued to growl ominously.

Brian's blow pipe was taken, and Beiste tied the boy's hands, leaving him in his ski-doo.

'You'll never get away with this,' shouted Brian furiously.

'The cops are on the way,' yelled Rohan.

'And they'll be here any moment,' snapped Nimal.

'Quit yapping and move,' snarled Clyde, his back towards the helicopter, his gun now trained on the boys as Nimal was pushed next to

Brian. 'Zulfi, Garbhan, Moire – get the first cage into the chopper, pronto. Beiste, tie these two and gag them – then get the bag of tranquillizers.'

Beiste dealt with Nimal, and turned to get Rohan, when – CRASH – Gràinne's cage toppled off the helicopter, right onto Zulfi's foot, and the man hopped around, yelling in anguish – while Garbhan and Moire, who had climbed into the helicopter to assist by pulling the cage, backed further into the machine, looking out fearfully.

Clyde and Beiste were distracted, and that was all Rohan needed. He aimed a karate kick at Clyde, felling him to his knees and sending the gun flying out of his hands. Rohan caught it, quickly put on the safety catch, and aimed it at Clyde.

'You won't shoot me,' snarled Clyde, rising to his feet.

'Try me!' snapped Rohan, holding the gun steady and taking careful aim. 'One move and you'll have a nasty flesh wound in your leg.'

'Beiste, Garbhan . . .' began Clyde.

Moire screamed, making everyone jump. 'Clyde, behind you!'

Clyde glanced over his shoulder and froze.

One side of Gràinne's cage was broken; the groggy animal had crawled out of it and was shaking her head, rapidly regaining her senses.

'Beiste, remove Nimal's gag – NOW – and untie him,' snapped Rohan, keeping his gun trained on Clyde.

'Hurry,' said Brian, sharply. 'Only he can calm Gràinne, and she's getting ready to spring at Clyde.'

Beiste hastily removed Nimal's gag, his hands shaking as he struggled to untie him.

Immediately, Nimal began speaking. 'Good girl, Gràinne. Stay calm, okay? I won't let anyone hurt you.'

The creature, recognizing a loved voice, turned her head to look for Nimal.

'Don't even *think* of moving, Clyde,' warned Rohan. 'She'll be on you in a jiffy.'

Beiste released Nimal and sank, petrified, to the floor.

Nimal, still talking calmly, moved slowly towards Gràinne.

Just then Gavan, Taran, Doilidh and Drostan arrived.

'Gav – there's a blow pipe and darts in my ski-doo,' said Brian quickly.

Taking in the situation at a glance, Gavan quickly loaded the blow pipe, but he couldn't shoot since Nimal was between them. Drostan and Taran covered Zulfi and Clyde, while Doilidh released Brian. Apart from Nimal's low tones, the only other sound was that of the helicopter engine. Niall, who had woken up completely and was prowling in his cage, also paused to listen to the mesmerizing voice.

'Nimal, move so that I can get a clear shot at Gràinne,' said Gavan, quietly.

Nimal, still talking to the crouching snow leopard, moved so that she had to turn her head to watch him; Gavan shot a tranquillizer into her rump and she swayed, dropping within a couple of minutes.

A sigh of relief swept the shed; but before they could do more than grab Zulfi and Clyde, the helicopter rose into the air.

'*Duck!*' yelled Drostan, and everyone instinctively ducked as the ramp, which was still down, barely missed their heads.

'Rohan! Careful – it's closing,' yelled Nimal, as his cousin, with a mighty leap, caught the edge of the ramp and began pulling himself up.

They watched anxiously, but Rohan had already scrambled into the helicopter, unseen by Moire and Garbhan, who had decided to flee justice.

'Come on, Brian, Hunter!' roared Nimal running towards a ski-doo. He put Hunter in the bubble and started the machine.

'B-but . . . where are you going?' shouted Drostan, as the boys turned their vehicles.

'To be in at the finish,' yelled Nimal. 'Here come the others and the cops – Drostan, tell the cops to get to the other side of the boundary wall at Cairns, near the castle, and look for two choppers. Mich and Gina, follow me!'

Mich and Gina, who were just arriving, didn't stop at the shed, but changed direction and raced after Nimal and Brian. Tumbler was in the bubble with Mich.

Drostan passed on the message to the police inspector who had just arrived with Dan, and the inspector immediately contacted his team.

*****

In the meantime, Anu, Amy and Umedh had been busy. They reached Cairns around 9:55.

'Park near the ruins – I'll be back,' said Umedh. 'I need something from the shed.' He joined them shortly, waving a toolkit and saying, 'Don't leave home without these – at least, not if you want to "fix" a chopper.'

They made their way cautiously to the cellar entrance – which was open – and found the Sco-Js. The boys were released and updated briefly on the situation at Burns; then all five raced through the passage, glad that despite the landslide, they could make their way through it easily.

'We've got to prevent the crooks escaping – just in case things don't go smoothly at the other end, and they return for their chopper,' said Anu.

'Whoa, nearly there – slow down,' said Umedh, who was in the lead.

They crept forward the last few metres, and Umedh peered out – the entrance was open. In the moonlight, he saw the helicopter parked not even fifteen metres away from the entrance. Clearly, nobody was around.

'Nice, large clearing – enough for three choppers,' said Umedh, as they emerged from the passage. 'Let's get to work, JEACs. We need to guard the passage so no unwanted people come through.'

'Amy and I will find a good hiding place close to it,' said Anu.

'Eadan and I'll find hiding places for the three of us,' said Cormag.

'And I'll operate on this beauty so that she can't start.'

'Good luck, buddy,' said Eadan.

By the time the boys had found good hiding places for themselves and Umedh, close to the helicopter, Umedh descended from it, grinning broadly.

'They won't be going anywhere in that baby,' he said, triumphantly waving a few wires in the air.

The others cheered and then stopped quickly as Amy hissed, 'Sshh – voices in the passage. Hang on – I'm sure that's Hunter.'

Hunter and Tumbler charged out of the entrance, followed by Gina, Mich, and Nimal, with Brian on his back.

'What's happening? Where's Rohan?' yelled the others.

'Brian, you tell them,' panted Nimal, lowering the boy onto a rock near Amy's hiding place.

'Thanks, Nimal,' said Brian. 'Moire and the pilot, Garbhan, have escaped in our KWCC chopper and will probably come here to get their machine. Rohan's in the chopper, too – he caught the ramp just as the chopper was taking off.'

'Is he okay? Did they see him?' gasped Amy.

'He scrambled inside before the ramp was completely drawn up. I doubt they saw him,' said Nimal.

'So where's the chopper?' asked Eadan.

'They took off in the wrong direction, but they'll soon find their way here,' said Nimal.

'There'll be a couple of police choppers arriving, too,' said Brian.

'There won't be room for more than two more choppers to land,' said Umedh. 'And since the crooks may try and make off in our chopper when theirs doesn't work, I'm going to try and disable it as well.'

'I hear a chopper,' yelled Nimal, calling Hunter urgently and depositing Brian under a bush.

They scattered in different directions, and everybody was well hidden by the time the KWCC helicopter arrived.

The helicopter landed awkwardly, backing the other machine. Moire scrambled out, ran to their machine, and clambered into the passenger seat.

'Hurry up, Garbhan! The cops will arrive soon – move, man, move!' she screeched.

Garbhan jumped out, searching for keys as he ran to his machine. He put the keys in the ignition – nothing happened. 'What the . . .' he muttered, trying again. 'Oh, shut up, Moire!' he yelled, as she screamed for him to hurry.

As soon as the crooks were in their helicopter, Umedh ran over to the other machine just as Rohan opened the door.

'Get back,' whispered Umedh, clambering in quickly.

'But we need to . . .' began Rohan, and then grinned. 'Did you disable it?'

'Yes, and I'll do this one, too,' chuckled Umedh.

'No need, yaar – I have the keys,' said Rohan, patting his pocket.

'Good man,' said Umedh. 'What next?'

'They've both got guns – so be careful.'

'The others are in the shrubbery,' said Umedh, 'and they'll help.'

'The crooks are coming back . . .' began Rohan, when Cormag and Eadan ran out of hiding, yelling loudly, and successfully distracting the crooks.

Moire and Garbhan turned swiftly to face the boys.

'How did you brats break free?' snarled Moire, as each of them pointed a gun at the boys.

'None of your business,' shouted Eadan, determined to keep the crooks facing him since he could see the other JEACs creeping up behind them.

'You won't escape,' yelled Cormag. 'The police will catch you.'

'We'll take you as hostages,' growled Garbhan, grabbing Cormag, who was closest to him, while Moire grabbed Eadan.

'Get 'em, Hunter! JEACs, to the rescue!' yelled Nimal, speeding towards the crooks from one side, Hunter bounding beside him.

The crooks gasped as children and dogs erupted from every direction, converging on them.

'Stay away!' bellowed Garbhan, as he and Moire backed towards the KWCC helicopter until they were close to the door. 'Call that dog off – one step closer, and we'll shoot your buddies.'

'No you won't!' shouted Rohan as he and Umedh leapt out of the helicopter, on top of Garbhan and Moire, felling them to the ground. The guns flew into the snow, and Nimal and Amy grabbed them quickly.

Cormag and Eadan were unhurt and wriggled away from the crooks who were face down in the snow, well guarded by dogs and JEACs.

Brian, shouting jubilantly, was brought over by Umedh, to join the group surrounding the crooks.

'And here come the cops,' said Rohan, looking up as two police helicopters came in sight.

One helicopter landed quickly. Policemen handcuffed the crooks and put them in the machine, which flew off so that the second one could land.

Inspector Jeffries jumped out. 'Excellent work, youngsters! You're wanted back at Ruthven so that we can get the complete story. My chopper won't take everyone so we'll have to use these two as well – Cesan can fly one and I'll fly the other.'

'Er . . . sorry, sir,' said Umedh, 'but I disabled their chopper.' He held out a handful of wires.

The inspector laughed so infectiously that the JEACs and the policemen could not help joining in. 'I'm just happy that you JEACs are on *our* side. Cesan can fix it in a jiffy – though I'm sure you could, too, young man.'

'Come and help me, laddie,' said Cesan, grinning at Umedh, and they went off to fix the machine.

The inspector telephoned Dan, informing him that they would be arriving shortly. Fifteen minutes later, all three helicopters were in the air, filled with JEACs, dogs and policemen, and when they landed at Ruthven, Dan was waiting to escort them into the castle.

'Everyone's longing to hear the complete story,' said Dan, ushering them into a large conference room where some of the staff, the policemen, and the crooks were assembled. 'Inspector J, since we figured you'd want to question the JEACs and deal with the crooks first, I informed the others that everything was okay, that we would prepare a wonderful dessert, and update them shortly.'

'Thanks, Dan. We'll get the basics and join you in the auditorium for the complete tale.'

'Sure, let us know when you're ready. Ailean and I will organize things,' said Jay, speaking for Ailean who was staring, speechlessly, at Clyde and Beiste. She pushed him out of the room.

Gina, Mich and Friseal approached Rohan.

'Do you need us for this part, Rohan?' asked Gina softly.

'Of course,' began Rohan. Then, seeing the anxious looks on their faces, he smiled, and continued, 'unless you need to be somewhere else doing something special – is that it?'

'Yes, please,' begged Mich.

'Okay, kiddos, where will you be?'

'In the library – with Friseal,' said Gina.

'I'll bring them to the auditorium when I hear the announcement,' said Friseal, winking at Rohan.

'Thanks,' said Rohan, and the trio hurried off.

'Where are . . .' began Amy, when the inspector called the meeting to order.

The JEACs took turns in describing what had happened, while a police officer recorded everything.

'And there's further evidence: the flints in Gràinne's enclosure, as well as this piece of meat, which I'm sure is poisoned,' said Nimal, pulling it out of his pocket.

'There's also Beiste's bag of darts, with the red tailpieces,' said Rohan. 'We hid it under a bush, and I'm sure you'll find some of his fingerprints on them.'

'You've done a brilliant job, JEACs – despite the danger involved,' said Inspector Jeffries, 'and I'm impressed. We'll check everything out, including the passage, draw up a report and ask you to look it over to ensure we've not missed anything.'

He turned to the crooks and said sternly, 'Do *you* have anything to say in your defence?'

No one said a word, and Clyde and Beiste kept their eyes on the floor. After the inspector issued instructions to his second-in-command, the crooks were taken away.

Everyone breathed a sigh of relief, and the inspector said, 'Shall we adjourn to the auditorium?'

'I'll make the announcement,' said Taog, who had listened in silence. 'It's a great pity that we had traitors in our midst, led astray by greed.'

'True, Taog,' said Dan. 'It's a lesson to every one of us.'

CHAPTER 20

Prince Charlie and Colonel Bogey

'Phew! Our snow leopards are safe from harm at last,' said Rohan, as the group moved towards the auditorium.

'Yes, thanks to you JEACs,' said Dan. 'Taran just called to say that they were back in their enclosures, and he was going to spend the night keeping an eye on Gràinne.'

'That's great. And where did the kiddies disappear to?' asked Amy.

'The library,' said Rohan. 'I think they were planning something.'

'A song and cartoons, perhaps?' smiled Anu.

'Probably,' said Brian. 'Can't wait to see what they've been up to.'

Friseal, Drostan, Mich and Gina joined the others outside the auditorium, and the JEACs gaped at the men: Friseal and Drostan carried bagpipes, and wore Prince Charlie outfits, which is the Scottish equivalent of black tie suits.

'Wow!' gasped Anu and Amy.

'Autographs later, ladies,' grinned Drostan.

'Absolutely!' said Anu, while the boys cheered.

'We've borrowed complete outfits for you lads, to wear at Brian's birthday party on the twenty-second, the day after tomorrow,' said Friseal.

'Super,' said Nimal, adding mischievously, 'Do you think I could learn how to play the bagpipes by then?'

'No fear, laddie – we'll not let you even hold one,' said Uallas, joining them. 'We'd rather our animals stayed *in* the conservation centre and aren't driven *away* by your endeavours.'

Everyone burst out laughing, and they entered the auditorium, which was crammed with people; everybody wanted to hear the tale.

Dan led the JEACs onto the stage, to join Robert McCale.

'We would like . . .' began Dan, and stopped.

The crowd shouted and cheered! They had been worried sick when Jay had informed them that their snow leopards were in danger, yet again, and it took Dan and Robert's best efforts to calm them down and leave matters to the JEACs, staff and police.

Dan joined in the cheering and then raised his hands for silence. 'JEACs – you're on.'

'Anu – you start,' said Rohan.

'Okay. I'll begin with a brief review of what everyone knows, and then the Sco-Js will continue with what occurred prior to our arrival at KWCC. After that, I'll take over the narration once more and involve all of you.'

The JEACs nodded and Anu spoke into the microphone, 'It all began when KWCC decided to help preserve snow leopards by breeding them in captivity. As we discovered, even conservation centres can be infiltrated by people greedy for money – though, thankfully, this is rare, and our centres, which are run by wonderful, dedicated staff, are safe places for animals.'

Anu went on with the tale, involving all the JEACs, who spoke clearly and concisely about their part in the adventure, leading up to the capture of the crooks. The crowd listened intently.

At the conclusion of the story, Anu wrapped up by saying, 'I understand the snow leopards are none the worse for their adventures and, thank goodness, they're all safely ensconced in their enclosures.'

There was absolute silence and then Gavan, who was seated on the edge of the stage, leapt to his feet and roared, 'Hurray for the JEACs!'

Once more, the room resounded with shouts of joy, as the JEACs were cheered with clapping, stamping of feet, whistling and shouting.

Once the crowd had quietened down, Robert McCale said, 'JEACs, I am honoured to know you, and am delighted by your dedication and valour in protecting animals, in this case, our beautiful snow leopards. Your group's mission statement and goals are superb, and I understand that 732 new members were recruited today. If every member recruits one other member, and they, in turn, recruit one more, we'll soon have thousands of JEACs in every country. You are the future leaders of our world – and the best way to lead is by example.

'Now, I have been informed that we have a special performance to conclude today's exciting fundraiser. Gina and Mich?'

The girls moved towards a microphone on one side of the stage as a beautiful picture of KWCC flashed onto the large screen; expectantly, they looked towards the main entrance to the auditorium. The crowd standing in the middle aisle parted quickly as bagpipes sounded.

Friseal and Drostan marched down the aisle, playing 'Colonel Bogey's March', and everyone started whistling in time to the well-known tune. When the men reached the stage, they stood behind Mich and Gina. Pictures depicting various scenes at KWCC flashed on the screen, the bagpipes continued playing, and the girls began to sing.

When we arrived at KWCC
We knew that there'd be tons to see,
But we were shocked to hear that
Snow leopards were killed for their bones and fur.

We were quite aggravated when
We heard about the killings, then
Brian told us what Eadan,
Cormag and he found, and we were appalled!

It made us really sore and mad.
We felt so very cross and sad.
And we knew that we had to
Discover who was the cause of this woe.

So we set out the crooks to catch.
For us JEACs they were no match,
And dar-ling Gràinne taught them

A lesson that they will never forget.

Snow leopards now are safe and sound
Our hearts with joy do now abound
So if you'd like to join us,
We'd be so happy, if all of you sing.

Thank you, to each and everyone
Come on, it's time to have some fun,
We'll have a jolly good time,
As we start singing and dancing around!

At the end of the song the crowd exploded with cheers and applause. But Gina and Mich beckoned the other JEACs; the words of the song were put up on another screen; and Friseal and Drostan began playing again. The auditorium rang with the song as everyone joined in – singing, whistling and clapping.

And now, let's bid the JEACs goodbye, and – HOLD IT! Is that a humongous chocolate cake I see before my eyes? Yes – Ceana has discovered their favourite dessert and has brought it onto the stage, ready for everyone to eat when they finish singing. Hurry up, JEACs!

And is there any chance that you'll be coming to Canada soon? We have superfantabulous chocolate cake here, too!

* * *

GLOSSARY

Word	Meaning
Advocate	A person who pleads a case on someone else's behalf
Amigos	Friends – Spanish
Anorexic	Extremely thin
APs	Aged Parents – acronym
ASAP	As Soon As Possible – acronym
ATV	All Terrain Vehicle
Aunty/aunties	Nimal uses it on the girls in mock respect
Bag of salt	The usual expression is 'to take something with a pinch of salt' – which means to believe only part of something
Balaclava	A close-fitting garment covering the whole head and neck except for parts of the face, typically made of wool
Biscuits	Cookies
Brekker	Breakfast – short form
Brill	Brilliant
Bro	Brother – short form
CAB	Clyde and Beiste – acronym
Canucks	Canadians – informal/slang term, origin uncertain
C-ite	People who live on conservation centres – fun word, pronounced see-ite
Chopper(s)	A casual word for helicopters
Confab	An informal private conversation or discussion
Conning	Deceiving someone by lying to them
Crèche	A nursery where babies and young children are cared for during the working day
Creep	A feeding enclosure for young animals, containing a long, narrow entrance so the mother can't get through, often installed in zoos or conservation centres which have breeding programmes
Cu	Dog – Gaelic
Delhi	The capital of India
Divvy up	Split up; divide up
Dorm	Dormitory – short form. A large bedroom for a number of people in a school or institution
Double, double toil and trouble!	'Double, double toil and trouble; fire burn, and cauldron bubble.' This is part of the original verse in William Shakespeare's play, *Macbeth*, while the three witches are stirring a boiling cauldron
English Lit.	English Literature – short form
Enid Blyton	Well-known British writer of children's fiction
Eureka	A cry of joy or satisfaction when one finds or discovers

Word	Meaning
	something
Exactimo	Exactly – fun usage
Dekko	Look – Hindi
Flip chart	A large pad of paper bound so that each page can be turned over at the top to reveal the next, used on a stand at presentations
Frostbite	Injury to body tissues caused by exposure to extreme cold, typically affecting the nose, fingers, or toes
Gaelic	A language of Scotland, pronounced *Gal-lik*
Germ/germs	Gentlemen – fun usage when saying 'ladies and germ'
Grey Man	A creature which resembles the Yeti (see Yeti below)
Heptad	A group of seven
Hols	Holidays – short form (vacation)
Hon	Honey – short form
Hubbub	A chaotic din caused by a crowd of people
Info	Information – short form
Keep your eyes peeled	Be on the alert; watch carefully or vigilantly for something
KWCC	Kinnaird Wildlife Conservation Centre– acronym
Laddie	Chiefly Scottish – informal for boy or young man
Lassie	Chiefly Scottish – a young girl or woman
Lift	Elevator
Lugs	Ears
Mater	Mother – Latin origin
Mes amis	My friends – French
Mobile phone	Cell phone
Moi	Me – French
Mr. Q	Code name for the inventor in the 007 movies
Muchas gracias	Thank you very much – Spanish
Nineteen to the dozen	Talks a lot – idiom
No problemo	No problem – fun usage of word 'problem'
Och	Used to express a range of emotions – Scottish or Irish
Panthera uncia	Scientific name for snow leopards; also Uncia uncia
Patron	A person who gives financial or other support to a person, organization, or cause
Pax	Peace
PC	Politically correct – acronym
Piggyback	A ride on someone's back and shoulders
Résumé	Curriculum vitae; a summary of your academic and work experience
Sco-Js	Scottish JEACs – abbreviated acronym

Word	Meaning
Sec	Second – short form
'Singin' in the kitchen'	An old song by Bobbie Bare
Situ	Situation – short form
Sotto voce	In a quiet voice, or as an aside – Italian
Tailpiece	The back end of a dart which stabilizes it
Tarp	Tarpaulin – short form
Texted	To send a text message via a mobile/cell phone
Toque	Knitted winter hat
Uncle	Umedh uses it on Nimal in mock respect
Veggies	Vegetables – short form
Video cams	Video camera – short form
Voilà	Expression used to call attention; to express satisfaction or approval – French
Whisht	Scottish and Irish for 'Hush'
Whoa	An expression of surprise
With a pinch of salt	That's the usual expression; however, an exaggerated version is to say 'with a whole bagful of salt'
WTs	Walkie-talkies – acronym
Yaar	Mate/buddy – most often used in India by males
Yeti	Abominable snowman – an ape-like creature said to live in the Himalayan mountains
Yum-a-licious	Combination of 'yummy' and 'delicious' – fun word

PRONUNCIATION GUIDE FOR SCOTTISH NAMES

In this book I have used a number of Gaelic names, thus a guide on pronunciation and meanings might be useful.

Name/Gender	Pronunciation	Meaning
Ailean – male	A lun; E lun	Rock, noble, or harmony
Beathag – female	BEH ak	Life
Beiste – male	BEST	Beast
Blàr – male	BLAWR	Field
Boisil – male	BO shil	No meaning found
Brian – male	BREE un	Strength
Catan – male	KAH tan	Small cat
Ceana – female	KEH na	Fair one
Doilidh – female	DOL ee	True desire
Drostan – male	DROST an	Offspring of Drost – possibly a Pictish name
Failbhe – male	FAL uh vuh	Either lively, spritely, or wolf-slayer
Friseal – male	FREE shul	Gaelic form of Fraser
Garbhan – male	GAR uv an	Rough
Gràinne – female	GRAW nya	Name of a Celtic goddess, meaning 'she who inspires terror', or derived from the word for grain, symbolizing fertility
Luag – male	LOO ak	Name of a Celtic sun god, meaning 'to win'
Moire – female	---	Bitter
Mòrag – female	MORE ak	Great
Niall – male	NEE ull	Champion, cloud, or vehement
Sorcha – female	SOR uh kha	Light, or brightness
Taog – male	TOOK	Poet, or philosopher
Taran – male	TA ran	Name of a sixth-century saint
Uallas – male	WAL lus	Foreigner
Uisdean – male	OOSH jun	Intelligent

AN AUTHOR AND FOUNDER'S ACCOLADE TO
JEACS – CAC – No. 1

From an *inspiration* to a *story*; from the story to a *series of books*;
from the books to a *book report* in a school;
from the book report to the *reality of an authentic group*,
namely, *JEACs – CAC – No. 1.*

I am absolutely delighted to introduce this enterprising, dedicated, and passionate group of young people! Congratulations: Aidan, Alexa, Alexandra, Bodie, Caelin, Carson, Charlie, Emma, Ethan, Georgia, Hannah, Jack, Jack, Jennah, Jennie, Jocelyn, Karina, Laila, Mackenzie, Owen, Peter, Robyn, Roman, Ryan, Sam, Samantha, Stephanie and Wallace, for being the first to form the group on 25 May 2012.

JEACs – CAC – No. 1, the first *real* group of JEACs was started by Laila, a nine-year-old girl. After reading my book *Peacock Feathers*, Laila was eager to do a book report at her school. She visited my website and sent me an email, asking if I was a Canadian author. I wrote back immediately, suggesting that we speak on the telephone. Laila, her mother, Melaney, and I had an interesting conversation during which Laila asked if she could start her own group of JEACs (she and her mother thought that the JEACs group already existed in reality, since they had both read *Peacock Feathers*).

Having decided that the report would be presented in the form of the "first-ever-in-the-world JEACs meeting", Laila set up an agenda and a call for membership. I was invited to attend the event as the "surprise guest" and to do a book signing, which I accepted! The school principal and Laila's classroom teacher supported her, and needless to say, the entire event was a huge success. The Grade 4 students were a super group who listened intently and asked pertinent questions. At the call for membership of the **JEACs – CAC – No. 1** group, more than half the class joined up enthusiastically.

At the conclusion of the event, Laila's teacher congratulated her on her superb presentation, and reminded the class that they, too, could achieve anything they set their minds to; that, since they were our future leaders, they should work hard in order to improve things; and that inspiration, discipline and determination, even in small things, could change the world and make it a better place. Laila received the applause and commendation she so richly deserved from her peers. I presented Laila with a certificate of recognition and a little silver elephant to signify that – like the elephant who never forgets – I would never forget this heart-warming event.

The book signing was a success too, and I donated a percentage of the sales to JEACs – CAC – No. 1, so that they could, in turn, donate it to a zoo or conservation centre of their choice. After their pizza lunch, I surprised the students with a chocolate cake – much to their delight!

I am thrilled that in 2013 and 2014 more groups of JEACs were formed – aided and supported by their parents, teachers, schools, family and friends. I look forward to groups forming globally and assisting in creating awareness of the importance of saving our planet. Conservation centres and zoos are striving to educate our world, and we need to do everything we can to assist them. It is, after all, our world!

Please contact me if you wish to know more about the JEACs and would like to set up a group, so that you can review the **Mandate for the JEACs**, receive your unique identity name and number, and become part of this global network. The JEACs groups are independent of one another.

Finally, in *Can Snow Leopards Roar?* I mention the setting up of **JEACs International Foundation**. I have always wanted to set up a foundation based on my books, and several years ago, I discussed the feasibility of doing so with like-minded friends who were in agreement; I therefore started the process by trade-marking the name **JEACs**. This project will take off at the right time! We currently have an Advisory Board in place, and they keep the groups, and myself on track!

Thank you for caring about our planet.

Amelia Lionheart
Author and Founder of **The JEACs**
Website: www.jeacs.com

ABOUT THE AUTHOR

Amelia Lionheart has been writing for many years and is the published author of four books for children. She has a diploma in writing from the Institute of Children's Literature, Connecticut, USA.

Amelia, who has lived and worked in several countries, believes very strongly in the conservation of wildlife and, in particular, the protection of endangered species. She is convinced that awareness of this issue, when imbued in children at an early age, is a vital step towards saving our planet.

As a member of several nature/wildlife preservation organizations, including the Durrell Wildlife Conservation Trust, she invites children and their families to become involved with local zoos and conservation centres and to support their important work, both by creating awareness and fundraising. To encourage this, she created a group called the 'Junior Environmentalists and Conservationists' (the JEACs) in the first book of her JEACs' series, *Peacock Feathers*. In the other books, the JEACs travel to various countries, having adventures while enlarging their group and encouraging local children to start groups of JEACs in their own countries. As of November 2013, Amelia has four *real* groups of JEACs in Canada. The JEACs continue to evolve.

Amelia's other interests include environmental issues, volunteer work and fundraising. She believes that if people from different countries explore the diversity of cultures and learn from one another, they will discover that they have more similarities than dissimilarities. Many of these ideas are included in her books.

Please check out http://www.jeacs.com, Amelia's website for children.